Hand to Hand

Other Books from Hatrack River Publications

Denise Tucker

HATRACK RIVER

P U B L I C A T I O N S

Cover art by Paul Mann
Cover and title design by James Fedor
This book was set in 16-point "Goudy" and 16-point "Tekton" from Adobe,
    using WordPerfect for Windows 6.1 and a Hewlett-Packard LaserJet 4
    Plus printer. It was then reduced and printed as approximately 12-
    point type on pH-neutral paper.
Printed by Publisher's Press, Salt Lake City UT
Sole distributor of books from Hatrack River Publications is:
    Publishers Distribution Center
    805 West 1700 South
    Salt Lake City UT 84104

First printing August 1996
10 9 8 7 6 5 4 3 2 1

Library of Congress Catalog Card Number: 96-77299

ISBN 1-887473-00-9

To my niece,
Samantha Lauren Tucker

Acknowledgments

Despite popular opinion, the process of writing a book is actually not a solitary endeavor. True, no one was nearby at midnight when I sat solemnly at my computer, madly typing away. However, there were many people who offered their expertise and assistance in getting this novel published.

First of all, my deepest appreciation to Scott and Kristine Card for their enthusiasm in publishing this story and for all their guidance in showing me "the ropes." My thanks to Kathleen Bellamy for preparing the manuscript — only she knows how well I really spell.

I am indebted to numerous people in Utah for their help in painting a reasonably accurate picture of Salt Lake City in the 1920s. My thanks to Margaret Adams at the Beehive House for her information on Brigham Young and historical buildings in downtown Salt Lake. I am grateful to Thomas Alexander at Brigham Young University, Dean May at the University of Utah, and John McCormick at Salt Lake Community College for their knowledge concerning the history of Salt Lake City. My thanks to James Allen and Thomas Alexander for their book *Mormons & Gentiles: A History of Salt Lake City*. This book was a great resource.

My thanks to the archivist at Bryn Mawr College for details regarding The Women of Summer program; to Bill Slaughter from the LDS Church Historical Department for his cheerful last-minute assistance regarding the layout of Sister Smith's gravesite; to George Givens and Dr. Marita Angleton for their knowledge of early American medicine; and especially to Bil and Peggy Card for reading the text and for going the extra mile (literally) to Salt Lake City to draw a much-needed map.

PART
ONE
Ginny

1

August 1902

Ginny lay in her bed, wide awake and shivering.

It wasn't cold weather causing her to shake so badly beneath the thin, white sheets. Outside, it was a hot evening in early August, and the Virginia night air blowing in through her bedroom window was just as hot and humid and sticky as the Virginia day air had been. The awful summer heat made Ginny restless, and in protest, she angrily kicked the sheets off her skinny legs. She tried to settle down, but it was hard to be still while listening to the sounds that made her so afraid.

Stop it, she thought.

Stop it! Stop it! Stop it!

But it didn't stop.

The angry voice of her drunken father in the kitchen downstairs kept yelling and yelling, and the unhappy voice of her mother yelled back, then pleaded, then wept. And these recurring sounds shook Ginny's soul.

She pulled the feather pillow out from under her head and put it over her face, holding the ends over her ears. She knew that she couldn't fall asleep like this, but it usually made her feel better. Why couldn't she sleep through it like Willie and Bessie? Willie was her little brother, just turned four years old. He was the baby of the family and too young to understand. Besides, once Willie was asleep, he stayed that way till morning. Bessie, her younger sister, was eight years old, just two years younger than she, and old enough to understand what was going on downstairs in the kitchen. But there Bessie lay in the bunk above her, softly snoring away in peace.

This really made Ginny mad, and she was sorely tempted to stretch her leg upwards and kick the underside of Bessie's bed real hard. She had done this before. Slowly, she lifted her right foot up carefully towards the bunk above. At that precise moment, a small yellow kitten named Cornbread jumped up on Ginny's bed and proceeded to attack her exposed left elbow.

Ginny reached out and pulled the kitten up to her chest.

"Stop it!" she insisted. At least the kitten obeyed her wishes. Insulted as only a cat can be, Cornbread pranced haughtily across Ginny's chest and curled up into a tiny ball on the bed beside her. Ginny felt guilty for yelling at the innocent kitten; she reached out and began rubbing her behind the ears. The kitten closed her eyes in ecstasy and starting purring. It was a comforting sound.

She put the pillow back underneath her head and closed her eyes and tried to remember happier times, days when her papa was well. Papa was a tobacco farmer, and their family lived on a small farm in rural Charlotte County, Virginia. They lived in a two-story white farmhouse that had a large open front porch and a screened-in back porch. Her earliest memories of Papa were sparkling summer evenings when she was four years old. Just before dinner, Mother would let her go out on the front porch swing and wait until she could see Papa walking down the road towards their house. Ginny would leap off the porch and run down the road to greet him as he returned from the tobacco fields.

Papa's hands would be stained brownish black, and his shirt would smell like tobacco leaves. She didn't mind the stains one bit, and she learned to like the funny smell of the tobacco. Papa would give her a big bear hug and then throw her up on his wide shoulders for a piggyback ride back to the house.

Another sweet memory came to Ginny's mind. It was that cold winter just before her little brother Willie was born, when it snowed and snowed and snowed. For many days school was canceled, and

Bessie and Ginny sat around the house after chores were done and complained there was nothing to do. Mother told Papa that she was sure that her children were going to die of cabin fever. That made Bessie scared. Bessie thought cabin fever must be like measles or scarlet fever, and she didn't like being sick.

One night, Papa and some of the neighbors decided to organize an evening sleigh riding party. The menfolk built a big roaring fire at the top of Hamner's Hill, and the grown-ups sat around the fire, drinking hot cider and talking happily while the children rode their wooden sleds down the steep embankment. Bessie's fears of being sick had came true that day. She had caught a bad cold playing outside without her mittens the day before, so Mother decided Bessie had to stay in with her.

That meant Ginny had Papa all to herself. Each time she got ready to ride, Papa would push her sled in a running start, and Ginny just squealed with fear and delight all the way down that snow-covered hill. Several times, Papa jumped on the back of the sled and rode down the hill with her. It was so much fun!

When she and Papa walked home, he held her hand and pointed out some of the star constellations to her, like Orion and Little Pleides and the Big Dipper. She liked Orion best. Papa told her it was a strong prince wearing a sword in the sky and that he watched over small children and young animals. After that, whenever she looked up into the sky and saw Orion, she felt safe inside.

The sound of shattering china startled Ginny and interrupted her pleasant thoughts. Mother must have thrown a dish again. She only did that when she was very, very angry at Papa. Three dinner plates and one salad bowl had been lost since Christmas. Ginny moaned and pushed the edges of the pillow up against her ears.

She thought back to "The Parade." Well, that's what Mother called it. Papa's younger brother, Abraham, and his family lived up in Lynchburg, Virginia. He wrote Papa a nice letter, inviting Papa's whole family to come up to town for a visit on the Fourth of July. Since it was the beginning of a new century, the year 1900, the city had planned an extra special Independence Day parade.

The news of the trip thrilled the children. Ginny was anxious to see Lynchburg, the big city she had heard so much about. Lynchburg was a river town, built on seven large, steep hills right beside the James River. Bessie was excited to see her cousin Elizabeth, Uncle Abraham's only child. That was because Bessie and Elizabeth were the same age and both had blond hair. They liked to pretend they were twins separated at birth by a tragic accident. They never explained what the accident was, but Bessie assured Ginny it was very "tragical." Two-year-old Willie didn't quite understand what it meant to go to the big city, but Papa explained that he would get to take a long ride in Papa's big wagon. That was enough to make Willie happy.

Uncle Abraham had sent written directions for them to meet him and his family right downtown where the parade was going to be, but somehow Papa got lost riding around down there on those steep hilly streets. By accident, they ended up on the parade route just before the parade started. Mother was so embarrassed that she held her head down and put her hands over her face, but Papa proudly drove their wagon and horses right down Main Street, waving and smiling and tipping his hat to the people lined up on the curb. The people thought the parade had started, and they yelled and smiled and waved right back. Mother swore she would never set foot in Lynchburg again. Papa and Uncle Abraham thought it was great fun. Ginny thought so, too.

Through the feather pillow, Ginny could hear her Papa yelling and hitting the kitchen table now with his fist. If Papa would only go to sleep, she thought anxiously, things would be okay again in the morning.

Go to sleep, Papa.

Just go to sleep.

Ginny squeezed her eyes shut and thought of the best memory she had of Papa when he was feeling better. It was old Hiram Blankenship's funeral. Old Hiram was something of a legend in their community. He was a Civil War veteran, having survived several of the biggest and last battles of "The War." For some reason, people in

Virginia didn't like calling it "The Civil War." "The War Between The States" was an awful lot to say in one breath, so folks just shortened it to "The War." If you started talking about "The War," folks knew exactly which war you were talking about.

Mother said Old Hiram had his horse shot right out from under him, but Old Hiram never got wounded. He was present at the surrender with General Lee at nearby Appomattox, and since he didn't have a horse, he had to walk home to Charlotte County.

He was a little man, not much taller than Mother, with a long white beard that reached below his waist. Mother said he used to tuck it under his belt when doing his carpentry work. Mother and Ginny were invited to lunch at his house once, and Old Hiram showed Ginny the old black boots he had worn in battle and the little prayer book which he swore protected him from the Yankee bullets. When Old Hiram died, the Widow Blankenship asked Papa to sing at the funeral.

Ginny could still clearly recall the images of that day in church as she sat in the second pew in her Sunday best. The minister's sister, Mabel Coffey, had come all the way down from Madison Heights to play the organ. At the end of the service, when the Reverend Coffey had finished his sermon, Papa stood up front next to a large wreath of red roses and sang "Amazing Grace." Ginny looked around and saw that a lot of people were crying while Papa was singing. Afterwards, she heard Mother say proudly to their neighbor, Mrs. Holt, that there wasn't a dry eye in the place when Papa sang.

That was not so long ago. But Papa got real sick last winter with the croup, and old Doc Davis had told him to drink a glass of whiskey for his cough each night before going to bed. Doc Davis said it would help him sleep. The doctor's cure worked. Papa slept well, and in no time, the cough went away. But the whiskey stayed. Papa continued to have one drink at night when he came home from the fields. Then it was two drinks. Then three. Then the fights with Mother started.

Ginny rolled over onto her stomach in frustration and threw her pillow on the floor. Cornbread saw this as an opportunity to regain lost territory, and the kitten promptly rose and climbed up on Ginny's back. Ginny didn't move. Why fight the kitten? She felt helpless against her Papa's drinking, against what was happening downstairs. It felt good to just lay there with the whole world and that kitten on her shoulders and to feel quite sorry for herself.

Week after week, the family situation was getting worse. Most nights she lay in her bed like this, feeling guilty for not doing anything to help. But what could she do? Children were to be seen and not heard when it came to grown-up problems. But Ginny did reason initially that if she would do more around the house to help Mother, without being asked, things might get better. Unfortunately, Ginny soon saw that nothing she did seemed to make any difference.

The worst part of it all was she couldn't talk to anyone about it. Since Bessie was pretending that nothing was wrong, she could hardly talk about it, and Willie was too young to understand or help. And Ginny knew things like drinking and fighting were not talked about outside the house. Mother did not speak of it to friends or to Reverend Coffey. So neither would Ginny.

Suddenly, there was silence.

The absence of sound from downstairs made Ginny bolt upright in her bed and sent Cornbread flying in the air. The kitten yowled in protest, landed on the hardwood floor, and then scurried underneath the bed to hide.

The quiet woke Bessie up from her deep sleep, and she sprang down from her bunk bed and threw herself into the bewildered arms of her older sister.

"Ginny, what's happening?" she asked with her big blue eyes wide with fright.

"I don't know," whispered Ginny anxiously. She stared at her sister, straining to hear what was happening downstairs. But no more sounds came. Just silence.

Bessie reached for Ginny's hand and held it tight. The two girls held each other close and continued to listen, but no more sounds came from the downstairs kitchen. Now Ginny wished that Papa would yell or that Mother would cry. Any of the sounds that usually frightened her would be a comfort now. The seconds seemed like minutes. Nothing. Nothing. Nothing.

"We better go see," Bessie said finally. She slid out of Ginny's bed and waited for her sister to take the lead.

Ginny reluctantly got out of her bed, ashamed that her younger sister was braver than she was. She put her lips tightly together, determined to not be afraid in front of her younger sister, and more than anything else, she promised herself she would not cry.

The two girls stepped carefully into the dark hallway and slowly walked together towards the back stairs. The old wall clock ticked loudly, still the only sound in the house. Ginny led the way, slowly making her way down the narrow staircase and holding Bessie's hand tightly for security.

She was the first to see Mother lying on the kitchen floor. She was unconscious. Her black hair, which fell in long tresses below her waist, was lying across the floor in a wild tangled mess. There was a small amount of blood on her face. It was a horrible scene, but what really frightened Ginny was the blood stains that appeared on the bottom half of her mother's thin, white nightgown. Mother was eight months pregnant. Ginny knew instantly what those stains meant. The baby was starting to come.

Bessie screamed, "She dead!" and rushed angrily towards their father, who was standing motionless with a lost expression on his face. His blond hair was matted against his brow, which was wet with perspiration, and his cheeks and eyes were an ugly shade of red. The strong smell of whiskey reached Ginny's nose, and the smell made her feel sick. Papa held a half-empty bottle of whiskey in one hand. There was blood on his other hand.

Bessie reached her father and began hitting him in the stomach with her little fists, crying uncontrollably. His daughter's screams acted like a splash of cold water on his face, cutting through the alcohol's numbing effect on his brain, and Papa's face contorted into a look of painful comprehension and utter anguish. He reached down and grabbed Bessie's hands.

Protective, angry feelings welled up inside Ginny. She felt alert as a mother cat, waiting to see what Papa would do, afraid he would hurt Bessie for hitting him, and more than ready to attack him if he did. But her father stood frozen. More feelings rose up inside Ginny, moving her to action. It took all the courage and anger she possessed to decide what to do. But, at last, she would do something. And she would not cry!

With determination, she walked over to the back door and opened it.

"Get out," she said in a harsh low voice that surprised her. It sounded very grown up.

Papa turned and looked at Ginny, but Ginny didn't move nor did she speak to him again. She just continued to hold the door open with the powerful authority of an angry child. Her father paused to look down at Bessie and at his wife. Then, he haltingly walked over to the table, picked up his crumpled hat, and walked out the back door. Ginny slammed the door behind him.

Louella moaned, and both girls rushed over to their battered mother. Ginny ordered Bessie to go immediately to the linen closet and get washcloths and towels while she poured water into a basin. Together the girls knelt and washed Mother's bruised face and hands, and slowly the woman opened her eyes.

"William?" asked Mother.

"He's gone," answered Ginny bitterly.

A look of hurt crossed Mother's face. Her hand went over her bulging stomach, and her head jerked back in response to the wave of pain.

"The baby . . ."

Bessie looked up at her sister frantically.

"The baby's coming?" asked Bessie, her eyes widening with understanding.

Ginny frowned. Being a farm girl, Bessie was already aware of the basic facts of life, yet she was too young to be allowed to help deliver this baby. Ginny had been present at several births with Mother and essentially knew how it was done. But she knew she couldn't do it all by herself. She would need help. She sighed as she thought of the first and best choice of action. Doc Davis lived several miles away. She knew how to ride a horse, but she couldn't leave Bessie and Mother alone for that long. There was only one other option.

Ginny stood up and pulled Bessie up with her.

"You stay with Mother, Bessie, and don't let her get up. I'm going to get Mrs. Holt. She's close by and the best midwife in the county."

Bessie nodded her head obediently, and Ginny dashed up the stairs to her room to change her clothes. She hurriedly tore off her white nightgown and then rushed around the room, frantically looking for her blue flower-print dress. Where was it? It took her a few moments before she spotted the edge of it sticking out from underneath her bed. It must have fallen down there when she kicked off her covers earlier. She pulled it out and discovered Cornbread curled up in a comfortable ball on top of the dress.

"Off!" she ordered, as she tossed the kitten off the dress. The kitten responded to this action by pointing its tail high in the air, turning around in a circle twice, and then walking out of the girl's bedroom headed in the direction of little Willie's room. There she could sleep undisturbed.

As Ginny changed, fearful thoughts began racing inside her head. Would Mother live? Sometimes women died in childbirth. Ginny was aware of that. Mrs. Ramsey died in April giving birth to twin boys. What would happen to them if Mother died? Would Papa come back?

Did she even want Papa to come back?

Her eyes began to moisten, but Ginny wiped them quickly. Not now! She needed to be brave for Mother. She would not let herself cry until Mother was safe.

As she was putting her shoes on, someone abruptly entered her room. Ginny jumped up defensively, fearing that perhaps her father had returned. Instead, a sleepy, four-year-old Willie walked into the room, dragging his tattered blanket behind him.

"Ginny, I thirsty," he whined. "I want a drink."

This was almost more than the ten-year-old girl could stand. She had been close to hysteria up till now, and the last thing she needed to do was worry about her little brother. Who would take care of him? She had to go get Mrs. Holt, and Bessie needed to stay with Mother. And Willie absolutely must not be allowed to see Mother in her condition downstairs.

Oddly enough, Willie's presence proved to be a gift, for it forced her to calm down. It made her stop worrying about the future in order to rationally think about what to do for her brother right this instant. The request for a drink was easily solved. There was a glass on her nightstand, and there was still fresh water in the washstand pitcher that she and Bessie used to wash their face and hands. That meant she didn't have to go downstairs for the drink. Ginny got the glass and poured a small amount of water in it for her brother. Willie took the glass and drank it all in several loud gulps. He handed the glass back to his sister and looked at her closely.

"You got your clothes on, Ginny. You going somewhere?"

She lovingly picked up her little brother and his blanket and carried him back to his room. "I'm going to Mrs. Holt's house, Willie. Bessie is terrible sick with a cough, and Mother needs me to go to Mrs. Holt's house for some medicine."

"Bessie's sick?"

"Yes," lied Ginny sweetly. "She has a very bad cold."

"Can I give her a kiss and make her feel better?" he asked sincerely. Willie loved his sister and he loved giving kisses.

"Oh, no, 'cause then you might get sick and then Mother would have to give you some medicine," replied Ginny wisely.

Willie made a face. He was persuaded. Loving or not, he hated medicine.

"Why don't you give me Bessie's kiss, and I'll give it to her later," said Ginny as she tucked Willie back into his bed. Cornbread appeared, jumping up onto Willie's small bed, and snuggled herself down into the covers at Willie's feet.

Willie smiled and reached up and kissed Ginny gently on the cheek twice.

"One's for you," he said.

"You're a good boy, Willie. Now, go to sleep and sweet dreams."

"Sweet dreams," answered Willie through a yawn.

Ginny stood for a few moments at his door until she could hear his breathing slow down into the quiet sounds of sleep. Thank goodness little children fall asleep almost instantly, she thought, closing the door securely.

Ginny lost no time in rushing back down to the kitchen. Bessie sat on the floor with Mother's head in her lap. Mother was awake and holding her daughter's hand.

"Mother, are you alright?" asked Ginny, kneeling beside her.

"Yes," said Mother weakly. "But the baby is coming tonight, Ginny. You must go and get help." Mother's request made Ginny feel good that she had made the right decision. Mother's face contorted with pain as another contraction gripped her bruised body. Ginny held her mother's hand tightly until the wave of pain stopped.

"I'm going now to Mrs. Holt's," assured Ginny.

"Hurry," said Louella. She turned her head and tried to smile at her oldest daughter.

"Hurry."

She ran as fast as her thin legs could carry her. Gratefully, there was a bright full moon hovering overhead to light the way down the winding dirt road that stretched between their house and the Holt's neighboring farm. The Holt place was at least twice as big as their farm, which was a good thing seeing that the Holts had nine children. Fortunately for Mr. Plunkett Holt, six of those children were strong, healthy boys who could work the land alongside him. The Holt children were Josiah, Mary Susan, the twins Elijah and Embro, Eliza, Kathleen, Benjamin, Jeremiah, and Jacob.

It was about half a mile between the two houses, and the Holts' large white farmhouse lay hidden back in a thick patch of pine trees.

To Ginny, it seemed like a castle, with a large round tower that Mother said was a turret built on one side. Eliza Holt, Ginny's best friend, had the round bedroom up in the turret, and sometimes the girls liked to pretend they were fairy-tale princesses locked inside some evil castle.

Ginny loved the Holts. Mr. Holt was a farmer like Papa, but he grew corn in his fields. He also had a big apple orchard, and Ginny and her family always helped them pick apples during the fall harvest. Ginny and Eliza loved to climb up the small apple trees, full of dark red fruit, and toss down apples to waiting hands and baskets below.

Like her husband, Mrs. Holt loved to garden, but her efforts centered on flowers and herbs. Once Mother said if God ever planted another Garden of Eden, he would put Mrs. Holt in charge of the roses.

Mrs. Holt's roses were the most beautiful part of their farm. They were everywhere. There were large white climbing roses growing on the brick gates at the main entrance to their property. At the side of the house, Mrs. Holt had her kitchen garden. It was a small square piece of land that Mr. Holt had set apart with a white picket fence. Inside, there were patches of tomatoes and green peppers and onions. There were buckets filled with different kinds of wild mint, and there were small patches of dill and oregano and thyme. Within her kitchen garden, Mrs. Holt planted large shrub roses in the four corners and more climbing roses along the sides of the fence. Ginny loved going there. It was wonderful to be surrounded by the smell of roses and peppermint. In the front, alongside a large porch that wrapped around both sides of the house, Mrs. Holt had planted her favorite roses. These roses only bloomed in the spring, but they had the strongest and sweetest scent.

Because of the pine trees, Ginny couldn't see the house until she was practically at the front gate, but the smell of the white roses on the gates greeted her and gave her the assurance that she had arrived at her destination. As she ran down the drive leading to the house, she was relieved to see light shining out from several of the downstairs windows. The Holts were still awake.

As Ginny approached the large house, she realized that the Holts were more than just awake. They must be entertaining company, for the sound of Mr. Holt's fiddle floated out upon the hot night air, and Ginny heard the happy sounds of singing and laughing and dancing when she reached the front porch.

She'll be coming 'round the mountain when she comes!
She'll be coming 'round the mountain when she comes!

Ginny bolted up the front porch steps and began pounding furiously on the screen door. The singing and fiddle playing stopped immediately, and a surprised-looking Mr. Holt soon peered out through the screen door. Ginny liked Mr. Holt. He was a plain man, tall and thin with grey hair and soft green eyes, and he had such a nice laugh. Sometimes he took time to play at the fairy-tale games with her and Eliza. He liked playing the part of the fire-breathing dragon.

"Virginia St. John!" he exclaimed with a whistle, opening the screen door and motioning for Ginny to step inside. "What in blue blazes are you doing out this time of night, child. Do your folks know where you are?"

Ginny grabbed Mr. Holt with both of her hands and shook him fervently. "Mr. Holt, you got to help us. Mother is having her baby! Now!" shouted Ginny. "Doc Davis is too far away. We need Mrs. Holt. Hurry!"

Mr. Holt smiled in understanding and patted Ginny on the back. "Now, now, don't fret so, child. Babies are born every day! I should know. Nine were born here in this very house. That's nothing too serious for a pretty girl like yourself to worry about . . ."

"We got to hurry, Mr. Holt," interrupted Ginny, "Mother isn't well. She needs help! She's . . ."

Before Ginny could explain further and before Mr. Holt could respond, Ann Holt breezed into the hallway from the back kitchen, carrying a large tray filled with several bowls of hot peach cobbler and vanilla ice cream. Besides Mother, Ginny thought Ann Holt was just about the prettiest woman in all of Charlotte County. She was tall and slender like her husband, but her hair hadn't turned grey yet like Mr. Holt's hair and beard had done. She had the most beautiful dark auburn hair that Ginny had ever seen.

Ann Holt stood there, holding her heavy tray, and stared at Ginny in amazement.

"Virginia dear, what's all this commotion about? What are you doing here late at night like this? Where's your Pa?"

Mr. Holt answered the first part of his wife's question before Ginny could reply.

"It seems Mrs. St. John is having her baby tonight, Mrs. Holt, and Virginia has come to ask for your help."

"Mother said to hurry," added Ginny quickly, hoping to move Mrs. Holt into action.

Instead, Mrs. Holt put down the tray and put her hands on her hips and continued to stare at the child.

"And where's your Pa?" she asked with a frown.

A terrible feeling suddenly came over Ginny. Her only concern had been getting help for Mother. Not until this moment did she realize she would have to explain what had happened. She looked around and discovered that there were several other people now standing in the doorway of the living room watching her. She recognized the three eldest Holt boys, Elijah, Embro, and Josiah. Josiah was almost eighteen, and he worked full time in the corn fields with his father. He was supposed to get married next Christmas to Sarah Simpson. Embro and Elijah were thirteen years old, and they loved horses. The Holts raised horses to sell, and it seemed that the twins were destined to take over this part of their father's estate. Mary Susan, the Holt's sixteen-year-old daughter, was also there, standing between the twins. She had often babysat Ginny and Bessie when they were little girls.

There was an older couple and two teenage girls standing there that Ginny did not know. She found it hard to speak in front of all these people.

"Papa's . . . Papa's gone," Ginny stammered.

Mr. and Mrs. Holt continued to look at her for further explanation. Why should she feel bad for Papa? She was still angry at him. What he did was wrong. Yet something deep inside her now wanted to hide the truth, to protect him. But she had to tell. Besides, once they saw Mother, they would know anyway.

"Papa was drunk and had a fight with Mother," she muttered, with her head down. "He hit her and hurt her real bad, and Papa left. I . . . I made him leave."

Mr. and Mrs. Holt exchanged knowing glances and said nothing at first. This made Ginny relax a little. Then Mr. Holt knelt down in front of Ginny and put his hands on her small shoulders. "It's okay, child, I think we understand now. You don't have to say another word. And don't you worry one little bit. We'll see to it that your mother is well taken care of."

Ann Holt removed her apron and excused herself from her company, explaining that she needed to go upstairs to get her midwifery things. As she left, Mr. Holt took Ginny by the hand and led her into the living room where the other people were gathered.

"Virginia, there are some folks here I'd like for you to meet. Virginia St. John, this is my sister Susanna Johnson and her husband Stephan and their two daughters Sophia and Martha. They are visiting us this week from Richmond." The older couple advanced and held out their hands in greeting.

Once the introductions were made, Mr. Holt took matters firmly in hand.

"Elijah, Embro, Louella St. John is . . . in need of a doctor immediately. I want the two of you to saddle up your horses and ride over to Doc Davis' place as fast as you can. Tell him it's an emergency. Bring him over to the St. John place as fast as you can."

Elijah and Embro agreed and left the room quickly. Ginny felt better already knowing they were going after Doc Davis. Both young men were excellent riders, and she knew that Embro's red horse, Cinnamon, was said to be the fastest in the county.

"Susanna," asked Mr. Holt, "would you mind staying here with Virginia and our children? I'd like to take Stephan with me. Mrs. St.

John has two small children that I think ought to stay here overnight. I'll take Stephan along to bring them back here promptly."

"I'll be happy to care for the children," said Mrs. Johnson warmly. "I'll just sit up with my knitting till Mr. Johnson brings them 'round."

"We'll sit up with you, Mother," said one of the teenage girls.

"Thank you, Sophia. You and Martha and Virginia can help me get a place ready in little Jacob's room for those two youngsters to sleep in."

"We can put Virginia in Eliza's room," suggested Mary Susan.

Ginny did not like what she was hearing. She didn't want to stay here and help Mrs. Johnson and her daughters. She grabbed Mr. Holt's hand and shook it in protest.

"Mr. Holt, I don't want to stay here. I want to go with you. I want to help Mrs. Holt with Mother's new baby."

Mr. Holt shook his head decidedly. "Virginia, I don't think so. You've been through so much already, child. I think it's better for you to stay here with Mrs. Johnson. We'll take good care of your Mother. You'll see."

But Ginny wouldn't be easily swayed.

"Mr. Holt, I saw what Papa did to Mother, and I was the one who threw him out of the house. I'm not going to stay here now and be tended! I want to be with Mother. She needs me."

Ginny thought she could see those kind green eyes of Mr. Holt get a little misty. He looked at her for a long moment and then relented.

"Alright, missy, you can go. But stay right here with the Johnsons while I go get the horses hitched up to the wagon. Josiah, will you give me a hand in the stable?"

Mr. Holt and Josiah left the room together, leaving Ginny alone with the others. She took a deep breath. Mother, she thought, help is coming. Hold on, Mother, for just a little bit longer.

Mrs. Johnson came over and put a reassuring arm around the girl.

"Don't worry, Virginia. Everything is going to be fine."

Against her will, Ginny turned and put her arms around this woman. She had been brave beyond her years for the last hour. She had faced her father and his sickness. She had seen her sweet mother abused and in pain. She had deceived her little brother and had told the terrible truth to these strangers.

From this night on, Ginny would have to be an adult in her family, to help Mother with running the house and with raising the children. Tonight, her childhood ended. But just for a few moments more, she wanted to feel like a child again.

Ginny closed her eyes and leaned her face on Mrs. Johnson's sturdy shoulder and cried.

2

August 1902

Ginny was grateful that the trip back to her house was both quick and quiet.

Mrs. Holt sat up front in the wagon next to her husband. She held on tightly to her husband's right arm as he clutched the dark leather reins, driving the horses to run at their fastest pace down the bumpy dirt road. Ginny sat in the back of the wagon with Mr. Johnson. The road was so rough in places that she had to grab the side of the wagon and hold on for dear life.

Surprisingly, Mr. Johnson didn't try to talk to Ginny, and that was just fine with her because she didn't want any sympathy or advice at the moment. She just wanted them to get home to Mother as fast as they could. Ginny was puzzled, however, at the fact that Mr. Johnson kept his eyes closed and his head bowed. He looked like he was asleep.

This bothered Ginny until she decided that Mr. Johnson must be praying. Perhaps that was exactly what she ought to be doing herself while she had the chance.

Ginny started to bow her head, but it felt wrong somehow. Bowing her head and folding her hands together was fine for normal prayers like "God is great and God is good . . ." and her nightly "God blesses," but this was not a normal situation. She felt her memorized prayers were all wrong. She needed to talk to God face to face.

Ginny decided she would look straight up into the sky and speak to him.

Ginny looked up. Despite the awful heat and humidity, it was a remarkably clear night, and the stars sparkled brightly overhead. The full moon seemed like a transparent blue ball in the sky. Ginny focused her eyes on the glowing moon as if it were God's face and whispered simply, "Dear God, please hear me. Mother needs your help now real bad. Please, please help Mother."

Many words weren't needed. Only feelings. Deep, human, desperate feelings.

When she finished, Ginny felt good inside. God must have heard.

In no time, they pulled up in front of Ginny's house, and Mr. Johnson jumped out of the wagon to tie up the horses while Mr. Holt helped Mrs. Holt down. Ginny started to leap out to run ahead with them, but something made her stop and wait for Mr. Johnson to come back and help her out of the wagon.

Fear. It was plain, old fear.

Ginny stared ahead at the dark house and the front door standing wide open. How badly was Mother injured? Would she survive the birth? Had Papa returned while they were gone? If so, what would he say to the Holts and Mr. Johnson? What would Mr. and Mrs. Holt say to Papa? What would Papa say to her?

The Holts rushed inside the house, and Mr. Johnson returned to the wagon. He held out his arms to Ginny and carefully lifted her out of the wagon. As they walked towards the house, Ginny didn't say anything to him. However, Mr. Johnson must have sensed what she was feeling because he reached down and took hold of one of Ginny's hands and held it tightly in his own.

When they reached the kitchen, Ginny saw Mr. Holt lifting Mother off the floor while Mrs. Holt held a much relieved little Bessie in her reassuring arms. Mother looked very pale but she was awake.

Ginny let go of Mr. Johnson's hand and rushed forward.

"Mother, Mother, are you alright?"

"Yes, Virginia," she whispered in a very weak voice. Mother reached out her hand, and Ginny grabbed it.

"Is anything broken?" asked Ginny fearfully of both her Mother and Mr. Holt.

Mother looked at Mrs. Holt sadly. "Just my pride . . ." Another wave of labor pains started as Mother gasped, reached for her bulging stomach, and held it tightly with her pale hands.

"Gently, Mr. Holt," cautioned the overseeing Mrs. Holt. "Gently. We must put her right to bed. Use the front stairs, dearest. The back stairs are much too narrow. I'll be up in a moment."

Mr. Holt carried Mother carefully out of the kitchen, and Mrs. Holt pulled a handkerchief out of her dress pocket and began wiping Bessie's tear-stained face.

"Bessie, you were such a very brave little girl tonight, and I'm right proud of you. Now don't fret anymore about your mother. Mr. Holt and I are here and we'll take good care of her till Doc Davis comes." Bessie smiled at Mrs. Holt's reassuring words, but those same words made Ginny very nervous. Bessie would believe it. Bessie would believe anything Mrs. Holt told her. Ginny would not. She knew things might not turn out so fine.

Ginny looked and saw Mr. Johnson standing in the hallway. Mrs. Holt directed Bessie's attention to him.

"Bessie, this is Mr. Johnson, my brother-in-law. He's going to take you and Willie back to my house. I thought it would be best for you two to spend the night there. So run upstairs, child, and get some play clothes for tomorrow. You and Kathleen can climb in our apple trees all day to your heart's content. And perhaps Mrs. Johnson will make you some hotcakes with my peach preserves for breakfast!"

The mention of little Kathleen and Mrs. Holt's peach preserves put a quick stop to Bessie's tears. She wiped her nose and then rushed up the back stairs to get her clothes.

"Ginny, would you be a dear and help your sister get her things together while I show Mr. Johnson the way upstairs to collect Willie?"

Ginny said she would help and followed Mrs. Holt up the stairs. In her bedroom, Ginny rushed around, gathering up Bessie's blue summer dress and shoes and socks. When they came back downstairs, Mr. Johnson was standing on the front porch with a sleeping four year old draped across his shoulder. Mr. Johnson took Bessie's hand and started walking toward the wagon.

As she left, Bessie turned and gave her sister a funny last look. Maybe Bessie understands after all, thought Ginny sadly. She suddenly felt sorry for her young sister. Ginny did her best to smile as she waved a big goodbye to Bessie as the wagon pulled slowly away.

As soon as the wagon and Bessie were well out of sight, Ginny turned and went straight upstairs to Mother's room to find Mother lying on her bed. Mrs. Holt was talking to Mother while sponging off her bruised face with a wet cloth. Mr. Holt was busy tying two long, white strips of cloth from an old sheet to the front of the bed. He took the ends of the strips and wrapped them carefully around Mother's wrists. Ginny had seen these strips of cloth before. They weren't tied so tightly as to hurt Mother. Instead, they were loose and provided Mother with something to grab and hold onto when the pains were real bad.

Just then, the birthing pains began again, and Mother cried out. Mrs. Holt spoke softly to Mother, encouraging her, comforting her. Mr. Holt took a damp washcloth and gently placed it across Mother's forehead. Mrs. Holt asked Ginny to go get Mother's fan to help cool her off. Mother had a beautiful paper fan that she used only for church. Ginny quickly got it out of Mother's chest of drawers and stood up close to the bed. She fanned steadily near Mother's face. Mother looked so miserable. It was so awfully hot in the room. Why did this baby have to be born in the worst part of summer? It was terribly hard to watch Mother struggle as she pulled hard on those strips of cloth. But Ginny stood firm in her determination to stay. Finally the pains stopped, and Mother quieted down.

"Close your eyes and rest, Louella," advised Mrs. Holt. "Save your strength between contractions."

Ginny stood at the foot of the bed watching.

"How long till the baby comes, Mrs. Holt?" asked Ginny.

"An hour or so, I think. Two hours at the most," she answered coldly. Mrs. Holt was staring at Mother's bruised face and swollen lips. Mrs. Holt looked very angry. Mr. Holt looked angry, too. Ginny felt ashamed. How could Papa do this to Mother?

Ginny heard rumbling noises coming from outside, and she rushed over to the front window to look out. She could see Embro riding Cinnamon at a hard gallop towards the house with an off-balanced Doc Davis desperately hanging on behind him in the saddle. In the distance, Ginny could see Elijah riding not far behind, carrying the doctor's black bag in his lap.

"Mrs. Holt, the twins are here with Doc Davis!"

"Glory be!" Mrs. Holt exclaimed.

"Thank heavens!" said Mr. Holt.

Ginny looked out the window again to watch the doctor and the twins. The doctor looked like he had barely crawled out of bed. His white hair was sticking straight up and out like a scarecrow's, and his shirt was buttoned up all wrong. By the look on his face, the doctor seemed right pleased to get off of Embro's horse and to put his feet down on solid ground again. Elijah rode up to the front porch and handed Doc Davis his black bag. The doctor thanked him quickly and rushed inside the house. It didn't take him but a moment to run up the stairs.

"How is she?" he asked Mrs. Holt when he entered Mother's bedroom.

"Weak but awake . . . and alone," answered Mrs. Holt.

Doc Davis looked at Mrs. Holt, and the two of them looked down at Mother and then back at each other.

"I see," said the doctor as he leaned over the bed and began speaking to Mother.

"Mrs. St. John? Mrs. St. John? It's Doctor Davis. I'm here now."

Mother opened her eyes and nodded her head. The pains started again, and this time, Ginny could barely watch.

"Just hold on, Mrs. St. John, hold on. Try not to push yet. Easy does it. That's right. Good."

Doc Davis spoke these words while kneeling by Mother's bedside. Mrs. Holt moved to the other side of the bed, and Mr. Holt stood right behind her, ready to do whatever was asked of him. Ginny closed her eyes this time till Mother's pains stopped.

"How did you find her?" Doc Davis asked Mrs. Holt.

"Lying on her back on the kitchen floor."

"Thank the stars in heaven she didn't fall forward. We would have lost her and the baby."

The doctor looked at Mother and paused.

"Any sign of William St. John yet?"

"No. No sign of him at all." Ginny didn't like the way Mrs. Holt's voice sounded. She had never heard her voice sound that way before.

"Well, it is a blessing you are here, Ann Holt. You are an angel of mercy and the best midwife in the county. I just wish we had three more just like you."

This comment made Mrs. Holt blush. The doctor straightened up and rubbed his hands across his head, trying to smooth his hair down.

"I could use a nice cup of tea about now. That should wake me up and calm me down. How on earth a gentle Christian woman like you, Ann Holt, raised such wildcats as Elijah and Embro I'll never know. I'm certain I lost my stomach somewhere between home and here. Embro jumped my fence, two ditches, and a fallen pine tree on the way over. Doesn't that boy believe in roads?"

"Only on Sundays," replied Mr. Holt proudly.

"You see, it's not my fault," countered Mrs. Holt. "It's their father who encourages this kind of behavior."

"I must admit that I did tell Embro to bring you over as fast as possible," chuckled Mr. Holt.

"Well, at least he is obedient," sighed Doc Davis. "Nevertheless, I fear my heart will never be the same." The doctor dramatically put his hand on his chest. "Next time, Plunkett, send Josiah over with a nice, safe wagon for me to ride in and send Embro with your wife on horseback directly to the patient instead."

The doctor then turned and spoke to Mother again.

"Try to relax, Mrs. St. John, while I finish examining you." As the doctor turned, he finally noticed Ginny standing by the window.

"What on earth is she doing here? This is no place for a child."

"I'm not a child!" cried Ginny.

The doctor shook his head and frowned.

"I'm ten years old and I've been to births before!" Ginny didn't care what Doc Davis had to say. She was not going back to the Holt house.

Mr. Holt stepped forward and came to Ginny's defense.

"Ginny . . . uh . . . explained it all to me earlier. She really wants to stay and help. And we told her that she could." Before Doc Davis had a chance to disagree, which it appeared he was going to do, Mr. Holt added, "It's *important* to her."

Doc Davis turned and looked at Mrs. Holt for support. Mrs. Holt looked up at the ceiling. He was clearly outnumbered and not going to get any help from her. The good doctor scowled.

"Alright, she can stay. But in the meantime, while I give her mother a thorough examination, perhaps Virginia and Mr. Holt can go downstairs and boil some water. Virginia, do you know how to boil water?"

"Yes, Doctor Davis, I can boil water."

"Excellent. Then I suggest that you take Mr. Holt downstairs and show him the way to the woodpile. He can get a fire going in the wood stove, and you can make me that cup of tea!"

Ginny and Mr. Holt went down the back stairs to the kitchen. She picked up the big metal pail used for hauling water, and the two of them went out the back door. Ginny pointed to where Papa's woodshed was, a small building next to the side of the house. Mr. Holt hurried over and disappeared inside to gather wood for the wood stove.

The family's well was at the back end of their property, on the other side of Mother's huge tomato garden. Ginny quickly made her way around the tall tomato plants, now heavy with red juicy fruit, to the stone well. A long time ago Papa had planted three maple trees around the well. At night, the well was almost hidden in the shadows of trees. Standing in the dark, Ginny set the silver-colored pail down on the ground and reached up to take off the lid that covered the well. Attached to the well was a thick rope and a small bucket.

Ginny let the bucket fall down into the well, then carefully she hauled it up full of water. She poured the water out into her pail. It would take three buckets full of well water to fill her metal pail. She let the bucket fall again and raised it the second time. As she began to pour out the water into her pail, a person stepped out from behind one of the trees and called her name.

"Ginny."

Ginny screamed.

It was her Papa. She knew he would come back. She just knew it. Her anger was strong, and she wanted to run right over and hit him as hard as Bessie had done. But her fear of him was greater than her anger. She was scared of him being so drunk, so she lifted up the pail of water, threw the water and the pail at him, and then took off running in the opposite direction, back towards the house for Mr. Holt.

Ginny arrived at the back porch the same time Mr. Holt stepped out of the woodshed with his arms full.

"Mr. Holt! Mr. Holt! It's Papa. He's come back! He's come back!" Ginny ran up to Mr. Holt and threw her arms around his waist. Mr. Holt dropped all the wood he had been carrying and held her tightly.

"He came back," cried Ginny wildly, "but I got him, Mr. Holt. I got him good!"

"No, she didn't, Pa," said a voice in the backyard. "She got me instead."

Ginny looked up and saw Elijah standing there dripping wet.

"Oh, Elijah," Ginny exclaimed with embarrassment. "Oh, Elijah, I thought . . . I was sure . . . I'm so sorry."

Mr. Holt looked over at his soaked son and laughed.

"It was all my fault, Pa," said Elijah apologetically. "I sort of sneaked up on her. I just wanted to know if she needed any help."

"Help? Her? Son, that young lady can handle just about anything that comes her way," replied Mr. Holt with a wide grin. "However, since it is in the middle of the night, you might be a gentleman and go back with her to the well. And, seeing that you've just scared the living daylights out of her, I suggest you should be the one to draw the water."

"Yes, Pa," muttered Elijah. "May I go with you, Ginny?"

"Of course, Elijah," said Ginny. Poor Elijah! He looked as pitiful as a drowned cat.

Still chuckling, Mr. Holt gathered up the logs and went into the kitchen, and Elijah humbly walked back to the well with Ginny. Ginny stood back and watched him work. She didn't know Elijah very well. Most of the time that she spent over at the Holts' place was spent with Eliza. Ginny and Eliza didn't play much with the boys except during apple-picking time or at Christmas. She didn't know what to say to him, and she was glad that he finally spoke first.

"How's your ma?" asked Elijah, as he dropped the bucket down for the second time into the deep well.

"I'm not sure," said Ginny truthfully. "They say she's going to be fine, but she looks bad to me. Doc Davis wanted me to leave while he examined her."

"Doc Davis and my ma will see to it that everything turns out alright. You'll see. Between the two of them, I think they've delivered every baby in the county," said Elijah with confidence. He leaned over and poured out the second bucket of water into the pail. Elijah's wet shirt clung to his chest, and Ginny could see the outline of his lean muscles through the white cloth. Like his father and his brothers, he was very strong even though he wasn't very big.

"Thanks for going after the doctor, Elijah," said Ginny gratefully. "I appreciate it."

"You're welcome," replied Elijah as he dropped the bucket down into the well for the last time.

Ginny moved a little closer to where Elijah was standing. He and Embro looked almost exactly the same. Same height. Same curly dark brown hair. Same smile. But Embro had brown eyes. Elijah's eyes were blue. Blue as Mother's prize irises.

Elijah stopped what he was doing and stared at Ginny.

"Something wrong, Ginny?"

"Elijah . . ." Ginny whispered, looking up into those deep blue eyes.

Elijah let go of the rope and let the bucket fall back into the well.

"What is it, Ginny?"

Ginny quickly turned away and looked down into the dark well.

"Elijah, has your pa ever hit your ma?"

Elijah didn't say anything at first. He stood quietly by Ginny's side and fiddled with the rope for a moment.

"No, Ginny, he hasn't," he said solemnly. "And I do believe that he would shoot the person who ever dared it."

His answer made her want to cry again. Elijah reached out and turned Ginny around so that she faced him.

"You've got to be strong, Ginny."

"I'm trying, Elijah, but it's just so hard. I can't help thinking Mother might die, and that makes me want to cry. What would happen to us if she died?" She could feel her tears falling down her cheeks.

"Ginny, do you know the story about Daniel and the lion's den?" asked Elijah seriously.

Elijah's question caught her off guard.

"Well, of course I do," she said defiantly.

"Remember how Daniel was thrown down into the pit, down into the dark, surrounded by the hungry lions, and left alone all night long?"

"I remember."

"Well, that's when the angels came, Ginny. Pa says that's when they always come. God saves them up for the most terrible times in our lives, and then that's when they come."

Elijah surprised Ginny by giving her a big brotherly bear hug.

"I guess that makes you an angel then," said Ginny wiping the tears off her face.

"Yeah, a very wet one," laughed Elijah. He let her go and gave her a big grin like his pa had done.

Ginny smiled. "I guess that makes us friends."

"Friends," agreed Elijah happily. "And don't you worry about your pa coming back and making trouble. Embro and I are standing guard. Embro's watching out front while I keep an eye on things here out back."

They finished drawing the water and returned to the house. Mr. Holt met them at the door.

"Ginny, I was just coming for you. Doc Davis just called down the stairs for you. The baby is coming *now*."

Ginny dashed back inside the house and up the stairs into Mother's room just in time to see her new little sister, Lillian Ruth St. John, come into the world.

3

August 1902

As soon as the baby was born, Mrs. Holt took Ginny firmly by the arm and put her straight to bed. Ginny didn't resist. She was so tired and relieved that she slipped quickly into a deep and restful sleep.

Ginny slept late the next morning. The sun was already high above the maple trees outside her bedroom window when she finally opened her eyes. The smell of freshly-baked biscuits and fried bacon drifted into her room, inviting her to breakfast. Realizing how hungry she was, Ginny jumped out of bed, washed her face and hands, and put on her summer dress.

Before going to breakfast, however, Ginny softly tiptoed down the hallway to Mother's bedroom door and peeked inside. She wanted to make sure everything was alright with Mother. Ginny saw her lying in bed sound asleep. The bruises on her face didn't look as bad as they did last night. Ginny stepped forward into the room slightly to look inside the crib at the foot of the bed. The new baby was also sleeping, wrapped up tight in a pink and white blanket. Ginny blew her new little sister a kiss and then silently slipped out of the room.

"There you are," said Mrs. Holt in greeting as Ginny appeared in the kitchen. "I was getting worried. No child of mine can sleep through the smell of my hot biscuits. I was just about to come up and check on you. Ready for some breakfast?"

"Yes, Ma'am," said Ginny as she sat down at the kitchen table. Mrs. Holt had the table set, and Ginny helped herself to hot biscuits, fried bacon, honey butter, fried apples, cold milk, and freshly-cut slices of tomato.

"How do you want your eggs?" asked Mrs. Holt, standing over the wood stove with two brown eggs in her hand.

"Scram . . . bled, please," said Ginny, with her mouth full of a hot buttered biscuit. Mrs. Holt's biscuits were delicious, and Ginny ate the first one in just two bites.

"You don't have to eat it all at once," declared Mrs. Holt. "We don't want it coming back up." The pan on the stove was red hot, and the eggs cooked quickly. Mrs. Holt stepped over to the table and put the scrambled eggs onto Ginny's plate. Once she had served Ginny, Mrs. Holt sat down at the table and helped herself to a biscuit.

"I checked on Mother before I came down," said Ginny. "She's sleeping now."

"Sleep's the best thing for her today. Sleep and plenty of good food. I'll take her up a plate after we've eaten. I was up just once during the night with your ma and the baby after you went to bed. Your ma is doing fine." Mrs. Holt smiled reassuringly and helped herself to a second biscuit.

"Is the doctor coming back?" asked Ginny.

"Been here already and gone. I'm surprised you slept through that. Your ma didn't like what he had to say and told him so. She's a proud woman, your ma."

"What did Doc Davis say?"

Mrs. Holt took a bite of biscuit and chewed it thoughtfully. "Well, he stood over your ma's bedside, shook his finger at her, and said, 'Louella St. John, you are not to leave this bed for two weeks. Do you hear? Except for taking care of your natural body functions, I don't want you moving a muscle until I say so.'"

"What did Mother say to that?" said Ginny anxiously.

"She said he was talking utter nonsense, that's what she said. She said she had a family to care for and a household to run and that she couldn't rightly do that while lying around in a soft bed all day like the Queen of England. But," said Mrs. Holt with a twinkle in her eye, "I put a stop to all that sort of talk. Would you like some more milk, my dear?"

"No, thank you. What did you do then, Mrs. Holt?"

"Why, I told the two of them that I would be taking care of things here, that's what. I told them that it was already settled. Mr. Holt and Mr. Johnson came by early this morning to milk the cow and tend to the horses, and we worked it out then. The Johnsons have decided to stay an extra week, and Susanna has offered to help Mary Susan take care of the kids and the house while I tend to things here. Not that Mary Susan couldn't do it all by herself, mind you. And Mr. Holt won't complain at having Mr. Johnson help with the harvest. An extra pair of hands is always welcome."

"Oh, Mrs. Holt, you're wonderful," cried Ginny happily. She jumped off her chair and rushed over to give Mrs. Holt a big hug and kiss. Mrs. Holt's face flushed pink with pleasure, and she patted Ginny's face tenderly.

"That's what good neighbors are for, my dear. Besides, I haven't forgotten that your ma practically moved in and lived at my house, cooking and cleaning, when my little Jeremiah was so ill two years ago. Why, I'd consider myself a regular heathen if I turned my back on her now and didn't return the favor." Mrs. Holt stood up and started clearing off the table. Ginny got her plate and cup and put them in the sink.

"What about Willie and Bessie?"

"Oh, they'll stay over at my house," said Mrs. Holt as she started washing the dishes. "Susanna's girls love tending children, and I suspect they're already fighting over Willie about now. They'll spoil him rotten, you'll see. Hand me that plate, Ginny. Mind you, there'll be no need to tend Bessie. She and Kathleen will go off and tend to each other from sun up to sun down. As long as someone remembers to feed them once in a while and to wash and put them to bed, they'll be just fine."

Ginny picked up a dish towel and started drying the dishes as she listened to Mrs. Holt.

"You'll stay here with me, of course. I wouldn't have it any other way."

"Can Eliza stay over, too?" asked Ginny.

"I'm afraid not, child. Eliza started sneezing something fierce last night, and I believe she's getting her usual summer cold. It seems to happen every August. The last thing we want to do is bring a sick child into this house. Your new little sister came early, Ginny. She's very tiny. We need to take extra care in keeping her well till she gets a little bigger."

Ginny frowned at this news. She was going to really miss being able to play with her best friend.

"There's plenty of work for us to do," consoled Mrs. Holt. "Besides looking out for your ma and your new baby sister, we need to start working in your ma's garden. The tomatoes are looking mighty ripe and ready for canning. We better pickle those cucumbers, too, before they take over the backyard. Where does your ma keep her canning jars?"

"Downstairs in the cellar," said Ginny.

"Well, then, I think your job today will be to bring all those jars upstairs and get them washed good and clean. As soon as Elijah gets back, I'll send him into town to buy new lids and rings at the store. We can spend tomorrow pickling and putting up the tomatoes."

"Elijah was here?" asked Ginny in surprise.

Mrs. Holt turned and smiled at Ginny. "He came by this morning with his pa. Mr. Holt has his hands full with the corn crop, so he suggested that Elijah come and help out with the livestock and chores here. I've made Elijah a bed on the living room sofa. He'll stay with us."

"Where is Elijah now?" asked Ginny.

"Oh, didn't I say? I sent him down to the chicken coop to gather the eggs."

Ginny dropped the dish towel on the floor and stared at Mrs. Holt.

"Oh, no," muttered Ginny.

"What's the matter, my dear?" said Mrs. Holt with a puzzled look on her face.

"Excuse me, Mrs. Holt, but I've got to go rescue him," said Ginny as she started running towards the kitchen door.

"But Ginny, he doesn't need any help. He's gathered eggs a million times," called Mrs. Holt after her.

"Not our eggs!" said Ginny.

At Mother's request, Papa had built the chicken coop on the far side of their property, at the bottom of the hill on the other side of the barn. Mother wanted it there because she said she didn't like listening to the sound of chickens clucking all day long while she worked in the kitchen. Got on her nerves, she said. Consequently, due to the distance, it took Ginny several minutes at a dead run to reach the chicken coop.

It was as she imagined. She found Elijah standing at the gate to the chicken coop. There were feathers everywhere. In front of him, a large, angry rooster blocked the entrance to the coop. Elijah had his hands on his hips, yelling something ridiculous at the rooster, and the rooster flapped his large wings in defiance, loudly answering him back.

"Stand back, Elijah, or Mr. Jefferson will scratch you!" yelled Ginny in warning.

Elijah turned towards Ginny, and she saw several long red marks on the left side of his face.

"He already did," said Elijah angrily.

Ginny quickly pulled her white lace handkerchief out of her dress pocket and gently held it up to Elijah's face to help stop the bleeding.

"I'm so sorry he hurt you. Mother says Mr. Jefferson is a hundred percent plain mean, that's all."

"She's absolutely right." Elijah frowned and pointed into the chicken coop. "Mr. Jefferson? Who in blue blazes named *that* after a president?"

Ginny winced. Curse little sisters. "Bessie did. She read in her history book that Thomas Jefferson was a redhead and thought it would be a good name for our very red-headed rooster."

"Hot-tempered, rude, red-headed monster, you mean. Well, someone should sit down and read the rest of that history book to that bird. Perhaps he would learn that his namesake was known to be a gentle statesman and diplomat."

Ginny grinned at this and stepped back to look at Elijah's face. He looked about as funny as he did the night before, standing there all flustered with chicken feathers in his hair and those scratches on his cheek. Ginny decided that she was going to like having Elijah as a friend.

"It's stopped bleeding now. We'll get your mother to put some liniment on it when we get back to the house," said Ginny. She turned and bent over to pick up a long, black stick that was lying on the ground next to the coop.

"Now let's get those eggs."

"You're not going in there," asked Elijah startled, with his eyes opening wide.

"Of course, silly. I do it all the time. Watch."

Ginny lifted the big black stick and rushed into the coop, waving the stick at the rooster while making a loud, obnoxious sound. The rooster flew up in the air and began hitting the stick with his wings, but Ginny kept poking the stick at him and making her angry sounds. Eventually, she had him backed into the corner of the coop, and the old bird finally gave up and landed quietly on the ground. Ginny dropped the stick and headed towards the hen house. Elijah cautiously followed her.

"What was that awful noise you made?" he asked laughing.

Ginny giggled. "I call it my Indian war cry. It works every time."

Elijah grabbed Ginny by the arm and turned her around to face him.

"Pa was right about you," he said in awe. "You can do anything."

*   *   *

During the next two weeks, Mrs. Holt and Elijah kept Ginny very busy and very happy. Each day started with Ginny and Mrs. Holt getting up early. Ginny would attend to Mother and her new sister, Lily, first thing while Mrs. Holt got the breakfast ready. Mother let Ginny bathe and dress Lily before Mother nursed her. Elijah would go out and milk the cow and feed the other livestock. Then Ginny, Elijah, and Mrs. Holt would sit down and have a wonderful breakfast together and plan what work needed to be done for that day.

Mrs. Holt had Ginny and Elijah do most of the work harvesting Mother's vegetable garden. During the first week, it took them four full days to get all the tomatoes picked and canned. Together, they succeeded in putting up ninety-six quarts of tomatoes, which Mother said would surely last them through the winter. Next, they picked the cucumbers and onions, and Mrs. Holt showed Ginny how to make bread-and-butter pickles. Elijah cut wood and kept the wood stove burning hot while Ginny and Mrs. Holt chopped the cucumbers and onions and prepared the pickling brine.

The second week Mrs. Holt handed Ginny and Elijah two milking stools and two large metal buckets and sent them out to pick the beans. The black-eyed peas were easiest, since they were bushy plants. The beans grew right on top of the plants. It was the lima beans and string beans that were hard to pick. In order to pick them, Ginny and Elijah had to sit on the milking stools and bend over because these beans grew underneath the bushes. They picked during the morning and then shelled in the afternoon while sitting on the front porch. Ginny and Elijah had contests to see who could shell a bucket of beans the fastest. Elijah always won with the green beans, but Ginny put him to shame when it came to the limas.

The only time Ginny didn't feel happy was in the late afternoons just before suppertime. This was usually a time when she was alone, because Elijah had to go tend the livestock again. Mrs. Holt insisted that Ginny should rest before suppertime and wouldn't hear of Ginny helping her in the kitchen. Ginny would first go upstairs and check on Mother. Then, cleaning up after working outside all day, she would sit in the swing while waiting for supper.

It was then and only then she would think about Papa. She would sit in the swing, just like she did when she was a little girl, and watch the road in front of her. She knew exactly what she was doing. She was waiting for him to come home.

No one spoke to her about Papa. Mrs. Holt didn't mention him. Elijah didn't talk about him. Nor did Mother talk about him.

Was she still angry?

Yes, but truth be told she wanted him to come back. She wanted him to come home and be her papa again.

The two weeks went by quickly, and the day finally came when Doc Davis said Mother could get out of bed. Mrs. Holt decided they should celebrate with a big cookout at the house before the Johnsons left and before she went back to her own home. Mother gratefully got out of bed, but she was still very weak. Elijah moved Mother's rocking chair into the kitchen, and Mother enjoyed talking to Mrs. Holt while Mrs. Holt cooked. She cooked a huge smoked ham and a big pot of black-eyed peas. Mother was able to sit up to the table and cut up a vegetable salad with fresh lettuce and tomatoes, and Mrs. Holt made apple dumplings. The Johnsons and the Holts arrived that evening with hot corn on the cob, stewed tomatoes, corn pudding, hot rolls, peach pie, and a gigantic watermelon.

The adults stayed inside and ate in the kitchen while all the children ate outside on the front porch. Bessie and Kathleen sat together in the swing, sharing their plates and their little girl secrets. Willie sat between the Johnson girls, and they took turns feeding and fussing over him. He never looked happier.

Ginny sat next to Elijah and Eliza on the front steps. Ginny was so glad to see Eliza and told her all about the past two weeks. Eliza laughed when Elijah told her how Ginny had thrown the well water at him. Eliza said she would have done the same thing.

It was a wonderful day, and Ginny didn't want this special time with Mrs. Holt and Elijah to be over. She wondered if Elijah would continue to be her friend. As the time came for the Holts to leave, Elijah told her what she wanted to hear.

"See you tomorrow, Ginny," he said smiling.

"You'll be back?" she asked.

"Hey, we've still got two rows of lima beans left to pick, and you know I wouldn't miss that for the world. Someday, I'm going to beat you at shelling limas, you know." He looked up and grinned at her.

"That's what he thinks," said Eliza. "We'll show him, won't we, Ginny?"

Ginny laughed and said goodbye to her friends.

Ginny went to bed early that night, happy until she thought about Papa. Two weeks had passed, and there had been no word of him. Nothing. She lay in her bed and pulled the sheets up over her head. He wasn't coming back. She just knew it. Life would be very different at her house from now on. Things would change.

Everything changed dramatically the very next day. Ginny, Eliza, and Elijah were out picking beans in the vegetable garden when Mother came outside.

"Elijah," she said, "would you do me a favor and hitch up the horses to the wagon. I need to ride over to your place."

Ginny jumped up excitedly. "Are you alright, Mother?"

"Heavens, I'm feeling fit as a fiddle," said Mother. "I'm still a bit weak, but I can manage a ride over to the Holt place. I just want to discuss something with Mrs. Holt, that's all. I shouldn't be gone more than an hour. Could you watch the baby and Willie, Ginny, till I get back?"

"Yes, Mother," replied Ginny willingly.

"I'll help, too," offered Eliza.

"Thank you, Eliza. That would be lovely."

"Do you want me to drive you over?" asked Elijah sincerely.

"No, thank you all the same. I only had a baby, Elijah, I am not an invalid."

Ginny and Eliza went into the house to babysit, and Elijah went out to the barn to hitch up the wagon. Mother rode away. As Elijah came inside, Willie announced that he was starving and demanded a snack. Eliza got Willie's hands and face washed while Ginny sliced pieces of leftover peach pie for everybody, which they took out on the front porch to eat. After they finished their pie, Elijah and Eliza sat on the front steps and played checkers, and Bessie played with her dolls. Willie sat in Elijah's lap and watched the game. Ginny sat in the rocking chair holding Lily in her lap and wondered what in the world Mother had to talk to Mrs. Holt about.

Soon Mother rode up in the front yard and carefully got herself out of the wagon. Elijah got up to take the wagon to the barn and unhitch the horses. He left as Mother climbed up the front steps and sat down in the rocking chair next to Ginny.

"Children, gather round. I've got some exciting news for you." Willie immediately got up and crawled onto Mother's lap, and Bessie cuddled up next to Mother's shoulder. Ginny stayed in her chair and rocked.

"I have decided to sell the farm," announced Mother.

"Oh, no!" exclaimed Eliza loudly. She rushed over and grabbed Ginny and held her tight.

"Sell our farm?" cried Bessie in disbelief. Ginny said nothing.

"That's what I said. Now, listen carefully, children. While lying in bed the last few days, I've done a lot of thinking. The country is no place for a single woman to raise a family all by herself. It's true that I've got good neighbors, but I can't depend on them for everything. They can't leave their fields to come plow mine nor can they run the farm for me."

"You don't think Papa will come back?" said Ginny softly.

"No, Ginny," sighed Mother. "I don't think he will. Your papa is a very proud man, just about as proud as I am. Truthfully, I still love him, and I reckon he still loves me. But what he did was wrong, and he knows it. And I know it. He can't come back, and that's that. I believe that he still loves you children with all his heart. Don't you ever doubt that for a moment."

Did he? Ginny wondered. Or did he love his whiskey more?

Mother continued. "So we'll have to get along as best we can without him. I went over today and offered to sell the farm to the

Holts. Our property lies next to theirs, and they can use the land for their horses and their orchards. I mentioned that Josiah is getting married this Christmas and that this house would make a good home for him and Sarah. The Holts liked the idea a lot and agreed to buy it."

"But, Mother, Mother," exclaimed Bessie, "where will we live?"

"The city is the place for us, Bess. I've thought hard and long about it. There's plenty of opportunities for us in the city. I can take in washing and sewing and I can fix hot meals for factory workers. There's the shoe factory and the sewing factory there. I figure with the money I can get from selling the farm and the money I could earn in the city, I'll be able to support this family all by myself."

A question rose in Ginny's mind that made her suddenly stop rocking her chair.

"What city are we moving to, Mother," she asked anxiously. "Roanoke? Richmond?"

Mother took in a deep breath and bit her lip. "No, Ginny. I've decided that we will move to Lynchburg."

Mother might as well have said they would move to the moon. Ginny couldn't believe it. Never, ever, in her wildest dreams, would Mother pick Lynchburg.

"Lynchburg? But, Mother, you said you'd never go back to Lynchburg ever again, not after 'The Parade.' Don't you remember?"

Mother got up out of the rocking chair and brushed off her skirt. "Actually, I believe that I said that I would never go to downtown Lynchburg again, Ginny. And I won't. I'll never set foot on Main Street or Court Street or Church Street. You just wait and see."

4

November 1902

Mother moved the family to Lynchburg before Thanksgiving.

They moved into a nice two-story house on Wadsworth Street. This house was a lot smaller than their country house, but Mother said she didn't mind at all. She said it would be a lot easier to keep clean. Like their old house in the country, there were three bedrooms. Ginny shared a room with Bessie, and Mother had Willie and Lily share her room. The third bedroom Mother made into a sewing room.

Mother immediately found work to support the family. The hosiery mill was nearby, and Mother set up a business fixing hot lunches for the hosiery mill workers. She would get up early every morning to start her baking and cooking. Ginny helped to tend Lily and Willie while Mother cooked. Ginny really enjoyed the morning time that she spent with her new little sister. Lily was a very good-natured baby. She hardly fussed at all.

At lunchtime, Mother and Willie would fill up Willie's wagon with the meals and then take them down to the mill. Willie soon became fast friends with the mill workers, and sometimes they gave him a penny tip or a piece of rock candy. On such occasions, Mother said Willie would skip happily all the way home.

Mother also decided to take in sewing and to raise chickens and cows. Raising livestock provided the needed eggs and milk and cream for both her family and her business. Ginny was given the job of collecting eggs, and Bessie was given the job of milking the cows. Ginny thought collecting the eggs here was pretty easy compared to what she was used to in the country, and she thought of Elijah every day when she gathered the eggs. She missed her friends so much. She didn't miss Mr. Jefferson. Mother had given him to Josiah and Sarah as a wedding present. Some present.

Ginny did not return to school. She was needed at home to tend and to help Mother around the house. Ginny didn't mind leaving school very much. She had finished the fifth grade, and that was more schooling than Mother or Papa had ever had. She could read and write and figure with numbers. What more schooling did a woman need? Mother did send Bessie back to school, much to Bessie's dismay. Bessie said she wanted to stay home and help Mother cook the mill lunches. Ginny thought Bessie just wanted to stay home was all.

When they left the country, Mrs. Holt had promised to write their family faithfully every week, describing in detail all the news of home. Mrs. Holt was president of the Methodist Women's Sewing Circle at the church, so she was in a position to know just about everyone's business. Like clockwork, Mrs. Holt's letters began arriving as promised, and Mother would save each precious letter to read to the family on Sundays after supper. Eliza began writing short letters to Ginny and sent them along with Mrs. Holt's letters. Elijah never wrote though, and Ginny worried that his promise of friendship had been short lived. But Mother assured her that it meant nothing.

Right away, Ginny and her family made new friends in Lynchburg. The Whittens were their next-door neighbors on Wadsworth Street. Mr. Whitten was a very quiet man who hardly spoke at all. When he did speak, it was usually in one- or two-word sentences. So far, Ginny had only heard him say things like "Morning," "Evening," "Yep," "Nope," "I declare," "Imagine that," "I reckon," "Praise God," and "Hell fire." Ginny noticed that he only said "Hell fire" when Mrs. Whitten wasn't nearby. Ginny figured Mrs. Whitten didn't approve of it. When the Whittens visited, Mr.

Whitten usually sat back in the corner of the living room in Mother's rocking chair and just listened.

In contrast, it seemed to Ginny that Mrs. Whitten never stopped talking. Ginny thought she must wake up each day with her mouth open, ready to say something. Mrs. Whitten had opinions on everything and loved expressing them. She especially took pleasure in telling tragic stories about her relatives. Three times Ginny had heard the story about Mrs. Whitten's parents and how they died in a big flu epidemic. The Whittens lived alone in their little red brick house. They had four grown children and lots of grandchildren who lived in different parts of Virginia.

At first, Ginny was very nervous about moving to the city, but December was full of celebrations that made the transition easier. Ginny turned eleven on December 9, and Mother had a wonderful birthday party for her. The Whittens were invited, and the entire Holt family came up from the country for her birthday and an early Christmas visit. Mrs. Whitten and Mother surprised Ginny with a beautiful new dress made of a shiny green material. The color reminded her of the dark pine trees of home. Mother had bought the fabric, and Mrs. Whitten had done the sewing secretly over at her house. They made Ginny try the dress on and show it off.

"Oh, how darling you look," exclaimed Mrs. Whitten excitedly. "That shade of green makes your eyes sparkle. Doesn't that dress make her eyes sparkle, sweetheart?"

"Yep," said Mr. Whitten.

"That dress makes me think of a dress my grandmother once had, a gorgeous green silk with a fancy lace collar. Her father had to go to Atlanta once on a business trip and had brought it back for her. That was just before the Civil War. He became a confederate soldier and was killed one week before the surrender. Just one week. Such a tragic loss! Left seven children fatherless and penniless. Grandmother struggled hard, but she didn't lose any of those children. Not a one! They all grew to adulthood."

"Praise God," added Mr. Whitten.

"Oh, that dress was a beautiful thing. Grandmother didn't have much after losing Grandfather, but she never would part with that dress. No, sir! When I was a little girl, Grandmother let me play dress-up in it once. Oh, I felt like a fairy princess wearing that ball gown. It's sad we don't have fancy balls like they used to have back then. Don't you think so, sweetheart?"

"Yep," said Mr. Whitten.

"She left the dress to me when she died. I still have it. It's up in the attic in Grandmother's cedar chest. I'll have to find it and show it to you sometime, Ginny. Promise you'll come over tomorrow, and we'll get it out. Turn around, dear. You know, I do believe your dress is the exact shade of green of Grandmother's ball gown. Don't you think so, sweetheart?"

"I reckon," said Mr. Whitten.

Besides the new dress, Ginny received a new black ribbon for her hair from Bessie, and Willie proudly gave her a piece of red penny candy he had picked out all by himself. The Holts gave Ginny a box of fancy writing papers that were decorated with pink roses. Mrs. Holt said it was a purely selfish gift. She said she wanted Ginny to write to her often. Ginny promised that she would. Mother baked an apple spice cake for the occasion, and Mr. Whitten and Mr. Holt made vanilla ice cream.

The best birthday present of all was seeing Eliza and Elijah. After the birthday party, she took them for a walk to show them around the neighborhood. They walked down past the hosiery mill and then up past the old fire station to Miller Park. Ginny showed them a large two-story brick building that stood on one side of the park. This was Miller Park School where Bessie attended. Right next to the school building was the library, a small, round, brick building with lots of glass windows. Ginny and Elijah put their faces up against a pane of glass and looked inside. Eliza was afraid to do it, for fear of being caught. The library was full of books, and this really impressed Elijah. He had never seen a library before.

After seeing the library, the three friends sat down to rest on a bench right next to a baseball field.

"Do they play real baseball games here?" asked Elijah anxiously. It was clear to Ginny that he had never seen one of those either.

"Oh, yes," said Ginny assuredly. "Mr. Whitten told us all about it. He says there's a game here every Saturday during the summer. He's promised to take me and Bessie and Willie to some games."

"Wow!" replied Elijah excitedly. "Maybe Pa and Ma would let me come up and go with you!"

"I'd rather go swimming," observed Eliza, looking across the park towards the public swimming pool. It was a large square cement pool with a painted blue bottom. Ginny and Eliza and Elijah had walked past it on the way to the library.

"I'll ask Mrs. Holt if both of you can come up next summer," said Ginny happily. "We can swim and go to the games and shop at the stores. You just can't imagine the stores here in Lynchburg. Mrs. Whitten took me and Bessie downtown last Saturday to go shopping with her."

Elijah wasn't too excited about shopping, but it sparked a real interest in Eliza, almost as much as the prospect of swimming in a cement pool. The three friends spent the rest of their day together making plans for the following summer.

Christmas came quickly. Ginny nearly fainted when Mother invited Uncle Abraham and his family over for Christmas dinner. There had been no word from Papa since he left last summer, and Mother didn't let them talk much about it. What would they say around Papa's brother? Would they talk about Papa? Ginny worried about this for days. On Christmas morning, Uncle Abraham and his family arrived early with armfuls of presents and food. Everything went along like normal, like nothing was wrong at all, until Uncle Abraham said the blessing on the food.

Willie opened his eyes, looked up at his uncle, and exclaimed, "He sounds like Papa."

There was a pause. A long silent pause. Ginny looked immediately at Mother, who kept her hands folded for prayer on the table and her eyes cast downward.

"I guess I do, Willie," said Uncle Abraham finally.

Willie put a big spoonful of mashed potatoes in his mouth, swallowed, then asked, "Where is my papa?"

"Willie, be quiet," said Bessie hastily. "Here, have some cranberries. You like them."

"I think," said Uncle Abraham seriously, "that now would be a good time for me to say a little something about your papa. Louella, may I?"

Ginny held her breath as Mother nodded her head.

Uncle Abraham spoke to the family. "After your papa left home, he came here to live with us for a while. He was very sad and very sick, children, and we did our best to take care of him. Now he's feeling a bit better and has gone down to Campbell County to live for a while. I got a letter from him just last week. He started working for the railroad and plans to stay there until spring. He hopes to buy some land and get back to tobacco farming."

A few second passed, then Mother spoke.

"The house and farm were in my name, Abraham. They were a gift from my father, and I had every right to sell them. They were mine, and I owe William nothing."

"I know, Louella."

"He told you?"

"Yes, he did."

"Well, I didn't want you to think that I had cheated him."

Uncle Abraham reached across the table and put his hand over Mother's folded hands.

"I have no hard feelings against you, Louella."

"Thank you, Abraham."

"I know that William misses you and the children very much, but I understand that things need to be the way they are."

That was all that was said about Papa. Then Christmas dinner and presents were enjoyed by everyone. Uncle Abraham and his family left the house that evening with smiles and kisses and good wishes. Ginny didn't say anything about it to Mother, but she could tell Mother was very glad to hear that Papa was doing better.

The Whittens invited the family to celebrate New Year's Day with them. Mrs. Whitten's oldest son and his small family were there visiting. They had a little boy named David who was the same age as Willie, and the two boys spent the whole day playing together.

Three days after New Year's, Willie woke up covered with red blistered spots on his arms, legs, face, and stomach. Mother took one look at him and declared that Willie had the chicken pox. This didn't seem to upset Mother too much, and Willie didn't feel very bad at all. He just complained a lot about the itching. But Mother did get awful worried when she noticed that Lily developed some spots on her face and arms the next day. Lily cried all day long, and Mother had trouble getting her to nurse. The day after that, Lily developed a fever and wouldn't eat at all. That evening, Mother sent Ginny over to get Mrs. Whitten for help. Mr. and Mrs. Whitten came immediately.

"Strip her down to just her diapers," ordered Mrs. Whitten as she rolled up her sleeves at the kitchen sink. "We need to start sponging her off with tepid water. That will help cool her off. It's the best thing in the world to break a fever."

Mr. Whitten looked at Lily and shook his head and spoke a complete sentence.

"I'm going for the doctor," he said.

He put his hat and coat on and went out the front door. Mrs. Whitten and Mother looked at each other, both astonished and very worried. This scared Bessie, and she started to cry. Mother gave Lily to Mrs. Whitten and took Bessie into the living room to calm her down. Then Mother asked Ginny if she would take Bessie and Willie upstairs and put them to bed.

When Ginny returned to the kitchen, Mother and Mrs. Whitten were standing over the kitchen table, working on Lily, washing off her arms, legs, and body with cool dish rags. Lily didn't seem to mind. She just lay there on her blanket, awake but very still. Lily's skin was breaking out with more rash. She looked just awful. Mother then tried to get her to drink a bottle filled with some water, but Lily wouldn't take it.

"I wish she would cry," said Mother in a whisper. Mother's voice shook.

"Courage, Louella, courage," said Mrs. Whitten wringing out a rag and handing it to Mother. "The Lord will provide. Now, give me that basin. I'm going to get some fresh water."

Mr. Whitten soon came back with the doctor, a tall, thin young man with dark glasses who introduced himself as Dr. Watkins. Mother described the baby's symptoms as the doctor examined Lily.

"She's extremely ill, Mrs. St. John," said the doctor solemnly when he finished looking at the baby. "The threat here isn't the illness so much as it is dehydration, and you know it doesn't take very long for an infant to become dehydrated. Her fever isn't dangerously high, but in this case, it seems to be enough to make her somewhat lethargic. It's very important that you continue to try to get fluids into her. If you can't get her to drink anything in the next twenty-four hours, I'm afraid the chances of her of surviving may not be very good. And, I must warn you, if she survives," he added gravely, "her skin will probably be badly scarred. This rash is running very deep into her skin. I've never seen such a bad case of chicken pox in an infant this young."

The doctor gathered up his coat and hat and prepared to leave. "Unfortunately, there isn't any medicine I can give you to cure this. The best thing we can do is wait it out. Keep up with the sponge baths and keep trying to get her to drink clear fluids. If you can get her fever to break, she'll feel more like eating. I'll come back tomorrow morning as soon as I can."

Mr. Whitten saw the doctor out. Mother sat down at the table and began to cry. Seeing this tore Ginny up inside. Mother rarely cried. She went over to Mother and put her arms around her and held her.

"Don't cry, Mother. Lily will be alright."

"Listen to the child, Louella," encouraged Mrs. Whitten. "You've got to keep your spirits up."

"I'm just so tired," Mother said softly as she pulled away from Ginny and wiped her eyes. "What's going to happen to us next?"

Mrs. Whitten picked Lily up off of the table and started rocking her gently in her arms.

"Whatever happens, Louella, you won't be alone. We'll be right here beside you. Isn't that right, sweetheart?"

Mr. Whitten sat down at the table and put his strong arm around Mother and said in the kindest voice, "Yep."

Despite Ginny's protests, Mother sent her up to bed. Ginny insisted on staying, but Mother refused. She said she needed Ginny to get a good night's sleep so that she could cook the mill workers' lunches and take them with Willie down to the factory the next day. Ginny went upstairs, put on her flannel nightgown, and reluctantly crawled into bed. She lay there for a few moments, awake and very warm underneath several heavy quilts while looking out her bedroom window.

Snow was beginning to fall. Ginny thought about last summer. Elijah had told her that the angels would come. As she drifted off to sleep, Ginny asked God to send them.

5

January 1903

Ginny awoke as the morning sun began to rise and cast its white winter light across her bedroom. As she pushed back the thick layers of quilts, she sensed something was queer. How odd. Her room was warm. Usually, Mother filled up the stove with wood at night just before going to bed, but the fire would go out sometime during the night and the house would be very cold in the morning. Sometimes, it was so cold in her room in the mornings that Ginny could actually see her breath as she jumped out of bed and hurriedly dressed.

Ginny slowly and sleepily got out of her bed, pondering and enjoying the warmth of the hardwood floor beneath her feet. Then she remembered. Lily was ill. Mother and the Whittens had stayed up all night with Lily. That's why it was so warm in her room. They had kept the wood stove burning.

Reluctantly, Ginny put on her dark winter dress and went downstairs, afraid that she would find matters worse. Perhaps Lily had even died during the night. Happily, Ginny found Mother sitting in the living room rocking chair, feeding Lily. The baby was awake and drinking. Ginny raced to Mother and knelt down beside her.

"Oh, Mother. Lily's eating."

"Yes, she is," said Mother through a weary yawn. "The crisis has passed, I think, but Lily is still a very sick little girl." Ginny held out her hands, and Mother gave Lily to her. Ginny kissed Lily's red face and hugged her gently. She was so happy. Lily was still alive.

Mother undid the brown ribbon that tied up her braided hair and shook her head to let it down. Her long black hair fell in thick waves across her shoulders and down into her lap. She rubbed her tired eyes and yawned again.

"Did you sleep well, Ginny?" she asked.

"Very well, Mother. Did you get any sleep?"

"A little. Lily's fever broke around three this morning, and she seemed to perk up right away. I got her to drink some then, and then she went right to sleep. Mrs. Whitten insisted that I lie down on the sofa and nap for an hour, which I gladly did. The Whittens woke me up about five o'clock and then they went home." Mother got up out of the rocking chair and stretched. "God bless our dear neighbors. We seem to always be blessed with them, don't we, Ginny? Thank the good Lord above for Mrs. Whitten's inexhaustible tongue. Her endless talking kept me awake and kept my spirits up."

Ginny looked at Lily, who was now sleeping soundly in her arms.

"Will she completely recover now?"

"I hope so. But we're not quite out of the woods yet, I'm afraid. She's still very weak, and her rash is worse. I've never seen such a rash on a child. Her skin is almost raw on her little arms. But I have hope now, Ginny, hope that I didn't have yesterday. All we can do now is take each day as it comes and see what happens."

For the most part, the rest of the morning seemed like any other morning. Mother made breakfast, got Bessie off to school, then she took Lily up to her room so they both could rest. Ginny tended Willie while cooking the mill lunches. The doctor came by to check on Lily late that morning, and he was more hopeful about her recovery. He brought an ointment he had made for Mother to put on Lily's skin. It would help reduce the itching. At lunchtime, Mother helped Ginny pack up the lunches, and Ginny took Willie with her down to the hosiery mill to deliver them. Willie enjoyed walking in the snow. When they returned, Mother put Willie down for his afternoon nap, and then she and Ginny sat down in the living room to do some sewing.

There was a unexpected knock on the front door.

"Good gracious, who could that be?" asked Mother in surprise.

"Most likely it's the Whittens coming to check on Lily," suggested Ginny as she put down the quilt square she had been working on and got up to answer to door.

Ginny found two men standing on their front porch. One man was quite tall and thin and had thick white hair. The other man was shorter and dark haired, and had very light blue eyes. The tall man smiled at Ginny, took off his hat, and said, "Good afternoon, young lady."

"Good afternoon," said Ginny warily. She turned around and looked back at Mother, who put down her sewing and got up from her rocking chair to come to the door.

"Good afternoon," she said politely. "I am Mrs. St. John. What can I do for you, gentlemen?"

The tall man answered, "Sister St. John, we are missionaries of the Church of Jesus Christ of Latter-day Saints. We are representatives of the Lord Jesus Christ, and we have been called to share the gospel in this area. My companion and I were walking through your neighborhood, and we felt impressed to stop at this house."

Mother gave these strangers an odd look.

"I see. Well, my home is always open to good Christian men and women. Are you hungry, gentlemen?" she asked sincerely. "You're welcome to come inside and rest awhile. It must be awfully hard to travel in ice and snow like this. I'd be happy to fix you a plate of food, if that's what you want."

The tall man smiled at Mother and shook his head.

"You misunderstand, Sister St. John. We are not here seeking for charity. We are here to serve you. As I said before, my companion and I were impressed to stop at this house."

Mother didn't respond to this. She just stared at the man. He stared right back. Ginny noticed there was a kind of glow about this strange man, especially in his face. She saw it in his eyes. Whoever he was, he was not a bad man. There was a warm feeling inside Ginny's chest just being near him.

The dark-haired man stepped forward and spoke. "As Elders in Israel, we are given the priesthood power to give blessings. Are there any in need in this household, Sister St. John? Are there any sick among you?"

Tears suddenly came to Mother's eyes. She reached out and took hold of Ginny's hand and held it tight.

"Yes, gentlemen, there is. My baby daughter is very ill. The fact is we were up all night last night with her, trying to get her fever to break. We were very afraid that we would lose her, but the Lord has spared her life. Her fever broke early this morning, but she is still very weak."

"May we see her?" asked the tall man humbly.

Mother opened the screen door and invited them inside. She asked for their coats and hats, and she gave the clothing to Ginny to put on the sofa. Then Mother, the strangers, and Ginny went back into the kitchen. Lily was there sleeping in the white wicker basket. Mother picked her up and showed her to the strangers.

"Sister St. John, why don't you sit down here in this chair and hold your daughter in your lap. That's good. Now, Sister, my companion is going to anoint your daughter's head with olive oil, and then I shall give her a blessing."

Ginny stood close to the kitchen table and watched as the dark-haired man knelt by Mother and opened a small glass vial of oil. He dropped several drops of oil on Lily's forehead. Carefully, he took his finger and rubbed the oil in a small circle over Lily's mottled scalp, then he placed both of his hands on Lily's head.

"What is the full name of this child?" he asked.

"Lillian Ruth St. John."

The dark-haired man bent his head and began to pray.

"Lillian Ruth St. John, by the power of the Holy Melchizedek priesthood which I hold and in the name of Jesus Christ, I anoint your head with oil . . ."

Ginny listened quietly as the man prayed.

The other man then knelt down by Mother. Both men placed their hands on Lily's head, and the tall man said another prayer. He said that Lily was a special spirit daughter of Heavenly Father and that she had come to earth at this particular time for a purpose. He promised Lily that she would live, and in the name of Jesus Christ, he commanded the illness to leave her body.

There were plenty of tears running down Ginny's face when the blessing was over, and that funny feeling of warmth inside came back again. The strangers stood up and said they must be on their way. Mother offered to give them some food, but they declined. Mother thanked them for the blessing, got up and put Lily back into the basket, then she and Ginny followed the men to the living room. Ginny handed the strangers their coats and hats. The dark-haired man shook Mother's hand and then shook Ginny's hand.

The tall man took Mother's hand and held it tightly.

"Sister St. John, do you own a bible?"

This question startled Mother.

"Why, yes, of course I do," she said.

The tall man let go of Mother's hand, reached inside his coat pocket, and pulled out a small dark book. He handed it to Mother.

"Sister St. John, I'd like to leave this book with you. It is a very precious book. It is a sacred record of the Lord's dealings with an ancient people who once lived on this American continent. It is a book much like the Bible, for it contains the fullness of the gospel of Jesus Christ and bears witness of Christ. I'd like for your baby girl to have it."

"Thank you kindly," said Mother. She opened the book and read the title aloud.

"The Book of . . . Mor . . . mon."

The strangers stepped outside on the front porch and said goodbye. Mother stood in the doorway and waved, watching as the men went down the porch steps and walked away.

"What a strange coincidence," said Mother softly to Ginny, as she closed the door, "for those men to show up today of all days."

"Mrs. Whitten says a coincidence is a wink from God," remarked Ginny.

"Mrs. Whitten says a lot of things," said Mother smiling, taking Ginny into her arms and giving her an affectionate hug.

"May I see the book?" asked Ginny.

Mother handed to book to Ginny, and Ginny sat down on the sofa to look at it.

"It's time for Lily to eat," announced Mother. "I'll go feed her, then I'll get supper started. You can stay here and read. How about some of my special vegetable soup?" Ginny said she would like that. Mother went back to the kitchen. Ginny opened the book and began turning the pages. It was a very old book. The inside page said it was a second edition printing. Ginny was disappointed that there weren't any pictures to look at, but there were funny names on the pages to read, words like "Nephi" and "Mosiah" and "Helaman."

Ginny heard Mother cry out.

"Oh, dear Lord!"

Ginny dropped the book on the floor and ran back to the kitchen as fast as she could. Something awful had happened to Lily. Something terrible. Ginny feared the worst. Lily was dead.

Ginny found Mother holding Lily in her arms, rocking back and forth in her chair, weeping.

"Mother, what's wrong? What's wrong?" cried Ginny. Still sobbing, Mother held Lily out for Ginny to see. Lily's eyes were wide open, bright and shining. Lily smiled up at Ginny and made a soft babbling noise. Ginny stared in disbelief. All of the scabs, the scars, the raw blisters, the ugly red marks that had been on Lily's face, arms, legs, and body were completely gone. Her skin was whole, as pure and white as an angel's wing.

Angels.

Those men weren't real men, thought Ginny excitedly. They were angels. They were real angels in disguise. What Elijah had said about Daniel and the lion's den had come true. I prayed for them, and God sent angels to help.

Mother's hands were shaking as she dried her face off with a dish towel.

"Virginia St. John, I want you to go find those men. I don't care if it takes the rest of the afternoon. Put your coat and hat on and go search outside until you find them. Check the neighbors' houses. Go up to the park. Check at the fire station. Go all the way down Fort Avenue if you have to. Look everywhere," she ordered in a trembling voice. "Just bring them back to me, Virginia, do you hear?"

Ginny rushed to do as Mother asked. She hurriedly put on her coat and hat, then she slipped on her boots. She dashed outside and down the porch steps. The snow had begun falling again, and a soft breeze was blowing the flakes around, making it very hard for Ginny to see very far down the road. She went over to the Whittens' house, thinking the strangers may have stopped there as well, but the Whittens hadn't seen them. Ginny hurriedly told them what had just happened, but she didn't stay to hear their response. Ginny ran up and down Wadsworth Street, checking with all the neighbors, but no one else had seen the men. She walked down to the hosiery mill. She walked all the way around Miller Park twice and up and down both sides of Fort Avenue. She stopped at the furniture store, the barber shop, and even walked around the old revolutionary war fort for which the avenue was named. Nothing. Not a trace of them.

The angels were gone.

6

May 1909

Virginia got out of the carriage and stared up at the house while Embro was busy getting her two traveling bags. How wonderful the old Holt house still looked to her. Before leaving for this trip, she had been afraid it would somehow look smaller or less beautiful to her now that she was a young woman of seventeen. It was hard to believe that it had been almost three years since her last summer stay with Eliza. She hated staying away so long, but her work at the shoe factory made it difficult to come for visits. Gratefully, the view of the house did not disappoint her. Mrs. Holt's old crimson roses were in full bloom and still wrapped themselves gracefully around the porch, welcoming stranger and friend alike into her home.

Virginia had barely put one foot on the front porch step when the screen door burst open, and a tall young woman with striking auburn hair dashed out of the house with open arms.

"Ginny! You're here at last!"

"Eliza!"

The two friends greeted and embraced each other gladly.

Virginia stood back and gazed happily at her dear friend.

"Eliza, I declare you look more and more like your mother with every passing year. What I'd give to have hair that color."

Eliza beamed at her friend's compliment. "Well, there's nothing wrong with your raven black tresses. You'll look simply beautiful in the pink bridesmaid's dress. Your dress is the last one we have to make, and we only have seven days left to make it!"

"Well, with the three of us sewing, it should be finished before the big day on Sunday. I still can't believe you're getting married!" exclaimed Virginia, taking hold of Eliza's arm as the two went inside the house. "You, a bride! I can't wait to meet this Henry of yours."

"He can't wait to meet you, either. He promised to come by right after supper."

"Doesn't it seem like yesterday that we were happy young girls without a care in the world, spending our summer hours at Miller Park with Elijah and Mr. Whitten, eating cotton candy and peanuts and watching baseball games?"

"What a wonderful summer. Elijah and I still talk about it," reflected Eliza.

Eliza then looked at Virginia seriously. "Virginia, dear, you look tired. It was a long ride from Lynchburg to here. Why don't you go upstairs and rest. Mother has Mary Susan's old room all ready for you."

A nap sounded like a good idea, and Virginia followed Eliza upstairs. She was not surprised to see that Mrs. Holt's redecorating efforts had extended themselves to the second floor of the house. Mary Susan's room was completely redone with a soft seafoam green and white striped bedspread and curtains. Eliza turned down the bed covers and refused to leave until Virginia was tucked beneath the covers. Almost as soon as Eliza had slipped out of the room and had closed the door, Virginia relaxed and drifted off to sleep.

"Why didn't you wake me up?" asked Virginia yawning as she walked into the kitchen.

Eliza turned and smiled at her friend, her cheeks flushed pink from standing over the hot stove.

"I was going to, but when I looked in, you were sound asleep. I just couldn't bring myself to disturb you."

"Well, what can I do to help you get dinner ready?" asked Virginia willingly.

"Not a thing. The fried chicken is done, the green beans are cooked, the potatoes are mashed, the gravy is made, and . . ." Eliza leaned over and opened the oven door, "the rolls are just about done."

"It smells wonderful."

Eliza looked into the oven, checked on the rolls, and then carefully took them out.

"Pa and Embro are down at the barn, feeding the horses. They'll be back in a few minutes. Why don't you go tell Elijah dinner is ready while I put the food on the table."

"Great," said Virginia. "Where is my old friend anyway? I haven't seen him all day."

"He's out on the front porch . . . sulking."

Eliza paused.

Virginia stared at her girlfriend.

"Sulking?"

"Well, I really shouldn't say anything . . ." Eliza paused again, with a look on her face that Virginia knew only to well. This look was one she and Eliza perfected as children. This look meant "ask me, ask me, ask me."

Virginia grinned. "Eliza, I *insist* that you tell me what's wrong with Elijah." Part of their old childhood game was to specifically use the word "insist" so that, if caught and later questioned, the informer could honestly say that the other person "insisted" on being told whatever it was that they were told.

Eliza hesitated for a moment, for effect only, before she spoke.

"Elijah told me not to say anything. He doesn't want to talk about it in the middle of the wedding and all, but you see, well, he and his girlfriend Frances Parker just broke up."

Virginia gasped. "Eliza, you're not serious."

"Very serious."

"What happened. She didn't . . ."

"She did. She dumped him. And it was awful, Ginny. Just plain awful."

"But Elijah last wrote me in February, and things were fine then," commented Virginia in disbelief.

"That was before little Miss Frances and her mother went for a visit to see distant relatives to Charleston, South Carolina," said Eliza bitterly. "Seems Miss Frances met a very distant cousin, an un-attached young man destined to inherit his father's entire fortune, if you catch my drift . . ."

"And she broke off with Elijah for him? For his money?"

"Came back home engaged!"

"No!"

"Yes! It just about broke Elijah's heart. I feel so bad. Here I am, deliriously happy and about to marry the love of my life, and I have to watch Elijah struggle so. Henry and I even talked about postponing the wedding, but Pa said no. Said Elijah would pull through. Pa's usually right about such things. But it's still hard to watch."

"Poor Elijah. He's such a good man. Frances Parker must be out of her living mind, if you ask me."

"Well, I'm glad you're here. Maybe you can cheer him up a bit."

"I'll do my best," said Virginia sincerely.

"I better go get this food on the table. Go get Elijah and bring him in. And promise you won't say a word."

"Not a word," assured Virginia.

"Promise me," demanded Eliza.

Virginia placed her hand solemnly over her heart.

"I'll be as silent as the grave."

Virginia found Elijah just where Eliza had said he would be, sitting alone in one of the front porch rockers, looking forlorn and miserable. He reminded Virginia of an abandoned old hound dog. Virginia's initial instinct was a maternal one. She should go and comfort her hurting friend. She would be gentle. She would be understanding. She would be kind.

But as she stared at Elijah, something stirred deep within her, something of a very different nature. As she continued to look at him, another course of action presented itself to her mind. No, she couldn't.

She just couldn't.

She had promised.

Besides, it would be so mean. She looked steadfastly at Elijah, his head bent over sadly, his hands folded pitifully in his lap. Poor thing.

But, maybe, just maybe, meanness would prove to be a really good medicine.

She'd do it.

With determination then, Virginia walked over to Elijah and plopped herself down in the rocking chair next to his.

"Hello, Elijah," said Virginia cheerfully.

"Hello, Ginny," muttered Elijah without much enthusiasm.

Virginia cleared her throat. Here goes.

"Well, Elijah," said Virginia brightly, "Eliza tells me that Frances Parker has gone and dumped you for a filthy rich cousin in Charleston."

Elijah was so startled that he practically fell out of the rocking chair. So far, so good, thought Virginia hopefully.

"What . . . did you . . . say?" sputtered Elijah.

"I said that Eliza told me that your high and mighty girlfriend has dumped you for someone else. Well, good riddance, if you ask me." Virginia made sure that there wasn't a shred of pity or sympathy in her voice. She didn't dare even look at Elijah as she said it. Instead, she gazed peacefully out at the red carpet of roses cascading up the front porch railings and took a deep breath. Those roses had the sweetest scent.

"I told Eliza . . ."

Virginia didn't give him a chance to finish his sentence. "You told Eliza not to tell me. And since when, my dear Elijah, has Eliza been able to keep anything really important a secret from me? Do you think that I'm an idiot and wouldn't notice you moaning and groaning and dragging around here, feeling sorry for yourself?"

"Well, no . . ."

"Or did you expect me to sit around all week, unable to guess just what it was that was troubling you?"

"Of course not. I . . ."

"I suppose that you want me to feel sorry for you. Well, I'm not sorry. Not one little bit."

At this point, Virginia did turn and look at Elijah face to face. His mouth was hanging open aghast, and those beautiful blue eyes of his were filled with tears. It was obvious now that he had been crying before she came. This almost undid Virginia. But she caught herself and continued her attack. It was for his own good.

"In fact, if you ask me, I'd say that you are the luckiest man alive."

"Lucky? Lucky? How can you say that I'm lucky? I just lost . . ."

". . . a shallow, two-faced, greedy, foolish excuse for a woman. That's exactly what you just lost. Tell me, is that what you want for a wife?"

Virginia stopped and stared intently at her friend. She didn't flinch as he angrily stared back at her. Elijah's face was flushed red now. He started to say something, then stopped. He looked back at her, with an ugly look of shock and rage. For a moment, just briefly, Virginia was afraid. Had she gone too far?

Then, suddenly, the expression on his face changed. It was a look of astonishment.

"You're doing it," he said in amazement.

His comment caught her off guard.

"Doing it? Doing what?" she asked puzzled.

"That . . . that thing you used to do with the old rooster. You're doing it . . . to me."

He was right. She had confronted Elijah as forcefully and directly as she had confronted Mr. Jefferson.

"Well," she asked cautiously, "did it work?"

Elijah gazed at her intently for a moment, then reluctantly sighed, wiped his eyes with his shirt sleeve, and finally grinned.

"Didn't it always?"

The wedding went off without a hitch. Eliza was a stunning bride, and Virginia had nothing but praise for her Henry. She liked him right off, as soon as she met him. As the two of them rode off for their honeymoon, Virginia felt assured that her friend would have a happy life with this young man.

Elijah's mood improved vastly after Virginia's shock treatment, and the two of them enjoyed the following week of vacation together. Elijah took Virginia riding on a new feisty mare. It was fun to ride through the open countryside again. They visited old friends and neighbors. One afternoon, Embro took them exploring, on horseback, of course, through a hidden wooded path up a small nearby hillside. They ate lots of Mrs. Holt's apple preserves and sang and talked till late into the evening.

On Saturday, the day before Virginia and her family were to return to Lynchburg, Mrs. Holt and Mother prepared a feast for dinner, a roasted turkey and dressing and sweet potatoes and cornbread and butterscotch pie. It was like Thanksgiving. After eating, Virginia asked Elijah if they could walk over to her old home. She had avoided it until now, but she wanted to go by and see the old place.

Everything looked so different. Some of the pine trees that used to separate the Holt farm and Mother's old house had been cut down, and a new farmhouse was under construction on the edge of Mother's property. Elijah said his pa was building it for one of his farmhands to live in now, but it would someday be given to one of his brothers or sisters when they got married. Virginia wondered if Elijah had been planning to live there with Frances Parker.

Virginia hardly recognized her old house. Papa had always kept it painted a sparkling pretty white when they lived there, but now it was painted a pale blue. The old woodshed had been torn down, and a small dog kennel stood in its place. The spot in the backyard where

Mother had grown her vegetable garden was bare and now had two long clotheslines standing on it.

Virginia was most heartbroken to see that Papa's maple trees had all been cut down. Young apple seedlings now stood in their place. The only thing that was the same was the old stone well.

"Oh, Elijah," moaned Virginia, leaning up against the well. "It's simply tragic about Papa's trees. They're all gone."

"Josiah had to cut them down, Virginia. Those trees got some kind of blight and turned all yellow last summer. There was no saving them."

"Well, I can still think it's tragic if I want to. They were like . . . like old friends." Virginia walked around the well and gazed across the backyard property. Bits and pieces of childhood memories flashed quickly through her mind. Elijah kept his distance, standing near the apple trees.

"You'll be happy to know," said Elijah cheerfully, "that the old chicken coop is still standing."

Virginia grinned. "Perhaps we should go see it."

"No, thanks. I still carry the scars from the last visit."

"Little scars," corrected Virginia.

"Deep, little scars," insisted Elijah.

Virginia laughed. "I miss Mr. Jefferson."

"I'm not surprised. He taught you well."

Virginia ignored his comment.

"Besides, I wouldn't want you to go near the place. You might find your old stick. Then I'd really be in trouble."

Virginia made a face at Elijah that made him laugh. She then reached over to lift the lid off the well and to peer down inside.

"I wish I had a nickel for every bucket of water I drew out of here," said Virginia wistfully. "I'd be rich as a king and would never have to work in that old shoe factory again."

"Well, I, for one, would gladly give a million dollars to have a certain pail of water that you once held," teased Elijah with a broad smile.

"You'll never let me live that down, will you?"

"Nope. Never," replied Elijah happily.

"Pig," retorted Virginia.

"Names, yet. Fair enough, I guess, since I did scare the living daylights out of you."

Virginia folded her arms and glared at him.

"I wasn't that scared."

Elijah didn't respond right away like she expected him to. He paused and looked steadily at Virginia for a moment. There was a strange look on his face. This made her nervous. He took a few steps towards her. She took a tiny step back.

"You know what? I am a fool," he said softly. "A total, complete fool."

He was staring into her eyes now. Virginia bit her lip.

"You are?" she said.

He took another step closer to her. She tried to take another little step back. Too late. The well was in her way. Darn.

"Yes. You were right, Virginia. I was a fool to fall in love with Frances Parker."

"You were?" she said faintly.

A strong, intense feeling surged through Virginia as Elijah spoke. It totally caught her by surprise. She had never felt this way about him before, and it practically scared the living daylights out of her. She could hardly breath as he took another step closer. She didn't try to step back this time. She took a little step forward instead.

"I should have seen it before now. I should have known. Here I was, mourning over Frances, when standing before me was a beautiful young woman, the bravest, strongest, best girl I've ever known and the best friend I ever had."

She didn't need to answer him. She couldn't. She only needed to close her eyes as Elijah bent down and his lips slowly met hers.

7

December 1909 – April 1920

Elijah proposed to Virginia on the following Christmas. To their dismay, however, Mother would not give her consent right away. She explained that she wanted Virginia to wait a few more years, until she was twenty-one.

This seemed so unfair to Virginia. She knew girls her age that were already married, like Eliza, for one. It made Virginia very cross with Mother, and she hardly spoke to her for several days after turning Elijah down. This hurt Mother deeply, but Virginia wouldn't listen to anything else Mother had to say. Mother had already explained to her and Elijah that after what she had been through with Papa and all, she would feel better if Virginia would wait. It wasn't that she didn't approve of Elijah. She said she wouldn't choose anyone else for her daughter. She already considered the Holts as family. But she just needed to be sure that Virginia was ready to take on the "burdens of married life."

Well, Virginia felt ready to take on those "burdens," thank you very much. Could it be any worse than the burdens she had already carried? Could the "realities of married life" be any more difficult than the realities she had already faced? For several weeks, Virginia lay in bed at night and thought very seriously about eloping. Just run away and get married. She was old enough. She didn't need permission. It might break Mother's heart if she did, but Virginia didn't care. Mother had already broken hers.

Virginia had almost made up her mind to defy Mother and go ahead with marrying Elijah. However, her anger subsided, and she soon saw the wisdom in Mother's advice. Losing Papa had been a terrible thing. Perhaps it would be better if she waited.

This meant it would be four more years before she could marry Elijah. Virginia passed the time working at the shoe factory and keeping up with her sewing. With a marriage to look forward to, she began working on things that she would need to set up housekeeping. For her nineteenth birthday, Mother gave her a beautiful cedar chest to keep her things in. Virginia and Bessie embroidered several pillowcases, and Mother made her a lovely tablecloth. Mrs. Whitten taught Virginia how to crochet, and Virginia began working on a delicate rose-patterned white crocheted bedspread. The stitches were so tiny that Virginia believed it would take her all the way up to her wedding day to finish it.

In the meantime, Elijah decided to spend his time getting an education. He went up to Charlottesville to the University of Virginia to study agriculture. This was the school that President Thomas Jefferson had founded a long time ago. Charlottesville was some sixty miles away, so Elijah could only come to visit on the holidays and in the summer. Now the lovers poured out their pent-up feelings with pen and paper.

Virginia thought the year 1913 would just never come. But eventually, the pages of the calendar turned to the appointed time, and she began actively planning her wedding. Many letters flowed between herself and Eliza and between Mrs. Holt and Mother, planning the details. The wedding would take place in the country at the old stone church. Reverend Coffey Sr. was dead and gone, but his son, the Reverend Coffey Jr., had taken over his father's old ministry. He would perform the ceremony. Bessie and Mary would be Virginia's bridesmaids, and she had asked Eliza to be the matron of honor. Elijah asked Embro to be his best man. Mrs. Whitten had volunteered to sew the bridesmaids' dresses and Virginia's wedding gown. Virginia asked Mr. Whitten if he would give her away. And, according to Mother's wish, Papa was not invited.

All was going smoothly.

Then, on November 2, tragedy struck.

Mr. Holt and Josiah had been working that afternoon breaking in a new stallion. In a moment of fright, the young horse bucked and threw Mr. Holt right off his back. Mr. Holt fell forward and landed on his head. It broke his neck. He died instantly.

News of Mr. Holt's death was a terrible shock. Mrs. Holt had to be practically carried to the funeral. Virginia stood with her arm tightly around Elijah during the service. She was as worried over Elijah as she was about Mrs. Holt. She had never seen Elijah look this way before. His face was so full of pain. After the funeral, Mother sent Virginia and the family back to Lynchburg while she stayed behind. Virginia would run the household while Mother was gone. Mrs. Holt was barely eating anything and hadn't slept for a week. Mother would not leave her. Mother would take care of her. She suggested that the wedding plans should be put off until Mrs. Holt regained her health. They would have to wait until summer.

Virginia wrote to Elijah almost every day during this dark time, hoping she would be able to comfort him in his grief. She learned that when someone you love is hurting, it makes you hurt just as much. It made her feel so helpless. It also made her love him even more. Slowly, very slowly, she saw the life and light return into his letters and into his face.

In the spring, Virginia and Mother and Mrs. Holt took up the belated wedding plans once again. But unexpected international events put off the wedding date once again. On June 28, 1914, a man was murdered across the ocean in Sarajevo. He was an Austrian archduke named Frances Ferdinand. His death was like an explosion, setting off a series of events in Europe that began a war. The world war.

Virginia would never forget the day in early July when she got a letter from Elijah, announcing that he had up and joined the U.S. Army! He wrote:

I know, my dearest Virginia, that this news must come as a deep blow, and I do not doubt that you will come after me with a big stick — I would not blame you. But, my love, I have the deepest feelings about the events unfolding in Europe. As a nation we are not committed yet, but we will be. I have no doubt President Wilson will make that move soon. And when he does, I shall go and fight for my dear country and family and you. I must do this, Virginia. My grandfather fought in the Civil War and my great-great grandfather fought in the Revolutionary War. How could I turn away? In good conscience, I cannot ask for you to wait for me, after you have waited for so long. You are so beautiful and deserving of a home and a family of your own. If you change your mind while I am away, I will release you from any obligation that you have to me. Only give me your love and your prayers and your approval, and pray for my success.

Virginia wasted no time in sending Elijah a short, terse reply to his letter. She spared no words in telling him just what she thought about his hasty decision and about "being released from obligations." She would wait alright. Until hell freezes over or words to that effect. August came, and instead of going to a church dressed in white, Virginia dressed in deepest black and went with Bessie and Mother and Eliza and Mrs. Holt to the railway station to see Elijah off. It was a bitter day, and Virginia was only able to hold back her tears until the train began moving away. Curse the German kaiser. As she stood on the station platform, waving and sobbing, Virginia vowed to earnestly pray every day for the kaiser's demise and for President Wilson's continued reluctance to commit the U.S. troops.

Virginia's prayers for the German leader's utter destruction unfortunately went unanswered; but for almost three years, to Virginia's delight, President Wilson hemmed and hawed and waited. Letters from Elijah were frequent and positive. He was full of anticipation. He actually wanted to fight. Virginia couldn't understand it. However, Bessie's only comment concerning the situation voiced Virginia's feelings exactly. Bessie just shook her head and said, "Men!"

What added to Virginia's consternation was that Embro decided to join his twin. If there would be war, he would fight, too. So, Embro went off to join his brother. They always did things together. Why should war be any different than riding horses or climbing apple trees or guarding a friend's house? The St. John and Holt households did their best to carry on with the daily chores of life, all the while anxiously reading the newspapers and fervently praying for the safe return of their loved ones.

The day Virginia feared most came in April 1917. Those hideous Germans deliberately sunk some U.S. ships. Then rumors began spreading that the Germans were encouraging Mexico to attack the United States. Finally, President Woodrow Wilson committed U.S. forces to the war, and Elijah got his wish. He was sent across the ocean to fight.

Once in Europe, letters from Elijah were few and far between. Virginia barely kept her sanity by sewing. Endlessly sewing. By now, she had finished her crocheted bedspread. She began another. For the guest room. For their guest room. When Elijah returns.

In the winter of 1918, Mother developed a cough. She said it was nothing, but it worried Virginia. Mother chose to ignore it. She said it would go away by spring. Spring came, then summer, then autumn, but Mother's cough didn't go away. It stayed. It got worse. Finally, Mother went to the doctor.

Virginia's worst suspicion came true.

Mother had consumption.

Virginia wrote the Holts immediately with the news, so she was not surprised to answer the door a few days later to find Josiah and Eliza standing on the front steps.

"Eliza! Josiah! How sweet of you two to come. Mother will appreciate it so. Did your mother send you?"

Josiah stood with his hat solemnly in his hands. Eliza stared sadly at Virginia.

"Yes, Virginia, Mother sent us," said Josiah solemnly.

"Well, then come in, and I'll tell Mother that you're here . . ."

"Ginny," Josiah interrupted.

Virginia stopped and looked at Josiah. The sound of his voice was strange. His face was pale. His eyes were red. His hands were trembling. He was holding a piece of paper. She looked at Eliza. Eliza was crying.

"Josiah, what's wrong?"

Then Josiah started to cry.

A feeling of stone cold dread rushed through Virginia's mind. She reached out and grabbed Josiah by the shoulders.

"Josiah, tell me," she cried.

"Mother received a telegram . . . Embro . . . Embro . . . has been critically injured. He was shot in both legs, Ginny. He's in a hospital somewhere in France. There was a real bad infection, and they had to amputate. Both legs, Ginny, *both legs.* He'll never ride again."

Virginia held Josiah in her arms. Eliza continued to cry. Dear, sweet Embro. Not to ride a horse again would be worse than death to him. Curse those Germans!

"It will be alright. You'll see. We'll take of him when he comes back, Josiah. He can come and live with Elijah and me."

Virginia looked into Josiah's eyes for confirmation, for hope.

Josiah shook his head.

"He's not coming back," whispered Eliza with a heartbreaking sob. "Elijah was killed in the same battle that injured Embro. In a forest called Argonne. Shot in the head . . ."

Josiah held out the telegram for Virginia to read, but she didn't see it.

She screamed and fainted dead away into his outstretched arms.

Virginia lay two weeks prostrate in bed. She had little memory of day or night.

She didn't want to eat.

She didn't want to drink.

She could only sleep or feel pain. Overwhelming pain. Her chest physically hurt, as if there was a throbbing dark toothache inside her heart. There was no color in the world around her. Everything was black. Everything was dead. She wanted to die.

But there were vivid dreams, images of the past, of Elijah as a boy, riding his horse. Of Elijah and her in each other's arms by the well. There were terrifying dreams of French forests, of exploding guns, of death. There were strange dreams of Elijah standing by her bed, assuring her that he was alright, for her to be at peace. But there was no peace. Only pain.

She had vague awareness of people sitting by her bed, speaking to her. Mother's voice. Eliza's voice. Bessie's voice. Mrs. Whitten's voice. The doctor's voice. But she could not see. She could not hear. She could only hurt.

Finally, she heard a voice that reached through the pain. It was Lily's young voice.

"And I will also be your light in the wilderness; and I will prepare the way before you, if it so be that ye shall keep my commandments; wherefore, inasmuch as ye shall keep my commandments ye shall be led towards the promised land; and ye shall know that it is by me that ye are led . . ."

"Lily?"

"I'm here, Ginny."

A small hand took her hand and held it tight. She could feel that through the pain. She clung to that hand.

"Don't leave me, Lily."

"I won't, Ginny."

Virginia pulled Lily's hand up to her chest and squeezed it with both of her hands. Held on to it for dear life.

"Stay with me, Lily."

"I will, Ginny," said Lily in tears. "I'll stay right here and keep reading to you out of my special book. Mother said those men came and healed me and gave me my book. So I thought I would read it to you. Maybe it will heal you, too, Ginny."

"I hope so, Lily . . ."

Virginia closed her eyes and tried to open her heart, to let in some light. Lily began to read again. "And I will also be your light in the wilderness . . ."

Virginia spent another week in bed. Often she wished to die, to be free from the pain. But almost against her will, the autumn sun continued to shine into her bedroom, the love of family and friends continued to surround her, and life returned to her broken heart. The pain subsided. She would live. She would go on.

Mother lived a year and a half after Elijah's death. She suffered greatly, and Virginia knew she should look upon Mother's passing as a blessing. But that was hard to do. With Mother and Elijah gone, Virginia felt extremely alone. One year after Mother's death, Virginia put the following in the Lynchburg newspaper:

In Memoriam
In sad but loving remembrance of my dear mother, Louella St. John, who departed this life one year ago today, April 15, 1920.

> In the graveyard, softly sleeping,
> Where the flowers gently wave,
> Lies the one I love so dearly
> In her lonely silent grave.
> Friends may think that I have forgotten her,
> And my wounded heart is healed,
> But they little know my sorrow
> That's within my heart concealed.
> God called her home; It was His will.
> But in my heart, I miss her still.
> Her memory is as dear to me today
> As in the hour she passed away.
>   — Her children.

Out of a sense of duty, Virginia cut out a copy of the poem from the newspaper and gave it to Uncle Abraham to send to Papa.

She was head of the family now.

PART
TWO
Lily

1

Summer 1923

Lily leaned over and gazed excitedly into the telescope lens. A fuzzy large white round object appeared before her.

"Can you see anything?" asked Charlotte breathlessly.

"Shhh," ordered Helen authoritatively. "Let her concentrate."

"It's not very clear," said Lily.

"Try looking with just one eye," suggested Pamela.

"You can adjust it by turning that knob there," offered Violet helpfully. "I couldn't see a thing until I turned that knob."

Lily stepped back for a moment to find the knob. Once it was secure in hand, she leaned over again and peered into the large black instrument that stood on the summer green lawn of Bryn Mawr College. The fuzzy round object gradually focused sharply before her, and Lily gazed in awe at the planet Jupiter and one of its circling moons.

"I see it! I see it!" she exclaimed happily. "Oh, wait till I write and tell Virginia about this!"

"I want to look," demanded Charlotte restlessly. "I haven't had a turn yet."

Lily reluctantly gave up her turn at the telescope and sat down on the cool grass with her new friends. A gentle June breeze blew across the lawn, bringing with it the powerful scent of blooming honeysuckle.

Lily took a deep breath, relishing the sweet summer scent, and closed her eyes in ecstasy. The beauty and peace of this campus was just overwhelming, a bold contrast to the cool, stark surroundings of the overall factory where she worked in Lynchburg, Virginia. She felt like she was in a dream.

It was a dream, really — an impossible dream for poor working women. She and ninety-nine other female industrial workers from across the United States and various countries across the world had been recruited and given scholarships to come to Pennsylvania to attend the two-month Summer School for Women Workers at the illustrious Bryn Mawr College.

Lily arrived on campus in early June that summer in 1923, full of anxiety and anticipation. This was just the third year that this summer school had been in operation, and it had been a real honor for Lily to be selected to attend. On the opening night, the founder and director of the program, Dean Hilda Worthington Smith, who was herself a graduate of Bryn Mawr, gave the opening address. She spoke passionately about the importance of self-government, social progress, and "non-violent revolutionary change." She painted horrifying pictures of the debilitating working conditions that existed in many parts of the world, along with the all-too-frequent working conditions of long hours and low pay experienced by the majority of female industrial workers. Lily could relate to these only too well. Dean Smith said that she was greatly concerned that such conditions dulled the minds of these noble women. She said, "My conviction grew that this type of school, having its roots in basic economic and social problems and reaching industrial workers through education, might, if well developed, be used as an instrument of social change."

Lily leaned back and looked up at the bright stars twinkling overhead. Well, one thing was for certain. She had changed. She had only been at the school for three weeks, but already she had felt the intoxicating sensation of a mind awakening.

She was taking a broad range of courses. Everyone was required to take classes in "modern industrial society," which included studies in economics, the labor movement, government, and industrial history. It was explained to all students that these classes were designed to help them become better workers in their communities.

Elective courses in the science area included physics, chemistry, astronomy, geology, and biology. Initially, Lily had been a bit nervous about taking some of these subjects. She had only completed the sixth grade in the public school before going to work in the sewing factory. However, she soon learned that the classes were non-vocational courses and had been created especially for them.

The biology course included relaxing nature walks around the surrounding campus, where the instructor would point out certain types of plant and animal life. More than once, Lily had witnessed one of the women actually burst into tears over seeing flowers that they had never seen before. The astronomy class, officially called "Women Under the Stars" set up this telescope on the lawn for nighttime viewing. This was undoubtedly Lily's favorite class.

In addition to the industrial and scientific courses, Lily and her associates were offered classes in literature, history, and art. Lily had chosen the literature class and was now thoroughly enjoying her first reading of Euripides' "Trojan Women."

Charlotte left the telescope and came over to sit down by Lily with a great sigh.

"What's the matter with you?" asked Lily kindly.

"I'm depressed."

"Why?"

Charlotte sighed again. "Science has spoiled the stars for me. Now I'll never be able to look at them again the same way knowing what they really are."

"I feel just the opposite," countered Helen bluntly. "Seeing stars has opened up the universe to me. To someone who will probably spend the rest of her life behind the high walls of a garment factory, that's really something."

Pamela came over and sat next to Charlotte, putting her arm around the unhappy young woman.

"Cheer up, Charlotte. If it helps, I've also felt depressed since coming to Bryn Mawr. I can't help but think about my sisters working in the factories and mills back home in New York who will never get such an opportunity as we've been given. I feel almost guilty."

"I've felt that way, too," said Charlotte sadly.

"Hush, you two," scolded Helen emphatically. "You're getting me depressed now. We simply can't afford to waste our time talking doom and gloom."

"She's right," chimed in Violet. "Let's talk about something else. Let's talk about our favorite class. Which one is your favorite, Pamela?"

"Literature. I'm falling in love with Shakespeare's plays."

"That's mine, too," added Helen delightedly. "I think I've fallen in love with Hamlet."

"The play or the prince?" quizzed Pamela with a smile.

"I'll never tell," said Helen.

"I like history best, I think," ventured Violet. "I like the stories of the ancient Greeks and Romans. Charlotte?"

Charlotte hesitated.

"Charlotte."

"I guess I like the recreational activities best," muttered Charlotte grudgingly. "I do like swimming, and I would like to learn how to play tennis."

"How about you, Lily?"

"I can't decide," said Lily truthfully. "I like all the academic classes. But I can tell you what I don't like. I can't stand that required course in hygiene and the two periods of corrective gymnastics!"

Just the mention of the course called corrective gymnastics sent all five young ladies into a fit of laughter.

"Have you heard about the lantern ceremony that takes place on the closing day of school?" asked Helen. "It sounds so wonderful. A marker of boulders is built in the cloister garden, and a fire is lit inside it at dusk. One of the instructors is dressed up and is representative of Wisdom. At Wisdom's call, the students approach as her hand-maidens. Each woman carries a lantern in her hands and lights it at the marker. Then they go out singing the school song, 'Shine, O Light.' This is to symbolize that each woman must carry back to her fellow workers the light she had gained at Bryn Mawr."

"How beautiful," whispered Lily. She tried to imagine herself walking down the garden passageway between the stone arches, carrying such a lantern. If only Virginia could be here to share this with her.

"Let's sing the school song," suggested Helen.

The five friends joined hands and voices as they began to sing the song, written for "The Women of Summer."

> Bryn Mawr, you called.
> We answer unafraid.
> Out of the factory
> We come to thee.
> Give us the tools,
> The tools of our trade.
> Give us the truth
> To set our spirits free.

*   *   *

Five weeks later, Lily St. John boarded a train heading back home. She sat down in her seat and immediately took off her traveling hat and gloves and put them into the empty seat beside her. Thank goodness no one was sitting next to her. She didn't feel at all like talking. She wanted to be totally alone and to relive in her mind every splendid, exciting, adventuresome moment of her summer at Bryn Mawr. She felt a sudden jerk, as the train started pulling slowly away from the station. She leaned over and looked out of the window, watching the train station platform gradually disappear and the green Pennsylvania countryside begin to roll past her.

Who ever would have thought that going to work at an overall factory as a seamstress would have led her to this, a whole summer of college study. But it had, and Lily sighed, pleased and very confident it was only the beginning of many wonderful adventures to come.

Virginia was so proud of her. How Lily missed her older sister. She reached over and pulled out a small stack of letters from her purse. She undid the thin blue ribbon that held them together and quickly looked through them, finding one of the last letters Virginia had sent to her that summer. Opening it, she pulled out a newspaper clipping that Virginia had enclosed. It was an article from the Lynchburg daily newspaper composed by a young reporter who had written Lily at Bryn Mawr for an interview.

> Miss St. John studied economics, science, and hygiene. She is an overall worker at A.C. Burrows Company and a member of the Y.W.C.A. Industrial Club. "The definite purpose of the school," Miss St. John said, "is to offer young women in industry the opportunity to study liberal subjects and to train themselves in clear thinking."

Lily smiled to herself as she reread it. Too bad the reporter had failed to print the remainder of her written interview, in which she went into great detail concerning her views that society did not value women who think for themselves. This "clear thinking" sentence had been a very good whitewash of that sentiment.

Lily stared out the window of the train, thinking about the young friends she had made at Bryn Mawr. She would miss Charlotte's complaining and Helen's energy and Pamela's kindness and Violet's music. Violet had such a wonderful singing voice.

One change that Lily had made, strongly suggested by Violet and highly encouraged by Helen, was short hair. Short hair was all the rage. Lily sat up straight in her seat and shook her head around, letting her new short cropped curls bounce up and down. What in the world will Virginia say when she sees I have cut all my hair off? It was positively too exciting to think about. She tossed her head around again in pure delight.

"A-hum," said a stiff male voice clearing his throat.

Startled, Lily looked up to see the train conductor, a short, fat, elderly man with a faded blue uniform standing in front of her compartment. His lips were pursed tightly together in a dark frown.

"Ticket, please," said the conductor in a disapproving voice.

How long had he been standing there? Lily decided she didn't want to know. She weakly smiled at the man while reaching for her purse. She quickly found her yellow ticket stub and handed it to the conductor. He properly punched the ticket and handed it back.

"Traveling alone?" he asked raising his eyebrows.

Lily nodded her head.

"Well, young lady, I see that you'll have to change trains in Washington," the conductor said slowly. "Nothing to worry about, though. All you have to do is follow the signs. If you get lost, dear, don't be afraid to go up to the ticket office for help. Somebody will show you where to catch your next train."

He sounded like he was instructing a helpless child. How demeaning. Lily's feelings of embarrassment quickly changed into feelings of anger. Here I've just finished studying economics, government, chemistry, and physics, thought Lily bitterly, and this man thinks I can't find my way through a train station by myself. The magic bubble of Bryn Mawr was bursting. Lily was back in the real world again.

Lily was mad at the conductor, but she was careful not to show her anger. She smiled and did something much more satisfying.

"Oh, thank you kindly, sir. I can't thank ya'll enough for hepping me," answered Lily with the sweetest, most pathetic southern drawl that she could muster. Then she batted her eyelashes at him.

The conductor look quite gratified. He tipped his hat, smiled at her, and left. Once he was out of sight, Lily immediately threw the ticket stub on the floor and mashed it with her boot.

She knew that she shouldn't let this man bother her.

Why did he have to treat her like a child?

Lily dreaded her trip south, knowing such behavior would be even more prevalent there. Maybe she *should* move up north and live in a big city. Violet was from Baltimore and Pamela was from New York, and both had extended such invitations to her.

Lily glanced over to the stack of letters lying on the seat beside her. No, she couldn't leave Virginia. Not now. Not after losing Bessie. Virginia still wasn't over that. A tear or two began to well up in Lily's eyes. She still wasn't over it either.

How long had it been now? Three years? Right after Mother's death, Bessie had run off and married that Walter Shultz. What a shock! Lily had been certain that Bessie had grown up like Virginia, sworn off of men for life. Bessie had been so negative toward any innocent fellow who foolishly but bravely cast his affections her way. And Walter Shultz of all people? Lily didn't think he was the least bit handsome, so short and stocky and every last inch of him that you could see covered with thick, dark hair. Because of his appearance, the young men at church had called him "The Dutchman."

Bessie and Walter had had two children right away, a boy and a girl. Then, Bessie got pregnant with a third child but delivered this baby prematurely. The baby died. So did Bessie.

Virginia had Bessie and the infant buried together in the city cemetery, not far away from Mother. Lily would never forget looking into that coffin, seeing Bessie lying there with that small child in her arms. Bessie looked like a fairy princess, with her golden hair curled about her face and wearing a lovely white dress. God only knows what Virginia paid for that gown.

To add insult to injury, old Walter Shultz had run off with another woman not six months after the funeral. What was the expression? *Before the funeral meats had turned cold?* The mere thought of it made Lily livid. Now Virginia was having to raise Bessie's two children by herself. Needless to say, the name "Walter Shultz" was not spoken aloud in Virginia's presence.

No, Lily told herself again, she just couldn't up and leave her older sister in pursuit of her own dreams. She had thought this over a hundred times at Bryn Mawr. It was her responsibility to go back to Lynchburg and help Virginia raise the children. She was all the family Virginia had now, particularly since Willie had gone and joined the navy.

She looked over at the pile of letters in the empty seat next to her. There were two letters there postmarked Jacksonville, Florida. They were from Willie.

She would not let herself think about him now. In defiance of her own anger, she got up, straightened out her skirt, took her purse and a small notebook, and marched straight back to the dining car. She ate alone, reading some essays from her notebook that had been written by several of the summer school students. One particularly touched Lily's heart.

> On its smooth green lawns, we are soothed and rested in mind and body, and the dull ache in our hearts slips from us and is lost. In the still hours of evening when the sun sets slowly in a haze of rose and gold, and soft grey shadows fall gently over the trees, a sense of eternity descends in a hush upon us.

A sense of eternity.

It was a beautiful phrase, and Lily savored it and her memories as she finished her dessert of chocolate pie and hot coffee. After supper was finished, she made her way back to her seat, desiring to take a short nap, but she found as she settled back down into her seat that she was unable to fight off her feelings any longer toward her absent brother.

Beast. After Virginia had lost her beau in the war, how on earth could Willie possibly go and do such a thing like joining the navy? What was he thinking?

Well, he wasn't thinking, concluded Lily reproachfully. That was the whole problem. Did Willie ever stop to think about what he was doing? He was always such a carefree spirit. At least there wasn't any war now, and her brother was stationed in Jacksonville. He said he wanted to see the world. Well, fine, dear brother, see it safely in Florida.

As she looked outside the window at the green countryside, Lily found her thoughts turning to a disturbing new direction. Why was she so mad at Willie? Was it just because he had deserted Virginia? Or was it possible that she was jealous? Willie was living his dream. He was seeing the world outside of little old Lynchburg, Virginia. But she was having to give up her dreams.

Am I envious, she wondered as she finally drifted off to sleep? The truth is I want more adventures like Bryn Mawr. I want to travel, to meet people, to see new things and new places. I want to be a woman of summer.

Despite the train conductor's misgivings, Lily was quite successful in changing trains without getting lost in Washington D.C. Soon she was stepping out onto the wide platform of the Lynchburg train station into Virginia's waiting arms.

"Lillian Ruth St. John, what in the world have you done to your hair?" exclaimed Virginia.

The two sisters walked off arm and arm, Lily full of stories which Virginia was most anxious to hear.

Lily returned to work right away and settled down to the business of being a dutiful aunt. It wasn't a hard job. Little Katherine and Hubert had completely won her heart, and she enjoyed doting over them. Katherine looked a lot like Bessie, with lots of blond curls and blue eyes. Thank the good Lord above Hubert looked very little like his father and more like his absent uncle Willie.

As she settled back into her daily routine, Lily's life stretched before her in her mind in a very predictable, uneventful course, and she mentally prepared herself for living such a life. And for over a year, her life modeled that mental image. But very unexpectedly and much sooner than she ever imagined, her much-wished-for opportunity to see the world presented itself at the factory. On a hot summer day in August 1924, she walked home in a daze and reluctantly told Virginia her news that night at dinner.

"Mr. Burrows himself called me into his office. Virginia, I was scared to death. I had never been into the owner's office before. I was afraid that I had done something wrong and that I was going to be fired. Imagine my shock when he told me about the new factory he is opening up out west. He plans to send out a small team of operators there to train the new workers. They'll stay for about a year. All expenses paid. I've heard he owns his own rail car, and the people he sends out west will ride in it. Imagine. A private train car. I hear it has velvet curtains!"

Lily sighed as she thought about those curtains. Virginia said nothing.

"I just can't believe that he wants me to go. He wants me to be the treasurer in charge of payroll. Imagine that."

Lily held Katherine in her arms and gave the little girl a long green bean to grab and eat.

"But of course, it's out of the question. I couldn't possibly go," she added unhappily.

Virginia frowned, concentrating her full attention for a moment on wiping up a large puddle of spilled milk in front of Hubert's plate.

"Do you want to go?" she finally asked solemnly.

"Well, I can't go and leave you alone with the children. That wouldn't be fair."

Virginia grimaced. "Life isn't fair, Lily. You will learn that soon enough. And you didn't answer my question. Do *you* want to go?"

Lily could never lie to Virginia.

"More than anything, Virginia."

"Then you shall go," said Virginia firmly.

"Virginia, I couldn't possibly . . ."

"Oh, yes, you could possibly. And," said Virginia holding up her hand before Lily could object, "I shall be the one to gladly pack your bags and put you on that train, come hell or high water."

"Virginia!" Lily exclaimed in disbelief. "You just said a swear word. Right in front of the children!"

Virginia wearily brushed back a wisp of hair from off her face.

"Lily, after all the misery this family has suffered, I'd stand up and swear in front of the devil himself if I thought it would bring one of us a chance at happiness."

Little Hubert got down from his chair and came over to Virginia, crawling up into her lap. He had finished eating all the food off of his plate, and now he began to finish what was left on Virginia's. Virginia lovingly stroked her hand across Hubert's small back.

"It's too late for me, Lily, but not for you. Go. Go and chase after all the fun and excitement you can. And don't you worry about us," she added with a sigh. "We'll be right here when you get back."

So it was decided.

Just like that.

Once the decision to go west was made, Lily was relieved to find that she wouldn't actually be leaving until after Christmas. She still felt somewhat guilty over leaving Virginia alone with the children, so she welcomed the autumn months to spend with her family.

Both she and Virginia worked full time, she working at the Burrows Overall Factory and Virginia working at the shoe factory. The Whittens kept the children during the day while they were gone. In the evenings, Lily took the responsibility of caring for Katherine and Hubert while Virginia got supper ready and attended to the evening chores. Lily often took the children up to Miller Park to play. Then she made sure the children got their nightly baths and that their teeth were properly brushed after supper was over. Finally, she had the delightful job of reading to them at bedtime. Frequently, she checked out story books from the library to read to them. Katherine liked stories about animals. Hubert liked everything. And, after her summer of college, Lily now checked out books of history and poetry for herself.

Christmas was especially sweet with the little ones. Old Mr. Whitten volunteered to play Santa Claus. Virginia made a wonderful red Santa suit for him to wear, and he promptly appeared on their doorstep early Christmas morning with a bag full of gifts. Katherine got a new dolly. Lily had spent many a late evening sewing little outfits for the doll, and she felt it was well worth it as she saw the look of joy on little Katherine's face. Hubert got a wooden train Mr. Whitten had made himself and several new picture books.

Willie had sent a big box full of gifts for everyone. Now that Lily was about to have her own adventures in traveling, her jealous feelings toward her brother had sharply faded.

Lily surprised Virginia with a new sewing box. She had Pamela buy it in New York and send it down. Virginia was still making beautiful crocheted bedspreads and tablecloths, and she needed a place to keep her needles and hooks and yarns.

The biggest surprise came when Santa announced that he had a really big present outside on the front porch. Would Lily mind helping him bring it in?

Lily put on her winter coat and walked out onto the front steps. There sat the most beautiful suitcase and matching traveling bag she had ever seen. It was designed in a tapestry pattern that was covered with big red roses. Lily turned to see Virginia standing at the door with a grin on her face.

"Merry Christmas, little sister," she said.

Two days later, Lily packed her new suitcase and bag and went down to the train station. She asked Virginia not to go with her. It would be too hard. Virginia agreed, and they said their goodbyes at the house.

Lily met her good friend, Mamie McGuire, at the station. Mamie would be traveling with her. They were the only two women making the journey. The rest of the team was made up of three men — two mechanics and one foreman. Mamie and Lily boarded Mr. Burrows' private car, which was just as fancy as Lily had imagined. She took her seat across from Mamie, over-awed at the thick, red velvet curtains hanging in the window. Lily vowed to write Virginia as soon as she arrived to tell her about those curtains. She would write about everything to Virginia.

Slowly, the train began to pull away from the station, and Lily settled down into her seat.

Another adventure was beginning.

Hopefully, it would be every bit as wonderful as Pennsylvania had been.

Lily was on her way at last to Salt Lake City.

2

January 1925

Lily loved her trip out west.

Before traveling to Salt Lake City, she had never been any further west than her own state of Virginia and her home in Lynchburg, which stood at the eastern base of the Blue Ridge mountains. On the train, she watched in amazement as the familiar mountains extended out into the lush rolling hills of West Virginia and then slowly began to disappear. The countryside grew progressively browner and flatter as she traveled through the central plains states. Eventually, she felt like she was riding across a large brown tabletop. This boring landscape seemed to go on forever. Then, quite suddenly, the majestic Rocky Mountains of Colorado broke the horizon, and Lily stared in awe at the famed sharp mountain peaks. The Rockies were unlike any of the mountains she had ever seen in Virginia, about twice the size of the Blue Ridge. They looked almost fairylike covered with January ice and snow.

Lily's train arrived in Utah early on a Saturday morning, January 2, at the railway station located in a city called Ogden, which was north of the Salt Lake Valley. She and the rest of Mr. Burrows' team left their private train car and transferred themselves and their belongings to a car that ran on an interurban railway connecting Ogden and Salt Lake City. Lily and Mamie were very excited to be so close to their final destination. They settled quickly into their seats, anxious for the train to leave the station.

Lily and Mamie found copies of the *Salt Lake Tribune* in their seats, and they passed the final moments of their long journey reading through the Utah newspaper.

"Look, Lily," observed Mamie excitedly, "they have a J.C. Penney store out here. That's one of my favorites."

"And there's also a Piggly Wiggly. Thank goodness for that. She hasn't said so, but I think Virginia has secretly worried herself sick with the notion that I might be staying in some sort of desert wilderness, far from the conveniences of modern civilization. I'll be sure to cut this advertisement out and send it home. Virginia does all her shopping at the Piggly Wiggly. This will be a comfort to her."

"What's a Z.C.M.I.?" asked Mamie with a puzzled look on her face. Lily leaned over and examined the full page ad, describing a marvelous after-Christmas sale of ladies' coats and hats.

"I don't know, Mamie. I've never heard of it before, but it sure looks nice. If it's going to stay as cold as this for several more months, I just might invest in the luxury of a second coat."

"Good idea," agreed Mamie. "What is the weather forecast anyway?"

Lily turned to the front page and read aloud. "Probably fair, little change in temperature."

Before the two friends finished reading the paper, the train entered the Salt Lake Valley and arrived at the station. Two gentlemen from Mr. Burrows' western factory were there to meet their party when they arrived. An older gentleman, a white-haired man named Mr. Bennion, greeted them enthusiastically and had all the detailed instructions regarding their living accommodations.

Lily and Mamie knew beforehand that arrangements had been made for them to stay in separate places. Lily would be staying at a boarding house northeast of downtown Salt Lake City with its famous Mormon temple square. She wanted to room with her friend Mamie, but there weren't any other available rooms at the place where Mamie was staying. Special arrangements had to be made for her friend. Mamie's legs were crippled from polio, so Mr. Burrows had wired ahead and seen to it that the place where Mamie stayed was very close to the factory.

The boarding house where Lily was staying was owned by two elderly sisters, Sarah and Elizabeth Decker. Sarah Decker had written Lily in early December, telling her of the arrangement. Mr. Bennion introduced the younger man to Lily as Silas Decker, a relative of the Decker sisters and a mechanic who would be working at the new factory. It turned out that he lived at the boarding house with his elderly relatives. He was a very handsome man; and looking at him, Lily was not as upset as she had been about not rooming with Mamie. Riding to work with Mr. Decker each morning was an exciting proposition.

Mr. Decker helped Mamie get her luggage safely loaded into a car that would take her to her new boarding house, then he loaded Lily and her two bags into his own vehicle. It was snowing lightly as they rode through downtown Salt Lake City, but Lily didn't mind. Salt Lake City reminded her a lot of Philadelphia. It was very large, with lots of businesses and elegant buildings. Big yellow electric streetcars ran down the metal railways in the middle of the streets. Mr. Decker took pride in pointing out the fancy street lights lining Main Street, remarking how Salt Lake City was one of the first U.S. cities to have carbon street lights. Lily was very excited when they rode past temple square. The famed grey granite temple sparkled boldly covered with the new fallen snow. Lily thought it was just beautiful.

"This is the Lion House," pointed out Mr. Decker, as they drove past a large stately home. He slowed the car down to a stop so that Lily could get a good look.

"I assume it's called that because of the lion statue on the second floor balcony?" observed Lily.

"Well, partly," said Mr. Decker. "Brigham Young, the second president of the Church, was known as 'the Lion of the Lord.' I think it's called the Lion House after him."

"So he lived there? This was Brigham Young's house?"

Mr. Decker hesitated, then politely cleared his throat.

"Uh, not exactly. He lived in the house right beside this one. It's called the Beehive House. Can you see the beehive on top?"

Lily nodded her head.

"Today, the Lion House is used for some sort of homemaking school for young women and the Beehive House is used as a girl's dormitory."

"But, Mr. Decker, you didn't say who originally built the Lion House."

Mr. Decker looked embarrassed. "Didn't I? Oh, well, you see, it was the living quarters for Brigham Young's plural wives and children."

"I see. He had a lot of wives?"

"Yes, quite a few."

"Well then," remarked Lily with keen interest. "Then perhaps it should have been called 'The Lioness House.'"

This comment seemed to take Mr. Decker aback. He actually turned sideways and stared at Lily for a long awkward moment.

"I think," he mused aloud, "that you will get along great with my Aunt Lizzie."

"Why is that, Mr. Decker? Was she married to Brigham Young?"

Mr. Decker threw back his head and laughed out loud, "No, Miss St. John, but she should have been. She should have been."

When Lily arrived at the Decker house, Mr. Decker formally introduced her to one of his two relatives, who greeted her warmly at the door.

"Welcome to Salt Lake," said Sarah Decker cordially, taking Lily's coat and hat. "And welcome to the Decker family. Make yourself at home."

Sarah Decker was the younger of the two sisters, a tall and matronly woman of sixty-five years. She appeared to still be in very good health, and Lily observed during her first week there that it was Sarah who did most of the housework and cooking. Her hair was dark with very little grey, and her small brown eyes sparkled with delight when showing off the beautiful home. Mr. Decker had bragged on his Aunt Sarah during the ride from the train station, saying she had the voice of an angel. She did have a lilting voice, clear as a bell.

"Thank you so much, Mrs. Decker. I'm sure I'll be very comfortable here," said Lily sincerely.

"Please call me Aunt Sarah," she insisted fervently. "We like to be very informal around here."

"Alright, Aunt Sarah," Lily replied smiling.

"And call me Silas," added Mr. Decker who followed her into the house carrying her luggage.

"Then you must call me Lily," she insisted as she followed Aunt Sarah upstairs to her new room. They had barely put her bags down when the other elderly sister entered the room, apparently very upset.

"Hurry up, Sarah, we'll be late. Silas, get the car!"

"Lizzie, this is our new boarder, Lily St. John, from Virginia . . ."

"The funeral starts in an hour, and I want to get a good seat!" said Lizzie passionately, ignoring Lily while banging her long black cane down hard on the floor.

Aunt Sarah turned and smiled weakly at Lily. "You'll have to forgive my sister, Lizzie. A friend of the family passed away this weekend, Brother Thomas Hooper, who sang in the Mormon Tabernacle Choir. Have you ever heard of the Mormon Tabernacle Choir? Oh, they're wonderful. You must go over to the tabernacle and hear the choir sing sometime while you're here. Perhaps Silas could take you. Anyway, Brother Hooper was a member of the Ensign Stake, and we're very good friends with his wife, Emily."

Lily looked at the other Decker sister with great curiosity. Elizabeth Decker or "Aunt Lizzie" was somewhere in her eighties. Exactly where in her eighties no one rightly knew, nor dared they ask. She was a real tiny thing, as small and petite as Lily. Lizzie's outer appearance was frail, with snow white hair, thin build, and thick glasses that made her eyes appear as big as an old owl's. However, "frail" was certainly not the word to describe Lizzie's personality. During her first week at the Decker house, Lily observed that she was curious, willful, stubborn, and loudly outspoken, almost to the point of rudeness. According to Silas, who continued to be quite a talker and a wealth of willing information, most people thought Lizzie was going senile and therefore made great allowances for her inappropriate verbal outbursts. But Silas confided to Lily that he was certain that Lizzie's mind wasn't that bad. She was still quite lucid at times, and consequently, it was not advisable to gossip much around her. She remembers. She also repeats gossip at the most inopportune occasions.

Lizzie always carried her heavy, black wooden cane around with her. Right away it was readily apparent to Lily that Lizzie didn't need this cane for walking. Aunt Lizzie could still get around very well on her own steam. The cane was Aunt Lizzie's way of getting people's attention and getting her point of view across forcefully. Silas advised Lily to sit or stand at a safe distance when Lizzie was "expressing" her opinions.

The house was charming, a large greystone Victorian, as beautiful as any Lily knew back in Virginia. It had a wide wraparound porch, and there was gold and purple stained glass in the front windows. There were three guest rooms in the house. Silas had one, and Lily had another. The third one was currently empty. Downstairs, there was a large formal living room that was on the right as you entered the front foyer. The kitchen was in the back. To the left was the dining room, the largest and most elegantly decorated room in the house.

The dining room contained a huge mahogany table. Sarah claimed it comfortably seated twelve, and in a pinch, could seat sixteen. There was a small but very delicate crystal chandelier hanging over the center of the table. It was an old fashioned one that still held candles, and Sarah joyed in lighting it just before supper. Clearly, it was Sarah's pride and joy. On weekends, Lily observed that Aunt Sarah dusted it at least twice a day.

At one end of the dining room, there was a huge china cabinet. It was filled with a numerous assortment of chinaware. Lily was surprised to see that none of the dishes matched.

"That is Lizzie's doing," explained Sarah with a mild note of exasperation in her voice. "In the early days, when it was hard to make a living out here in the valley, she started out with plates in this one pattern." Sarah pointed out a simple white plate with a plain gold rim. "When the day came that she finally could afford another place setting, she couldn't find this exact pattern in the local stores, so she chose that one, the bright floral blue and white one on the second shelf. Over time she chose another, then another, then another. Now having a table set with china that doesn't match is a Decker family tradition. Go ahead and pick out your favorite, my dear. It will be yours as long as you stay here."

Lily chose a white plate decorated with little blue and purple violets around the rim.

"That was one of my favorites," said Aunt Sarah obviously very pleased. She gave Lily a little hug and then took the plate and put it back in the kitchen.

Lily had been at the Decker house for almost a week when she made quite a startling discovery. Sarah and Lizzie were not "sisters" in the normal sense of the word, not like she and Virginia were. It turned out that they had once been married to the same man. At the same time. They were the last remnants of the old Mormon polygamist families. They were sister-wives.

"I hope you aren't too terribly shocked, my dear," said Aunt Sarah bluntly as she handed Lily a plate with an apricot fruit salad at dinner that evening. "Polygamy got a lot of bad press back east. No telling what you've heard. Silas shouldn't have told you. Shame on you, Silas. Sometimes, my dear boy, I think you stir up trouble just for pure pleasure."

Silas beamed a broad smile at his "aunt" as she handed him his salad.

"I was planning to tell you myself, Lily, but honestly I've been so busy around here that I plumb forgot. I hope you like apricots. We grow and dry our own. There are five apricot trees out back. Wait till you see them this summer. Nothing like apricot salad and apricot cobbler in the dead of winter."

"I love apricots, thank you. And as far as polygamy is concerned, Mrs. Decker, I really don't have an opinion. I know so little about it," replied Lily politely. It was true. Other than her own experience at her birth, she had not ever met another Mormon till now nor had she heard much about them.

"But I do know something about Mormons," added Lily airily. "I was healed by Mormon missionaries when I was a baby."

Three pairs of very interested eyes suddenly stared intently at Lily. This attention made her a bit nervous. She cleared her throat and continued to explain.

"My mother moved herself and our family up to the city when I was just a little baby. I got very sick, and it happened that two Mormon men stopped at the house. Mother said they put their hands on my head and said a prayer and I was completely healed. Mother said they were missionaries, but my sister Virginia believes they were angels."

"It was two of the Three Nephites!" declared Aunt Lizzie excitedly.

"Don't be silly, Lizzie," scolded Aunt Sarah.

"Three Nephites?" asked Lily confused.

"Mormon folklore, my dear," assured Aunt Sarah. "Would you like some sugar on top of your apricots. I'm afraid they are a bit tart."

"Now, Aunt Sarah, don't completely discredit Aunt Lizzie. Maybe it was the Three Nephites. When Lily was a little baby, the likelihood of Mormon missionaries being back east in her town was extremely slim. If I'm not mistaken, the entire eastern United States was a single mission back then. Do you know what the odds of Mormon missionaries being in her state, in her town, on her front doorstep, at that exact moment, would be? And, don't forget, Aunt Sarah, we do believe in angels."

"Well, I didn't say we didn't," said Aunt Sarah contentiously, "I just don't believe half of those Three Nephite stories that I hear."

Silas grinned at his aunt. Lily could see he really did enjoy stirring up trouble.

"The Mormon missionaries left me a Book of Mormon. It's really an old one. I brought it with me on this trip."

Again, all eyes were fixed on Lily. This time, Silas cautiously addressed her.

"Would you mind showing it to us?" asked Silas.

"Why, I'd be happy to," said Lily. Lily excused herself from the table and ran upstairs to her room to retrieve the book. She returned to the dining room and handed it to Silas. He inspected the outside of the book first, then he carefully opened it.

"Aunt Sarah. Aunt Lizzie. You won't believe this. This book is a second edition."

Lily watched as all three Deckers stared transfixed at her special book. Clearly, they seemed to value it very much.

"Did you ever read the Book of Mormon, Lily?" asked Silas.

"Parts of it a long time ago, but I never really understood it much," confessed Lily.

"Well," said Silas, smiling at her as he handed the book back, "perhaps, sometime, we could explain it to you."

Lily said that would be nice.

"What church do you belong to, Lily?" asked Aunt Sarah.

"Methodist. Virginia is mostly protestant — Baptists, Methodists, and Presbyterians. I guess that's why I never heard much about your church. And believe me, the protestants spend so much time fighting amongst themselves that they hardly have time to talk much about the Mormons."

"Don't have time to bad mouth the Mormons? Well, I never thought I'd live to see that day! My dear, just remember that if you do happen to hear any gossip about the Church or 'The Principle' — that's what we called plural marriage — I advise you to not believe half of it. Unless you lived it yourself, you don't know."

Aunt Sarah looked over at Aunt Lizzie, clearly wanting Lizzie to contribute something to the conversation. But Lizzie blinked innocently at her and quietly began eating her salad. Lily wondered if Lizzie ever spoke when you wanted her to.

Disappointed, Aunt Sarah continued. "Granted, 'The Principle' was a hard way of life. I won't deny it, my dear. It was that.
Sharing your husband with another woman takes more courage and
unselfishness than most humans are capable of. But, I have to also
admit that it had its advantages as well. With the right man and the
right women and the right religious convictions, there was a love and
sense of family that I dare say few people on this earth shall ever
know."

"Does your church still practice polygamy?" asked Lily as she
nibbled on the delicious yellow fruit.

"Good gracious, no," said Aunt Sarah bitterly. "The U.S.
government took care of that. You see, Washington didn't want
Utah with all its Mormons to become a state, so they created a law
that was designed to put our best men in jail."

"Aunt Sarah, I believe it was a little more complicated than
that," corrected Silas mildly.

"How would you know, Silas. You weren't even born yet. I
lived through it. Those were horrible days, my dear. Simply horrible.
Hiding and watching and waiting. Breaking up whole families. Our
Mr. Decker spent some time in jail, God rest his soul."

"Curse the U.S. marshalls!" declared Aunt Lizzie unexpectedly,
banging her hand down squarely on the table, just missing her glass
and Aunt Sarah's salad plate. Aunt Sarah quickly reached out and
managed to catch Aunt Lizzie's glass of milk, as it began to tip over.

"Let's not talk about the marshalls, Lizzie. It always gives you
a sour stomach. Here, have some more walnuts on your salad. My
Adam brought them up just this morning. Aren't they lovely? Now,
as I was saying, the U.S. law was changed, and we Mormons believe
in obeying the law. We are a law-abiding people, Lily. Never doubt
that for a moment. Obedience is an important principle in our faith.
We especially believe in following our living prophet. So when
President Woodruff announced the practice would be stopped, it was
stopped."

"Just like that?" asked Lily.

"Just like that."

"Follow the prophet!" Aunt Lizzie cried. This time the glass of milk didn't survive Lizzie's sentiments. Aunt Sarah sighed, got up from the table, and started mopping up the spilled milk with Aunt Lizzie's napkin.

"Tell me about your polygamist family," said Lily.

"Oh, don't get her started on the family history," moaned Silas. "We'll be here all night."

"Hush, Silas, or you won't get dessert," warned Aunt Sarah.

"Why don't I show her the family albums after supper instead," he offered.

"You'll do no such thing. If anybody shows her the family albums, it will be me. Now, let's see. Our Mormon family history begins with Mr. James Decker and his first wife, Caroline, who joined the Church in England way back in 1860. They were from the county of Kent, just outside London town. They immigrated to the U.S. in '63 and arrived here in the Salt Lake Valley in June of that same year. James was twenty-two years old, and Caroline was barely twenty. James was a gifted carpenter, so there was plenty of work waiting for him to do in the valley when they arrived. There was a great deal of building going on with so many families immigrating to Utah. James made the most beautiful furniture."

Aunt Sarah gazed at the dining room cabinet with affection and then continued her story. "With so many converts moving out west, they couldn't all live in this valley. President Young — that would be Brigham Young, have you heard of him, my dear? — he sent some of them right off to Mexico or Arizona or Canada to live. Such a wonderful man, President Young. When I was a little girl, I sat on his lap once and pulled his beard. Mother was so embarrassed, but he just laughed and laughed."

"I want more milk," demanded Aunt Lizzie with a frown.

"Not till you finish your salad, Lizzie. You've been filling up on milk lately and not eating your dinner properly. You're thin enough as it is. I'll get you another glass after I serve the roast beef. I hope you like roast beef, Lily dear."

"Oh, yes, very much. My mother used to make it all the time for Sunday dinner when I was growing up. Please continue the story. You were talking about James and Caroline."

Aunt Sarah sat back down and picked up a walnut and chewed it thoughtfully.

"Well, James and Caroline were lucky enough to not get sent off to some corner of Arizona or Idaho to live. James would have died a death living in Idaho. I know! If you think it's cold here, you should go there some January. Horrible winters. Simply horrible. And the only thing they ever grow there to eat is potatoes . . ."

"James and Caroline?" encouraged Silas quietly.

"What? Oh, yes, James and Caroline. They built their first house right here in downtown Salt Lake. You probably passed it on the ride in. Silas, you'll have to take Lily out on a Sunday drive sometime and show her Caroline's old house. They had five girls, all of them redheads like their mother. Beautiful girls. The neighbor-hood boys just fought over those girls, let me tell you. Dear Caroline died in 1898, just three months after James died. Doctor said it was her blood pressure, but I say it was a broken heart. Caroline just couldn't live a day without James. She wasn't as strong as Lizzie and myself."

"I had the first son!" announced Aunt Lizzie loudly, flashing with a broad smile at Lily. Lily smiled back. She sure liked Aunt Lizzie, and it seemed that the old woman was growing fond of her.

"Hush, Lizzie, I'm telling the story. Eat your walnuts. I was just getting to you anyway. Elizabeth was the first plural wife. She met James and Caroline here in Salt Lake while she was working as a school teacher. I think Caroline's oldest daughter was one of her pupils. Anyway, she married James in '65, and they had five boys and a girl. She and Caroline didn't get along at all, I'm afraid. It took Caroline a long while to get used to the idea of polygamy, and I think she always resented Lizzie somewhat for being the first plural wife."

"I named all my boys with J's after James — Joshua, Jeremiah, Jonathon, Jared, and Jacob!" added Lizzie proudly. She looked over at Lily with a pleased look on her face and blinked her eyes with satisfaction.

"That's lovely. And did you name your daughter with a J, too?" asked Lily.

"Nope. She's named Eliza . . . after *her.*"

"Her?" Confused, Lily looked at Aunt Sarah and Silas for clarification. Aunt Sarah looked distressed. Silas successfully ignored Lily's stare while somehow managing to soundly step on her right foot underneath the table. He then whispered sideways, "Don't ask. I'll explain later."

Aunt Lizzie opened her mouth to speak, but Aunt Sarah hurriedly resumed her narrative.

"Now let's see, where were we? I remember. I was just getting to Madeliene. Madeliene was next. Oh, she was a beauty, that girl was. Raven black hair and eyes the color of a bright blue October sky. She said she got her looks from her Welsh mother. We never met her mother, I'm sorry to say. She died and was buried out on the trail crossing the plains with the pioneers . . ."

Silas politely coughed.

Aunt Sarah glared. "You're dangerously close to losing your dessert, young man. I'll finish my story in my own good time. Back to Madeliene. I declare men would literally stop in their tracks and stare when she walked by. Poor thing. She only had two boys, Eli and Hiram. She died so young. Pneumonia in '70. She was only twenty-five. Lizzie took her two boys in and raised them herself."

Lily glanced at Aunt Lizzie. Lizzie didn't seem to be paying attention anymore to Sarah's speech. Her head was bent over her salad plate, and her entire focus was on slicing up her one remaining apricot.

"The same thing happened in my family. I had a sister Bessie . . . that died quite recently," said Lily softly. "She was very young also. Now my sister Virginia is raising Bessie's two children."

"I'm sorry," whispered Silas sincerely. Lily looked at him and smiled. Before now, Lily would say that she had an innate distrust of handsome men. This belief wasn't born from personal experience, but Virginia and Bessie had warned her often enough about the dangers of pretty man. Her sisters had taught her such men were most often vain and selfish. But Silas wasn't like that at all. He was different. He seemed open and humorous and very kind.

Aunt Sarah looked at Lily for a moment and then spoke with a mild voice with powerful conviction. "You needn't worry about your Bessie. She lives in the spirit world now, a place as real and beautiful as this snow-covered valley. She's not alone either. She's surrounded by family, your ancestors of days long ago. And someday, someday, I promise that you will see her again. In the gospel, we learn that families are eternal. That's what Mormonism is all about, my dear Lily. *That's what it's all about.*"

Sarah's words touched Lily deeply, and Lily felt her eyes moisten. She took a deep breath and brushed her eyes quickly with her hand. Silas quietly handed her his handkerchief.

"You haven't told me about you, Aunt Sarah," said Lily, wanting to get the topic back to the Decker family.

Aunt Sarah blushed with pleasure. "I was the last to marry James. We were married in 1878. Seems like only yesterday." Sarah gazed up into the chandelier for a moment. Lily wondered if the chandelier as well as the china cabinet had been a present from James Decker.

Aunt Sarah continued, "We had nine children. Two sets of twins! Twins run in my family. I used Old Testament names for all my children — Adam, Seth, Noah, Benjamin, Daniel, Eve, Rachel, Naomi, and Ruth."

Lily opened her mouth to ask a question, but Silas somehow was able to answer it before she could speak.

"That makes 22 children in all, and now there are 75 grandchildren, and as of last Thanksgiving, fourteen great-grandchildren."

"Who's grandchild are you?" inquired Lily innocently.

Silas got a funny look on his face.

"He's *my* grandson," answered Lizzie proudly.

Sarah frowned. "Don't be silly, Lizzie. You know perfectly well Silas is my grandson. He's Daniel's youngest child."

"Is not," exclaimed Lizzie, banging her cane on the floor in the direction dangerously close to Sarah's feet. "He's Eli's youngest. Lord, I should know my own grandson."

"Lizzie! If I have told you once, I have told you a thousand times, I will not have you take the Lord's name in vain at my supper table."

"Your table? Your table? James made this table for me as an anniversary present." She slammed her hand down on the table. Her empty milk glass fell over again.

"Well, he made me the china cabinet."

Silas butted in. "Aunt Sarah! Aunt Lizzie! Stop fighting this instant."

The two ladies immediately quieted and turned very innocent faces towards the young man.

"Fighting?" said Aunt Lizzie in astonishment. "We were not fighting, sweetheart. We were *bickering*."

"There's a difference," added Aunt Sarah in support.

Silas glared at his aunts and shook his head, letting them know he didn't buy it one bit. Lily struggled to keep a straight face. She didn't dare look at them any longer, for fear of giggling. She concentrated on her apricots.

"We've about finished with our salads, Aunt Sarah. How about that roast beef?" suggested Silas heartily.

Aunt Sarah rose and collected all the salad plates.

"Come with me, Lizzie, I need your help in the kitchen."

"I don't want to go in the kitchen. I want to stay with Lily."

"But I need your help mashing the potatoes."

Lizzie's eyes twinkled. "Can I use your new silver serving fork to mash them?"

Aunt Sarah sighed. "Yes, you can use my new fork."

Aunt Lizzie clapped her hands, got up, and hobbled after Aunt Sarah into the kitchen. Lily finally turned to Silas and giggled.

"They are precious, Silas."

"And they can drive you crazy if you live with them long enough."

Lily glanced over to make sure the door to the kitchen was completely closed, then she leaned over and whispered, "Well?"

"Well, what?"

"Who's grandson are you? Lizzie's or Sarah's?"

"Neither. I'm Madeliene's grandson."

"You're Madeliene's grandson!" exclaimed Lily in surprise.

Silas placed his finger to his lips and cautioned Lily to keep her voice down. "Hush, Miss St. John. Do you want to cause a war?"

"Don't they know?"

"Well, actually, I'm not really sure. And there is somewhat of a logical explanation, you see. When Madeliene died, Aunt Lizzie took her two little boys in to raise. So, naturally, Lizzie thinks of Madeliene's children and grandchildren as her own. As for Sarah, well, her son Daniel's boy, Joseph, and I are the same age and were best friends growing up. We were inseparable. I spent as much time at Daniel's house as I did my own. So, I guess Sarah thinks of me as hers."

Lily stared at Silas for a minute, then said, "Why don't you just tell them?"

Silas grinned. "What? And spoil their fun?"

"Fun? You call their fighting . . ."

"Bickering."

"Excuse me, their bickering, fun?"

"Of course, that's how they express their love for each other."

Lily eyed Silas suspiciously.

"Believe it or not, Lily, they are truly devoted to each other. A bit of advice: Don't ever, ever let Aunt Sarah hear you say a wrong word against Aunt Lizzie. She'll throw you out of the house in a heartbeat. I've seen her do it. About three years ago, they took in a railroad man as a boarder. One night he sat right where you are sitting and made a wisecrack about Aunt Lizzie's cane. Sarah marched over and grabbed him by the ear and said . . . well, I can't repeat exactly what she said, although I was most shocked to learn that such words existed in her vocabulary. She led him, ear first, out the front door, and then she marched upstairs and tossed his clothes and toothbrush and suitcase out the bedroom window. If I live to be a hundred, I shall never forget the sight of that man's long red underwear flying across the front yard!

"You see," continued Silas, "Sarah literally owes her life to Lizzie. When the law changed and plural marriage was banned, Sarah and her large family were left penniless. Grandpa James was thrown in jail and was not able to provide for his four families for several years. Aunt Lizzie took Sarah and her nine children into her home. This home. This house and everything in it belongs to Lizzie."

"Except the cabinet and the chandelier."

"Exactly."

"How could Lizzie afford all this?"

"Aunt Lizzie came from money. Big money. She was the only child of a wealthy family back east in New York state. Her parents both died before she joined the Church. If it wasn't for Aunt Lizzie, I doubt half of the family would have survived. She supported everyone while Grandpa was in jail."

"And who, pray tell, is *her*? My bruised foot and I would sincerely like to know," asked Lily.

Silas' face blushed red. "Sorry about that. As bad as Aunt Sarah is about rambling, she is no match for Aunt Lizzie. If you get Aunt Lizzie talking about Aunt Eliza, you might as well cancel your plans for the rest of the evening."

"Aunt Eliza? My sister has a best friend named Eliza back home. This one sounds like another plural wife."

"She was that and more. Much more. If early Mormons had ever decided to elect a Queen, she'd be it. She was quite the character in our history. She was married to Joseph Smith the prophet. Heard of him?"

"I'm afraid not," said Lily.

Silas smiled at her. "Well, I'll have to tell you about him as well. Anyway, she was married to Joseph. Then after he was killed, she was married to President Brigham Young. One of his 'lionesses' I believe you would say. All the early sisters adored her. Brigham they feared. Eliza they loved. She had quite the reputation for leading the sisters with her poetry and prophecy. She and Aunt Lizzie were good friends, and Lizzie religiously goes over to Aunt Eliza's graveside the first Sunday of every month for a 'chat.' She talks to Eliza as if she were still alive. Very strange. I have no doubt she'll drag you over there someday. If she does, just smile and go along with her."

"I will. I might even bring flowers. I'd like to meet this Aunt Eliza."

Silas turned and looked seriously at Lily. Just then, Aunt Sarah and Aunt Lizzie entered the dining room, with Aunt Lizzie carrying a bowl of hot mashed potatoes and Aunt Sarah carrying a large plate filled with sliced roast beef and baked carrots and onions. Everyone filled up their plates. Conversation lagged for a while, then Silas brought up a new subject for discussion.

"Aunt Sarah. Aunt Lizzie. Guess what I bought today?"

"No telling with you, Silas, my dear," said Aunt Sarah heartily.

"A motorcycle."

Aunt Sarah's face turned pale.

"Good Lord above . . ."

"Sarah, dear," piped up Aunt Lizzie. "If I've told you once, I've told you a thousand times, don't use the Lord's name in vain at the supper table."

Silas and Lily looked at each other.

They couldn't stand it any longer.

They both laughed.

3

April 1925

"What is that, Lily dear?" asked Aunt Sarah cheerfully, as she looked up from her knitting as Lily entered the sunny living room.

"A new purse," said Lily proudly, pulling a striking brown leather pocketbook out of a package to show Aunt Sarah. "Mamie and I went shopping downtown to the Z.C.M.I. store this afternoon. Do you like it?"

"It's lovely, dear," said Aunt Sarah, admiring Lily's purchase. "But why a new purse? I thought you just got a new one last month."

Lily sat down on the sofa next to Aunt Lizzie, who was helping Aunt Sarah wind woolen skeins of dark blue yarn into tight round balls.

"I did. And it's already worn out. Being the treasurer at the new factory, I'm in charge of the payroll each month. The money comes in silver dollars, you know, and I have to carry all that money around on payday. My purses wear out in no time flat."

"Well, be careful, dear," warned Aunt Sarah. "You might pull a muscle carrying all that money around. How did things go this week at the factory?"

"Okay, I guess. All of the sewing equipment has been installed and is running properly so far. Mamie and I have just finished training about a dozen new seamstresses, and we'll have another twenty or so to train before the end of summer. All of our seamstresses are Mormons, and they do such good work."

"Industry was something early Mormon women were known for, Lily dear. They went to medical school and opened businesses and grew silk worms to make their own silk. They made this desert blossom as a rose."

"Amazing. And what are you making?" asked Lily with interest.

Aunt Sarah stopped knitting and held up her work.

"It's going to be a sweater for my grandson Jeremiah. He's serving a mission up in Canada. Spring and summer are awfully short up there. He'll be needing this come September."

"Beautiful," said Lily, admiring Aunt Sarah's work. "My sister Virginia loves to knit, too. She's very talented. You should see the two white bedspreads she has made, one for me and one for herself."

"She must be a very patient woman. Bedspreads take forever. I prefer sweaters and mittens. How's your friend Mamie? I was so glad that she could come to dinner last Sunday."

"She's fine. She seems to really be enjoying this April sunshine. I think the Utah snow was quite hard on her legs, though she never complains a bit."

"You'll have to take her swimming in the Great Salt Lake this summer. The salt water will do her circulation good."

"I swam in the Salt Lake once," added Aunt Lizzie with a smile. Lily smiled back and reached over to give Aunt Lizzie a loving pat on the hand.

"We're already planning on it, Aunt Sarah," said Lily. "Silas and his friends have promised to take a bunch of us gals from the factory swimming sometime in June."

Aunt Sarah looked at Lily over her knitting in surprise.

"June? But isn't that when you plan to go on your trip to California?"

"Oh, no!" said Lily. She reached over, picked up a skein of yarn from Aunt Lizzie's lap and started the process of winding another ball. "Our trip to California isn't scheduled till the first of August. Did I tell you that Mamie and I are taking a cruise? Isn't that wonderful? I got some information about the ocean liner in the mail just yesterday. We are sailing on a steamship called 'The Yale and Harvard' from San Francisco all to way down to San Diego."

"I get seasick," announced Lizzie loudly.

Aunt Sarah frowned with disapproval. "Lizzie, you've never been in a boat in your entire life."

"Yes, I have."

"When?" asked Aunt Sarah drily, eying her skeptically.

Aunt Lizzie blinked at Lily and Aunt Sarah.

"A very long time ago."

Aunt Sarah sighed and shook her head.

"I got a letter from my sister this morning in the mail," said Lily.

"Virginia doing well?" asked Aunt Sarah.

"Oh, yes. She reports that little Katherine and Hubert are shooting up like weeds, and that she just got a letter from Willie. He's doing well wherever he is right now in China."

"China?" exclaimed Aunt Sarah in surprise. "You didn't tell me he was overseas! I thought he was still in Florida."

"Didn't I?" said Lily thoughtfully. "I thought I had said. He just got stationed in China for this coming year. I think it sounds awfully exciting. When I was a student at Bryn Mawr, I met some women from other countries — England, Russia, Germany. I decided then and there that I wanted to travel abroad. Willie's hoping for an assignment in Hawaii after this. Who knows? Perhaps I could get to visit him there. I can't wait to write to him about sailing on a cruise ship. Now he won't be the only St. John to ever set foot on a boat in the Pacific Ocean!"

"Lily, Lizzie and I are going to the Salt Lake Theatre tonight. Would you like to go with us? Baroness Elspeth Von Rhoden is performing. She's quite a famous singer."

Before Lily could answer, she heard a rather strange, loud, roaring sound suddenly approaching the front of the house. The noise startled Aunt Sarah, and it made Aunt Lizzie drop her ball of yarn, which went rolling quickly across the hardwood floor.

"What on earth?" said Aunt Sarah.

Lily jumped up from the sofa and dashed over to the front window. She parted the dainty white Irish lace curtains and looked out onto the front lawn.

"It's Silas!" she shouted excitedly. "Come see. He's finally gotten that new motorcycle he ordered!"

"Heaven help us," said Aunt Sarah, getting off her rocking chair and walking over to stand behind Lily. They looked out the window and saw Silas sitting on a large silvery metal object which looked like a very large bicycle to Lily. He looked up at her standing at the window, beamed a broad smile, and waved. Lily merrily waved back.

"What's that ugly big thing attached to the side?" asked Aunt Sarah with displeasure.

"It's called a sidecar, Aunt Sarah," informed Lily.

"He didn't say anything to me about buying a sidecar."

"Oh, they're the latest thing. Silas showed me pictures of them in one of his magazines. They're made for a passenger to ride in. Silas has promised to take me on a grand tour of Utah this summer in that sidecar. I can't wait."

Aunt Sarah look worried.

"Won't that be a bit dangerous, dear?"

"Oh, no, Aunt Sarah, they're quite safe. People ride in them all the time. I understand they're very popular in Europe."

"Well, I can't imagine they'd ever be very popular out here," Aunt Sarah said decidedly.

"Silas, I want to ride," an earnest voice called out.

Aunt Sarah gasped, and Lily turned around in time to see that Aunt Lizzie was off the sofa and well on her way out the front door.

"Lizzie, wait . . ." called Lily, heading after the elderly woman.

"Elizabeth Margaret Decker, you'll do no such thing," cried Aunt Sarah, running after her.

Lily and Aunt Sarah caught up with Aunt Lizzie just as she began going down the front steps. Each grabbed an arm and held on tight to the determined elderly woman.

"Let go," said Aunt Lizzie, impatiently squirming. "I want to go for a ride in Silas' new motorcycle."

"It's out of the question," insisted Aunt Sarah.

"But I want to."

"You simply can't, Lizzie dear," protested Aunt Sarah. "Be reasonable."

"I don't want to be reasonable. I want to go riding," said Aunt Lizzie defiantly.

"Elizabeth! Be still. You absolutely cannot do such a thing! Think about your poor hip!"

Aunt Lizzie's temper and nostrils flared. "My poor hip? That old hip walked across the plains!"

The mere mention of "crossing the plains" made Aunt Sarah's face flush pink. Lily had witnessed several incidents over the past few months where mentioning this history of walking across the American midwest to get to the Salt Lake Valley proved to be a real source of contention between the two sisters. It was a real badge of honor that Aunt Lizzie sometimes held over Aunt Sarah. Aunt Sarah had been comfortably born in the West. Aunt Lizzie, on the other hand, like many other early Mormons, had arrived by the powers of her own two feet, pushing all her possessions and rations in a small wagon called a handcart. And no one mentioned, but it was understood, that Aunt Lizzie didn't have to walk. She had been rich enough to purchase other means of transportation. This issue, more than anything, was a sore spot with Aunt Sarah.

Aunt Sarah let go of Aunt Lizzie and crossly folded her arms.

"Fine," she said hotly, "break your hip. See if I care." And with that, she turned and marched back inside the house.

By this time, Silas had climbed off his new motorcycle, turned the engine off, and made his way across the front yard and up the porch steps. He stood in front of Aunt Lizzie and angrily shook his finger at her.

"Shame on you," he said sharply. "You've hurt Aunt Sarah's feelings. And just for doing that, I have half a mind not to take you riding on my motorcycle this afternoon."

Lily could see that Silas was not teasing Aunt Lizzie this time, like he usually did when she misbehaved, but that he was genuinely mad. Aunt Lizzie blinked her big eyes sadly and looked quite ashamed.

"I'm sorry, Silas," she whispered, sounding like a scolded child.

Silas gazed at her intently.

"You should be," he said firmly. He reached over, took Aunt Lizzie's chin in his hand and lifted her face up. "Promise me that you will make up with Aunt Sarah right away."

"I promise."

Tenderly, he brushed away several tears that had fallen down Aunt Lizzie's cheeks.

"And that you'll be good for the rest of the day?"

Aunt Lizzie smiled sweetly at her grandnephew.

"I'll be very good, Silas," she said sincerely.

"Well, then, I guess you can go for a little ride after all."

Aunt Lizzie's face beamed bright with pleasure, both for being forgiven and for ultimately getting her way.

"Let's go right now!" she said excitedly.

Lily and Silas helped Aunt Lizzie down the front steps and out towards the motorcycle. Lily stood back as Silas picked Aunt Lizzie up and put her into the sidecar. Once properly placed, Lily stepped up and arranged Aunt Lizzie's thick, white shawl securely around the old woman's shoulders. She didn't want the old woman to catch cold. Silas got onto the motorcycle and started up the engine. It roared loud and strong, and Aunt Lizzie laughed and clapped her hands happily at the sound.

"Silas!" shouted Lily over the engine noise.

"Yes?"

"Do be careful."

Silas grinned with delight.

"Don't worry. I'll go real slow."

"But Silas," complained Aunt Lizzie bitterly, "I want to go fast."

Silas ignored Aunt Lizzie's request and gingerly started the motorcycle rolling slowly down the street. Lily watched fascinated as he reached the end of the street and turned the motorcycle around by going in a large semi-circle. They rode slowly back, and as they passed the house, Aunt Lizzie looked up at the second story of the house and waved fervently. Lily glanced up in time to see the front bedroom window curtains quickly fall shut.

"Whee!" said Aunt Lizzie.

Silas took Lizzie up and down the street two more times. As Lily watched them ride by, she thought about her feelings for Silas. He was such a good man. Over the past three months, they had become best friends. Each morning, they would ride into work together on the yellow Utah Light and Transit streetcar, and then they rode back together in the late afternoon when work was over. During those times, she and Silas had wonderful conversations together. She told him all about her family and the South and her experiences at Bryn Mawr. He, in turn, told her much about himself, his family, and his church.

He told her about the beginnings of the Mormon Church, way back in the early 1820s, about the prophet Joseph Smith's vision of God and Jesus Christ. He told her all about how her Book of Mormon came to be. It was a remarkable story of an angel named Moroni who came to the young Joseph and led him to the ancient gold records nearby and how Joseph translated those records. That was the angel who was depicted on top of the grey temple. He told her about how Joseph and his brother Hyrum were shot and killed by mobs and how Brigham Young then led the persecuted Saints out to the Salt Lake Valley.

Lily found it all very interesting. But she found herself resisting it and in turn, resisting her growing affection for Silas. He was attracted to her, she could tell, but he wasn't pushing. Not yet, anyway. But Lily's strong ties to Lynchburg and her sister and her past and her Methodist upbringing stood in her way. Could she give that all up? Would she be asked to?

Aunt Lizzie didn't want to get out of the sidecar when the ride was over, but Silas gently reminded her that she had promised to be good.

"Go inside now and set things right with Aunt Sarah," ordered Silas simply. Lily assisted Aunt Lizzie back up the front porch stairs and waited till she had gone inside the house. Then Lily dashed back out front to the waiting motorcycle.

"Hop in," said Silas.

Lily did just that.

"Where are we going?" she asked breathlessly.

"I thought we would make a big circle inside the city today. I'm still learning how to change the gears on this thing. I think I've got a good handle on it, but I want more practice before we start making our grand trips around the state. I want to take you down to Provo. Since you are such a nut about colleges, you must see the Brigham Young campus. We can go to Ogden. Some of my Decker uncles live there that I think you would like meeting. Logan is a sweet little town and very beautiful in the summertime, and I want you to see the Mormon temple there. It sits way up on a lovely hillside."

"Don't forget the mountains," urged Lily. "I want to explore lots of canyons, too."

"Consider it done! Ready?"

"Ready. And Silas!"

"Yes?"

"One more thing before we go."

Silas leaned over closer to hear Lily better.

"Go real fast."

4

July 1925

Before coming to Utah, the only holiday Lily had ever known to celebrate during the month of July was Independence Day. Now her stay in Utah was affording her the opportunity to experience firsthand a unique Mormon summer holiday — Pioneer Day. Lily thought the Pioneer Day activities were very similar to Independence Day celebrations held back in Virginia. Both occasions were filled with picnics and parades and sentimental speeches. However, other events, like horse races at the Salt Lake City fair grounds, bathing at Saltair resort, and a baseball game at Bonneville Park, were also available to enjoy.

The particular Mormon church that the Decker family attended, which they called their "ward," had a special outing planned on this Pioneer Day in which whole families were invited to a picnic at Liberty Park. Everyone was asked to dress up like pioneers. Aunt Sarah and Lily had a lot of fun going up into the dusty attic and going through trunks of old clothes. Aunt Sarah, Aunt Lizzie, and Lily chose old calico dresses and white ruffled bonnets. Silas found a pair of pants and shirt that had belonged to Grandpa Decker, and Aunt Sarah broke out in tears when she saw him in it.

They had their picnic lunch right between two lush flower beds. Lily and Silas spread an old quilt on the ground, then situated Aunt Lizzie carefully in its center. Food was arranged around her, and then

Lily and Silas and Aunt Sarah sat down on the quilt corners. Several of the Decker grandchildren and great-grandchildren joined in on the celebration, so that Lily saw that they were soon surrounded by other quilts full of Deckers.

"I want some of Lily's fried chicken," ordered Aunt Lizzie impatiently. Lily had made her landladies a special "southern" style dinner back in May for Mother's Day, and Aunt Lizzie had been hooked on Lily's fried chicken ever since. Lily handed the dish of chicken over to Aunt Sarah, who was fixing a plate for Aunt Lizzie.

"You must give me your recipe, Lily," said Aunt Sarah, putting a crisp chicken breast onto the china plate. "I can see I'll be needing it." What Aunt Sarah didn't say, but Lily knew that she meant, was that she would need it after Lily was gone. But Aunt Sarah never discussed Lily's leaving in the fall.

Lily didn't want to discuss it either. It was going to be very hard to leave Salt Lake City.

Once Aunt Lizzie's plate and mouth were full, the rest of the group settled down for a pleasant lunch. Lily helped herself to chicken and fresh rolls and potato salad and pickles and fresh apricots, which she and Silas had picked from the backyard. A couple of great-grandchildren came around, carrying samples of other dishes and desserts sent over by daughters and daughters-in-law, and Lily found that her plate was soon running out of room. One great-grandchild, a little girl about five years old, stayed and crawled up into Aunt Sarah's lap, fully enjoying Aunt Sarah's attention and fresh-baked peach pie.

When lunch was over, while Aunt Sarah and Aunt Lizzie visited with their posterity, Silas and Lily decided to go for a walk around the park. They strolled aimlessly, enjoying the background music of the Hawkins military band.

"This bonnet is too hot," complained Lily bitterly.

"But you wear it well, Miss St. John. It becomes you," responded Silas wickedly.

"Easy for you to say. You're not the one wearing it." Lily pulled it off of her head and ran her fingers through her damp dark curls.

"I thought you liked hats," teased Silas cheerfully.

"Why do you say that?"

"You're always buying them."

"No, I'm always buying handbags. Mamie buys the hats."

"Mamie buys everything," laughed Silas.

"You should see the dresses she's purchased for our cruise. There must be over a dozen. She has more dresses than we have days aboard ship!"

"Everything set for your California trip?" asked Silas.

"Almost. But, surprise, surprise, Mamie wants to go shopping at Z.C.M.I. again before we leave. She wants to get another traveling bag. I think she's planning on buying lots of souvenirs and wants something spacious to carry them home in. She wanted to go today, but we couldn't since everything in Salt Lake is shut down for the pioneer celebration."

"Well, never fear. The stores will surely open their doors to you both early tomorrow morning."

Lily laughed. "You know, I'm worried that Mamie is getting much too attached to that Z.C.M.I. store. The way she shops there, I wonder if she'll want to go back to Virginia."

"Well, I, for one, would vote wholeheartedly that you both stay permanently."

Lily felt her face flush. This was getting more and more difficult. Her friendship with Silas continued to deepen, despite her own concerns. Almost every weekend since he got his motorcycle last April, they had spent their free Saturdays taking day trips up and down the valley. Lily bought several pairs of knickers for riding and exploring, much to the shock of Aunt Sarah, who preferred dresses for young women for all occasions. Needless to say, Aunt Lizzie loved the knickers and immediately demanded a pair of her own.

Their latest adventure had been rock climbing up Emigration Canyon. Lily and Silas rode up together, and Mamie and several friends tagged along by car. One of Silas' friends brought along a camera and took lots of pictures of them crawling around the rocks. They had had a wonderful time, too wonderful perhaps. And Silas, bless his heart, was still so patient. He hadn't voiced his feelings yet, but he didn't need to. When he looked at her, his eyes were brim full with his affection and adoration.

"When do you leave?" asked Silas.

"September," owned Lily solemnly.

Her response shook Silas out of his serious mood. He grinned. "No, not that. I mean when do you leave for California."

"Oh . . . Friday. We leave Friday."

"From Ogden?"

"Yes, we'll catch the Union Pacific rail from there to take us to San Francisco."

"Well, you must send me a postcard and tell me what the Pacific Ocean looks like."

"I will."

Conversation, which was usually so easy between them, lagged. They were silent as they continued to walk, a silence which made Lily feel very unsettled.

"Let's go sit on one of those benches and listen to the band for a while," she finally suggested. "I think I've walked enough to work off that last piece of Aunt Sarah's peach pie."

"Good idea," conceded Silas heartily. "The newspaper this morning said that Miss Laurinda Brewerton was going to be a soprano soloist this afternoon. Aunt Sarah says she's really good. I'd like to hear her."

"Great. Let's go then."

Almost automatically, rather subconsciously, Silas reached for her hand and took it firmly into his own. The contact sent a physical spark of feelings through Lily that she both enjoyed and feared at the same time.

This was getting much too hard.

This was getting much too nice.

Lily didn't sleep well that night. She dreamed vivid dreams. In one dream, she saw herself on the deck of a large ocean linear. Silas was standing beside her, dressed in a handsome black suit with a bouquet of red roses in his hand. Lily looked out over the side of the ship and saw her sister Virginia standing on the dock, weeping and waving a white handkerchief. The ship began to pull out of the harbor, and Lily held onto the railing tightly with one hand and waved a sad goodbye to Virginia with the other. In another dream, she found herself back home in Miller Park. She was walking quietly along one of the garden paths until suddenly she heard the loud sounds of two women quarreling. She ran along the path toward the noise. She came up to a large stream of water with a bridge built across it. On the bridge, she saw Mrs. Whitten and Aunt Lizzie fighting. Mrs. Whitten was wielding her favorite rolling pin, and Aunt Lizzie was swinging her black cane. Across the bridge, on the other side of the stream, Silas was standing, laughing, surrounded by several small children dressed in white.

Lily awoke on Saturday morning, exhausted. She hardly spoke at all to anyone at breakfast, complaining of a headache, and went back to bed immediately. Aunt Sarah was duly perplexed and peeked into her room several times to check on her. Silas mildly knocked on her door at lunchtime, and asked through the door if she were hungry. She replied that she was not. He then gently asked if she was still interested in going for a ride that afternoon up to Brighton Canyon. She was not. She suggested that he take Mamie instead. Silas left, not asking any more questions.

Lily spent the day in bed, alternately lying down to think about her situation and then sitting up to read in order to not think about her situation. Neither activity made her feel any better. By dinnertime, she knew she had to get up and put on a good face. She dressed and went downstairs with many smiles and assurances that she was just fine. But it was all a lie.

She slept better Saturday night. This was probably due to the fact that she had completely exhausted her mind the day before. She did not dream much this night, and she woke up feeling somewhat refreshed. She got up and dressed and went down to breakfast in a more composed frame of mind. When she entered the dining room, Aunt Sarah and Aunt Lizzie were there at the table, waiting for her.

"Good morning, Lily."

"Morning, Aunt Sarah. Good morning, Aunt Lizzie."

"How are you feeling, dear," Aunt Sarah asked with concern as she handed Lily a plate of hot fresh waffles.

Lily took two waffles and put them down on her plate, then handed the plate to Aunt Lizzie.

"Much better, thanks."

Aunt Sarah's face relaxed into a look of genuine relief.

"Well, you look better. Nothing like a good night's sleep for what ails you! What would you like on your waffles? There's maple syrup and there's fresh peaches."

Lily sighed. Must there always be a choice?

"I don't know," she said brooding.

"I want both!" said Aunt Lizzie firmly.

Both. Well, there's another option. But I can't have both, thought Lily bitterly. Unless God could move both the state and the sister named Virginia out to the Salt Lake Valley in two months.

"Lily?"

"Oh, I'm sorry, Aunt Sarah. I was just lost in thought. I guess I'll have the peaches. They look delicious."

"They're wonderful. My daughter Ruth's husband brought them by yesterday afternoon. They have quite a few fruit trees on their property. She makes the best peach preserves. I'll be sure to open a jar for lunch."

"Sounds . . . wonderful," said Lily, while taking a big bite of waffle dripping with peach juice. It tasted heavenly.

"Would you like to read the paper? Lizzie and I have already read it."

Lily said she would, and Aunt Sarah handed her the crumpled copy of the *Salt Lake Tribune*.

"Oh, there's a piece about a woman jumping off a sixth floor window in Boston, some terribly rich woman. It's down at the bottom of the page. Horrible. Lizzie and I were just talking about it before you came down. All that money, and yet she was completely miserable."

"Money . . . doesn't make . . . you happy," said Lizzie with her mouth full. "People do."

"I didn't say that money made people happy," protested Aunt Sarah hastily. "I didn't say that at all. I meant that it's just awful that this woman should be so unhappy to throw herself out a window to her death. What's the world coming to?"

"The end," answered Aunt Lizzie plainly.

Aunt Sarah rolled her eyes at this comment, and they finished their meal in silence. Breakfast completed, Aunt Sarah got up to start clearing the table.

"Hurry and drink your milk," she advised Aunt Lizzie as she picked up Lily's plate and empty glass. "I don't want to be late for church."

Aunt Lizzie gulped down the last few swallows of milk from her glass and handed her dishes up to Aunt Sarah's waiting hands.

"I'm not going to church," said Aunt Lizzie.

Aunt Sarah's mouth dropped open. Unless desperately ill, Aunt Lizzie never missed church. Aunt Sarah hurriedly put the plates down on the table and put her hand across Aunt Lizzie's brow.

"Elizabeth, are you feeling poorly? Do you have a fever?"

"No, I do not have a fever. I caught Lily's headache."

Aunt Sarah frowned.

"You can't catch a headache."

"I did," said Aunt Lizzie matter-of-factly. "And I'm spending the day on the living room sofa." With that, she got up, took her cane, and hobbled out of the dining room. Aunt Sarah watched her leave with a mixed look of concern and disapproval on her face, shook her head, then gathered up the dishes and went out to the kitchen. Lily decided to stay in the dining room while she finished reading the *Tribune*, and she relaxed and made herself comfortable in her chair. Aunt Sarah finished up in the kitchen, hurriedly took off her apron as she walked back into the dining room, and bid Lily a hasty farewell.

"I'll see you at lunch. Silas has the car. He had to go to a meeting early this morning before church. I'm going to ride to church with the Ericksons next door and then will ride home with Silas afterwards. Do me a favor and keep an eye on Lizzie."

Lily promised that she would, and Aunt Sarah sailed out of the house. Everything got very quiet, and Lily focused her full attention on reading the rest of the paper. She was in the middle of enjoying an article announcing the opening of the second summer term at the University of Utah when she heard the sound of Aunt Lizzie's hobbled steps and tapping cane headed towards the dining room. She looked up to see the old woman, wearing her Sunday black lace shawl and black gloves. Aunt Lizzie was holding Lily's new white hat and gloves and briskly handed them to her.

"Put these on and come with me," ordered Aunt Lizzie.

"What . . ."

"We have to be back before Sarah comes home."

With that brief and unclear explanation, Aunt Lizzie turned and hobbled out.

Lily was stunned and called after her.

"Aunt Lizzie, wait . . ."

"Hurry up, Lily. We have to catch the 9:15 rail."

It was clear that Aunt Lizzie was not going to wait. Having promised to keep an eye on her and fearful of whatever it was that she had planned, Lily dropped the paper, grabbed her hat and gloves, and hurried out of the room to catch her elderly friend at the front door.

"Aunt Lizzie, I thought you had a headache," said Lily anxiously, as she helped the woman down the front steps.

Aunt Lizzie turned and patted Lily affectionately on the cheek.

"Lily, dear, don't be silly. You can't catch a headache."

They got off the rail at the Eagle Gate, at the corner of State Street and South Temple. Although it was just about mid-morning, it was already very sunny and hot. Both streets, which were usually very congested with downtown business traffic and commuters, were essentially empty. Most of Salt Lake was at church or was still in bed.

"We're going that way," said Aunt Lizzie, pointing her cane east. Lily took the woman by the elbow, and they slowly started walking up South Temple. Lily didn't bother asking just where they were going. She had essentially figured that out on the ride over. As Silas had warned several months earlier, Aunt Lizzie was finally taking Lily to meet *her*.

After walking for about a block, they came upon a small cemetery, tucked away unobtrusively behind several houses. Lizzie boldly proceeded to walk through someone's backyard to a small entrance to the graveyard.

"Most people use the entrance on First Avenue," she said simply, "but I always use this one. That way I don't have to walk so far."

The cemetery was surrounded by a high, ornate, black iron fence. Lily opened the gate, and the two of them went inside.

"Go over there first," directed Aunt Lizzie, pointing to a marker. Lily let Aunt Lizzie lead her. When they drew near, Lily looked at the name on the gravestone and openly gasped.

"Why, it's him!" she exclaimed.

The stone read, BRIGHAM YOUNG.

"You look shocked, my dear," observed Aunt Lizzie.

"I'm sorry. I'm just a little surprised, that's all."

"Whatever for?"

"Well, I guess I expected something more grand for 'The Lion of the Lord.' I mean, several times when Silas has taken me riding all around Salt Lake, we've gone around the city cemetery. There are some very majestic markers up there, beautiful things. I guess I just assumed that *he* would be there, too. This marker, this place . . . well, it's so secluded, so . . ."

"Humble?"

"Yes, that's it."

Aunt Lizzie stared down at the marker thoughtfully.

"That's because he was a humble man, in spite of all his wealth and position and power. If not, he wouldn't have been a prophet. And *she* wouldn't have had a thing to do with him."

Aunt Lizzie stared at the stone for a few minutes more, and Lily wondered what was going through her friend's mind. What memories of the past did this little garden cemetery stir within her? Lily remained quiet, not wishing to disturb Aunt Lizzie's reverie.

Finally, Aunt Lizzie turned and walked toward a large, white marker. They walked slowly around the flat stone lying in the ground. Lily read the name that graced the top of the marker.

ELIZA R. SNOW SMITH.

Aunt Lizzie leaned heavily on Lily's arm as she carefully lowered herself down to her knees, leaned over, and laid her hand lovingly on the stone.

"Hello, Eliza," she whispered softly in the gentlest voice that Lily had ever heard come out of Aunt Lizzie. Lily knelt beside her friend, gazing quietly at the touching scene.

"Eliza, I've brought a new friend for you to meet. You'd like her. She's smart and strong and full of life. Just like you were."

Aunt Lizzie looked up at Lily and beamed an approving smile.

"Say hello, Lily," she said.

"Hello, Aunt Eliza," said Lily tenderly. Lily half expected to hear a reply, but the only sound she heard in response was the call of a small sparrow perched up in a nearby shrub.

Aunt Lizzie reached over and squeezed Lily's arm tightly.

"Tell me more about Aunt Eliza," asked Lily in a hushed voice. Aunt Lizzie leaned over again and slowly stroked her hand across the stone. It seemed to give her strength, to connect her with another time and place. Her voice and her countenance seemed to light up. Her face glowed.

"You remind me a lot of Eliza, Lily. She was petite and had dark hair like you. She was gracious and so intelligent. She had the same passion for learning as you do. She wrote beautiful poems that seized our hearts, making the sisters of the Church completely devoted to her."

Aunt Lizzie paused for a moment, as if she were out of breath. This alarmed Lily for a brief second. She put her arm around the elderly woman. But Aunt Lizzie wasn't feeling ill. Aunt Lizzie was on fire.

"She was our president, our prophetess, our priestess! She labored among the sisters and among the poor and among the children. She was the best of our generation . . . and now she is almost forgotten. How could they ever forget her? How could they?"

Aunt Lizzie looked up at Lily, with tears streaming down her face.

"I promised that I would never forget her. Never!"

Lily felt a few tears tickling down her own face as well.

"And you haven't," she said assuringly.

Aunt Lizzie wiped away her tears with her gloved hand and sniffed loudly.

"And it makes me just furious when they do remember. They refer to her as 'Eliza R. Snow' as if she were an old maid, a girl who never got married." Aunt Lizzie took her cane and banged it angrily at the top of the gravestone.

"Is that the name of an old maid?"

Lily shook her head no.

"That's her name! They can't even remember that right!"

Lily waited a moment for Aunt Lizzie to settle back down before asking a question.

"What do you think she would like to be called?"

Aunt Lizzie pulled out a handkerchief from her purse and loudly blew her nose.

"That's easy," she sniffed sharply. "I think she would like to be called by either her Christian name as 'Eliza' or 'Aunt Eliza' or by the name that truly reflects who she was then and who she is now in eternity."

"And what is that?"

Aunt Lizzie looked up at Lily and smiled with satisfaction.

"Sister Smith."

Lily looked down at the cold stone and pondered what Aunt Lizzie had said.

"Aunt Lizzie, I believe you are right."

"She was a woman who possessed a great light inside. And you are like her in that regard, Lily. But her place was here among us. And your place is not."

This statement caught Lily totally off guard and struck a nerve at the very center of her present worries. But how did Aunt Lizzie know? Lily looked to see Aunt Lizzie staring at her. Her eyes sparkled behind the thick glasses, and her face seemed to shine in the morning sun.

"You are a very special person, Lily St. John, placed on the earth in the days of the restoration. And the Church has touched your life twice for a special purpose. Now you have to go back with that light. You have to go back."

Aunt Lizzie stopped speaking and suddenly bowed her head, as if she were exhausted. She took a deep breath and sighed.

"Go outside and wait for me by the gate, Lily," she said quietly. "I need to talk to Eliza alone for a while."

Lily didn't argue or ask any questions. She got up off her knees and slipped out of the small garden cemetery. She was surprised to see that her hands were shaking. Her whole body was shaking. She folded her arms tightly around her chest and started walking up and down the sidewalk, trying to calm down.

But she couldn't.

Aunt Lizzie's words rang in her mind over and over again, and Lily remembered back to the day of her graduation from Bryn Mawr, when she walked as one of Wisdom's daughters through the historic columned courtyard, holding a brightly trimmed lamp high in her hands.

How did Lizzie know?

5

August 1925

"I can't," said Lily.

"Yes, you can," said Mamie.

"No, I can't."

"Lily, you must," urged Mamie emphatically.

Lily bit her lip perplexed and shook her head.

"No, really, I can't do this."

Mamie placed a firm, reassuring hand on Lily's shoulder and continued her insistent persuasion.

"Lily, it's your decision, but I say it's a wonderful choice. Take it."

Lily looked at her friend and sighed.

"Well, if you think . . ."

This was all the encouragement Mamie needed. She handed the blue-beaded dress to the waiting store clerk.

"She'll take it," said Mamie triumphantly.

The grey-haired saleswoman congratulated Lily on her purchase and took the money Lily held out with her trembling hand.

"But, Mamie, twenty-five dollars for a dress? Virginia would die a death if she were here."

"Well, Virginia is not here, thank the good Lord. And I, for one, will not let you not buy that dress. It's absolutely darling on you and perfect for tonight's dance. Mr. Decker will fall where he stands when he gets one good look at you in that!"

"But do you think it's too much for the occasion? I mean, is it too dressy for the barbecue?"

"It will be perfect. Nothing is too fancy for a ball at Saltair, and you're sure to be the belle of the ball tonight. I can just see you and Silas doing the foxtrot across the dance floor, all eyes on you and your sparkling new dress."

"The prospect of such scrutiny doesn't give me much comfort, Mamie. Suppose I trip or something?"

Mamie's eyes widened.

"Shoes!" she exclaimed excitedly. "Now we have to find the perfect pair to match the dress."

"But . . ."

Mamie grabbed Lily by the hand as soon as the saleswoman handed Lily the bag containing her new ball gown and dragged Lily out of the Boston Store. Lily struggled to shift her package and purse comfortably around in her other hand while trying to keep up with her friend. How did Mamie do it? In the enthusiasm and excitement of shopping, her friend's handicap seemed to disappear. She could hobble along the downtown sidewalks at a pace that challenged Lily. In this respect, mused Lily humorously, Mamie was a lot like Aunt Lizzie. Aunt Lizzie hobbled as well, but it was not advisable to leave her alone for long. She and her cane could wander off anywhere in no time flat.

"If we hurry, we can hit Z.C.M.I. before lunch. They always have the best sales!"

"But, Mamie," shouted Lily as they made their way up the congested sidewalk, "we don't have time. I promised to be home by one. Silas is taking me out to the fairgrounds this afternoon. We're going to the Frontier Roundup."

"Oh, Lily. There's always time to shop!"

Despite Lily's misgivings, Mamie's declaration proved to be true, and they were successful in finding the needed shoes, in catching the needed train, and in arriving home by the needed time. Lily literally ran inside the house, threw her purchases on top of her bed, madly changed into her favorite pair of knickers and a white blouse, and even managed to run a comb through her wild curls before going downstairs for a quick bite of lunch. Aunt Sarah had a cold sandwich and some sliced fruit waiting for her, and a waiting Silas shared her company while they ate.

They rode over to the fair grounds on the motorcycle and spent the entire hot Saturday afternoon enjoying the events. Silas bought two tickets for the grandstand, which gave them a great view of the championship rodeo. Lily had never been to a rodeo before, so Silas had to provide her with some detailed explanations before each event. There was calf roping, steer roping, steer wrestling, and a bucking championship. The bucking contest looked quite painful. Riding around Utah in the motorcycle sidecar had more than once left Lily with bruises on her backside, and she wondered about the possible size of the bruises these fellows would be waking up to tomorrow morning.

After the riding events were completed, she and Silas walked aimlessly around the fairgrounds. Silas bought her some pink cotton candy and some peanuts, which she generously shared with him. She bought a souvenir for Virginia at one of the trade booths. It was a small square piece of leather that was painted with a picture of a rose and a lovely poem.

When she and Silas got home, Aunt Sarah had dinner and a surprise waiting. She had gone down to the drugstore that afternoon on an errand and had picked up the pictures of Lily's California trip. Lily clapped her hands for joy. They sat down to dinner immediately and sipped their vegetable soup while passing around the photographs.

"What's this one," asked Aunt Sarah intrigued.

"That's taken at Mission Dolores in San Francisco. We went there on the day we arrived. Isn't it lovely? There were so many different kinds of flowers in the gardens. And so many birds!"

"I want to see," demanded Aunt Lizzie impatiently.

"You've hardly looked at the last one I handed you," observed Aunt Sarah with disapproval.

"Yes, I did."

Aunt Sarah's eyes narrowed.

"What was it?" she quizzed.

"A picture of Lily."

Silas laughed.

"Good guess, Aunt Lizzie."

Aunt Lizzie beamed.

Silas let out a yelp.

"Oh, I love this one! I get to keep this!" he said and clutched the photo to his heart.

"Let me see," chorused Lily and Aunt Sarah together, both reaching madly for the picture. Silas teased and fought both of them off, refusing for a moment to let either of them examine the print while they protested loudly.

Finally, Silas held up the picture for both of them to see. It was a picture of Lily, dressed in a very modern dress and hat, sitting right on top of a huge ostrich.

"Why, it's Mr. Jinx!" said Lily.

"This bird has a name?" asked Silas, amused.

"Yes, Silas, you remember. I told you about going to the Cawston Ostrich Farm. We went there the same day we went to Chinatown."

Aunt Sarah successfully snatched the picture away from Silas and examined it more closely.

"Lily, you actually got on top of that thing?" she asked, shocked. "Wasn't it dangerous?"

"Oh, no, not really. There was a handler nearby. Lots of people had their picture taken with Mr. Jinx."

"With Mr. Jinx or on Mr. Jinx? Please clarify," asked Silas drily.

"Oh, hush, Silas. Eat your soup," ordered Aunt Sarah firmly before Lily could reply to Silas' teasing. "You'll give us all indigestion."

Happily, they finished eating their dinner and looking at Lily's photos. Then, Lily excused herself and went upstairs to get ready for the barbecue. She took an extra long time with her toilet, primping her makeup and hair leisurely. Tonight was the first official date that she and Silas had had since she returned from California, and she wanted to look especially pretty.

As she put the finishing touches of lipstick on her lips, she wondered what would happen tonight. Tensions and tenderness were extremely high when she left almost three weeks ago. If she hadn't gone to California when she did, she feared her remaining resistance to Silas' affection would have completely given way. Not that giving in to Silas' affection would be a bad thing. It appeared to be a very pleasant proposition. But was she ready to follow where such feelings would lead?

California proved to be a wonderful getaway, and she spent many moments on the deck of the Yale and Harvard steamship pondering the situation. When she had returned to Salt Lake, she had not made a final decision either way, but she had determined to be open to both options. Perhaps that, in itself, was a very big step. Before that, she had simply fought her feelings for Silas. When she put on her dress and stockings and slipped on her new shoes, she resolved to be open to whatever happened. She splashed on a tiny bit of cologne that Virginia had given her last Christmas and gathered up her handbag and gloves. She was ready!

When she came down the stairs, Mamie's prediction essentially came true. Silas didn't exactly fall where he stood, but he did look at Lily with an amazed look on his face and let out a sort of wolf whistle.

"Lillian Ruth St. John, you look fabulous!" He reached for her hand and placed a princely kiss upon it. Lily smiled with satisfaction. She was positively pleased with herself.

Silas had procured the use of the Decker family car for the occasion, and with great ceremony, he led Lily out of the house and up to the door of the big black automobile. Aunt Sarah and Aunt Lizzie stood on the porch and waved goodbye heartily to them as they drove away.

The Saltair resort was packed with a huge crowd of patrons that evening when Lily and Silas arrived. Lily loved seeing the lavish Moorish building at night. Lit up, with its large round center dome and rounded towers, it looked like a fairy-tale castle floating out upon the water. She and Silas walked hurriedly out along the dock, anxious to get inside. There were several extraordinary events happening that night at Saltair. There was the buffalo barbecue, made from the meat of three buffalos shot by Governor George H. Dern. This barbecue was being held as part of the annual outing of the state's Young Men's Democratic Club. There were boxing exhibitions, which Lily had absolutely no interest in viewing. What was of interest to her was the prize foxtrot contest and the music of the popular Salt Lake band, The Ambassadors.

Just as they entered the large dancing pavilion, the main attraction of the evening was just getting under way. The famed dancers, Armand and Lorraine of San Francisco, the originators of the newest dance craze, the Charleston, were on hand to give a thirty minute official demonstration.

"Come on! You have to see this!" urged Lily excitedly, tugging Silas by the hand and working her way up closer to the front of the crowd. "I saw this dance on board ship while in California. It's spreading like wildfire from coast to coast. Everyone is doing it!"

They edged up to the front of the crowd and watched spellbound as the two famous dancers shimmied and shook to the new dance step. The onlookers cheered and clapped enthusiastically when the performance was over and then filled up the dance floor themselves to try out the latest craze.

"Is this right?" yelled Silas over the music, unsure of his movements.

"Perfect!" Lily yelled back with enthusiasm. They made a decent attempt at the dance, and Lily felt very fashionable as she hopped and twisted around her escort in her bouncing beaded outfit. When the Charleston music finished, the band played other popular tunes — first a foxtrot, then a waltz. Now Silas seemed much more confident and took Lily masterfully in his arms around the dance floor. Lily swirled happily across the floor. She simply couldn't imagine a more beautiful night.

The evening hours slipped quickly by between the dance floor and the large dining room, where they retired on several occasions for refreshment. When the dance was over, Lily didn't want the night to end and frankly said so to Silas.

"How about a drive up to the capitol?" he suggested.

"That would be divine," said Lily wistfully.

"Your wish is my command," said Silas.

They rode up the hill on the north part of the city where the large state capitol building stood, majestically overlooking the city. On top of the hill, there was a beautiful view of the valley, full of its sparkling night lights, and of the shining moon and stars overhead. Surrounded by brightly-glowing street lights and tall trees, it was the perfect place for a late-night walk. They parked the car and got out. They chatted for a while, discussing the dance and who they did and did not see there. Eventually, Lily begged for a moment's rest and stopped to lean against a towering willow tree.

"I should never have allowed Mamie to talk me into buying a new pair of shoes. My feet are killing me," Lily complained. She leaned over and slipped her shoes off. The green grass underneath the tree felt cool and refreshing, and she wiggled her toes in relief.

"Well, it's your own fault," argued Silas playfully. "You didn't have to dance every dance!"

"Oh, yes, I did. Every single, solitary one! I made a promise to Virginia to have all the fun and excitement that I could while I was here."

Silas grinned at her clearly enlightened.

"I see. But did you have to almost kill me in the process? I fear that various and sundry limbs of mine will soon not be able to move due to an overabundance of sore muscles."

"You can't blame that on me," criticized Lily. "You didn't have to dance every dance with me."

Silas put his hand across his chest as if wounded.

"What? And let some other fellow have that pleasure? With you by far outshining every other young lady in grace and beauty? Perish the thought, Miss St. John. Tonight, at least, for a few moments, you were completely mine."

Lily laughed at this.

Silas did not. Instead, Silas stared. Deep into her eyes he stared.

Lily attempted to start the conversation again. "Didn't you just love Armand and Lorraine? I've never seen such performers. The way that she moved. It was incredible . . ."

Silas kept staring. This made talking extremely difficult. Lily looked away, to the left.

"I can't wait to show Virginia how to do the Charleston. Virginia loves to dance. She's such a good dancer . . ."

Lily looked back. Silas' eyes looked lovingly over her face, her hair, her eyes, her lips. Lily looked to the right.

"Didn't the Ambassadors sound good tonight? I wish Mamie could have been there to hear them play. She loves music. She's quite a good singer, you know. At home, she sings in the church choir . . ."

Lily looked back at Silas and shut up.

He didn't say anything, didn't move, didn't touch her. He just looked intently, as if he were studying her face, memorizing every detail. The suspense was overwhelming, electrifying, and the seconds seemed to be endless.

Why didn't he kiss her?

Finally, after what felt like an eternity, when she was at a point of either screaming or grabbing him herself, Silas leaned towards her slowly and gently brushed his lips across hers. She responded by melting into his arms, giving herself over fully to her deep affection for him.

They didn't talk much as they drove back to the house. Words didn't seem necessary. Silas held her hand tightly, and she leaned her head over against his shoulder. She was very happy.

When they arrived at the house, Silas parked the car in front of the house and shut off the engine. He lifted her face up to his and kissed her again.

"Lily?"

"Yes, Silas."

"Lily, you are supposed to leave Utah in two weeks."

"Don't talk about that now," she insisted, kissing his cheek softly.

Silas pulled away and looked at her seriously.

"Lily, we must talk about it now. I don't want you to go." He looked down at her hand that he held tightly in his own, then looked at her again.

"I want you to stay, Lily."

Lily sat back and studied his face carefully. Such a statement could only mean one thing, and she felt her heart racing as she asked him, "Silas, what are you saying?"

"That I never want you to leave, Lily. That I love you dearly, with all my heart and soul. That I want you to stay and become my wife."

Lily clutched his hand tightly as he proposed. Now she had to decide, to face the decision that she knew was inevitably coming. Saying yes meant saying goodbye to home and family, to the pink Virginia dogwoods and luscious pines, to the rolling mountains of the Blue Ridge. How could she leave that all behind?

Yet, how could she say no? In this moment, as she looked at Silas, she knew what it was she had been fighting for so long.

She loved him, too.

"Yes, Silas, I will marry you."

Now Mamie's prediction of complete collapse seemed about to come true. Silas looked so surprised that Lily felt sure he would fall forward and faint dead away in her arms.

"You will? You'll marry me?" His voice sounded incredulous, and he grabbed her up and held her so tightly in his arms she found it almost difficult to breath. After several minutes of happy hugging and kissing, during which time Lily was successful in catching a few breaths of air, Silas let go of her.

"Wait till Aunt Sarah and Aunt Lizzie hear the news. Shall I tell them or would you like that honor?" he asked with delight.

"We'll both tell them, I think," suggested Lily.

"And then we'll call Virginia on the telephone right afterwards."

"Across the country? But, Silas, that would be so expensive."

Silas took both of Lily's hands and kissed them tenderly.

"Who cares what it costs if it makes you happy. You've made me happy, Lily. I'm the happiest man in the world right now."

Lily liked hearing that and showed Silas her appreciation with another kiss.

"Lily?"

"Yes, Silas."

"What do think about shopping for a ring tomorrow?"

"Tomorrow is Sunday, Silas. All the big department stores are closed."

"Oh. Okay, how about the next day."

"We have to go to work on Monday, Silas. We'll go next Saturday, and if you don't mind, we'll take Mamie with us. She can sniff out a sale at a hundred paces."

Silas grinned merrily.

"Sounds great. Let's start making the wedding plans right away," said Silas excitedly. "You can start thinking about what kind of dress you would like, and we can get brochures on places we could go for our honeymoon. Where would you like to go for a honeymoon, dearest?"

The question startled Lily.

"I don't know, Silas," she laughed. "I've never thought about planning a honeymoon before."

"Well, don't worry. We have lots of time to plan and to prepare while we're waiting."

The last part of his statement puzzled Lily. What did he mean?

"Waiting?"

"You know."

"No, I don't know. What is this 'waiting' that are you talking about."

Silas smiled at her sheepishly. "Lily, we'll have to wait awhile before we can get married in the temple. It's some sort of guideline for new converts. You'll have to be a member for a while before you can get a temple recommend."

Convert? Member? Temple recommend? Suddenly, it dawned on Lily what Silas was referring to, and a sick cold feeling rushed through her entire body.

"Silas, I said I would marry you. I said nothing about joining your church."

Silas stared at her blankly, his smile quickly fading.

"But I thought . . ."

"Well, you thought wrong. Do I have to be a Mormon for us to get married?" she asked plainly.

"No," owned Silas reluctantly.

"Well, then, what does it matter. We don't have to get married in your temple. We can have the wedding here at the house."

Silas looked torn, terribly torn inside.

"I want a temple marriage, Lily. It's very important to me."

Lily folded her arms across her chest, beginning to feel angry inside.

"Wait a minute here. I am willing to leave my sister, Virginia, and my niece and nephew, and my hometown — all that I love dearly, in order to marry you. I am willing to make that sacrifice in order to be with you. I don't see why you can't make a sacrifice for me as well."

"But, Lily, I can't give up my religion," he exclaimed sharply.

"And yet, that's exactly what you're asking me to do,"
her voice and temper flared. A sharp look of pain fell across his face.

"But the Church has touched your life, Lily, as a child, and now . . ."

"Yes, it has, and I am very grateful. Living here in Salt Lake has helped me to learn a lot about your church and your people. I have a high estimation of both. But, Silas, I was born a Methodist. My sister is a Methodist. My brother is a Methodist. My mother was a Methodist. All of my grandparents were Methodist. I was born a Methodist, and I am a Methodist, and I will die a Methodist."

"Lily!" Silas reached out for her, but she pushed him away.

"This is awful," he moaned. "If only you would —"

"I think," she interrupted bitterly, "that we have said enough. Perhaps we better go inside. It's getting late."

6

December 1925

There was a knock on Lily's door.

"Come in," she said lethargically.

The door slowly opened, and Virginia entered the room, carrying a tray of food in her steady hands.

"I've brought you some lunch," she said, setting the tray down on top of the chest of drawers. "There's some hot potato soup, and there's buttermilk biscuits, fresh from the oven. And there's strawberry jam."

Lily didn't need a detailed announcement of what was on the menu. The steam from the hot soup rose up, filling her room with its delicious aroma. And the smell of bread baking had already reached her room many minutes before Virginia had arrived.

"Thank you," said Lily absently. "I'll eat it later."

Virginia gazed at her sister critically.

"No, you won't. You'll just lie there and brood and let everything get cold."

Lily closed her eyes and sighed. She didn't want company. She wanted to be alone with her misery. Virginia was caring for her like she was a child. Ever since Walter Shultz and his new wife decided to take custody of Katherine and Hubert again, Virginia was without someone to care for. Now she had Lily to fuss and worry about. Not that under different circumstances Lily would have minded. But grief and depression draw you in, make you want to hide. And Lily wanted to hide on the weekends when she was off work. But, glancing up at her sister, Lily saw that Virginia showed no clear signs of leaving.

"If I promise to eat everything, will you go? I want to be by myself this afternoon."

Denying her request, Virginia crossed her arms and sat down squarely on the bed beside Lily.

"Why don't I believe you?" she mused boldly. And before Lily could respond, Virginia answered her own question. "Perhaps because I have felt this way once myself?"

Lily winced. It hurt to hear Virginia speak of her past pain and compare it to Lily's present heartache. Virginia had lost so much. But, then again, so had she.

"Are you going to spend every weekend in your room brooding?"

Lily didn't answer but looked at her sister instead with eyes full of sadness.

"I should have never insisted that you go out west," said Virginia shaking her head with regret. "It was a mistake."

Lily sat up quickly and reached out for her sister's hand.

"Oh, no, Virginia. Don't say that. It wasn't a mistake. It was wonderful."

"You call this wonderful?" said Virginia drily. "Then I'd hate to see what horrible looks like."

Lily bent her head and finally let out a sound that was a mix of a sob and a groan.

"You don't understand."

Virginia put her hand under Lily's chin and lifted it up.

"Yes, Lily, I think I understand very well. You had a marvelous adventure, traveling across the country, seeing new and exciting places, and meeting new and exciting people. And on top of all that, you fell madly in love."

Lily tried to hold back the tears, but she couldn't. They started to fall down her cheeks.

"It breaks my heart to see you hurting so much," said Virginia sincerely. She looked around the bed and saw an open letter lying on top of the quilted bedspread.

"Another letter from him?"

Lily nodded yes.

"What did it say?"

Lily sat up straight in her bed, searched for and found a much needed handkerchief, and blew her nose hard.

"The same thing they always say. 'Lily, I love you. Lily, I want to marry you. Lily, please come back.'"

Virginia picked it up and eyed it carefully.

"How many does this make so far?"

"I don't know. Four or five, I think."

"Have you written anything in response?"

"No. But his aunts have written me twice, and I wrote them back."

"Are you going to write to him?"

Lily took the letter out of Virginia's hands and threw it on the floor in anger and frustration.

"What would be the point? What can I say different than I said last summer or when I left Utah in September? It's impossible, Virginia. I don't want him to go against his principles. That would make him less of the good man that he is. It would be wrong. And I can't change my religious beliefs simply because I love him and want to marry him. I would be joining a church, a good church, for the wrong reasons. It's useless."

Virginia studied her sister's face with an intense look of concern and love.

"Until now," she said reflectively, "I used to think that death was the worst thing that could separate two people in love." She paused briefly, her old anguish close to the surface in her quivering voice. "But this has changed that opinion. At least I can still think of Elijah as my own. We would have married if he had lived. I see now there are other barriers worse than death. And I am terribly, terribly sorry."

Lily could hold back her grief no longer, and she threw herself into her sister's sure arms, weeping. Virginia held her tightly, gently rocking her as if she were a tiny child, as Lily gave full vent to her feelings. When the wave of emotion passed, Lily pulled back and blew her nose again and wiped her face.

Virginia stood up and moved the tray from the chest of drawers to the nightstand beside Lily's bed.

"Eat something. It will make you feel better. Promise?"

Lily nodded her promise, and Virginia smiled and left the room.

About an hour later, there was a knock on the door.

Lily was still lying down on her bed, this time almost asleep.

"Don't worry about lunch," she called out in a drowsy voice. "I ate every bite."

The door briskly opened, and Mamie hobbled into the room, all bundled up in her matching brown hat and coat.

"Splendid. I'm so happy to hear it," she said heartily. "Now I wonder what you'll do with your dinner!"

Surprised, Lily sat up in bed and welcomed her friend dutifully.

"Hello, Mamie, how nice to see you. You look lovely today."

"Thank you. I only wish I could say the same thing about you," replied Mamie candidly. Lily eyed her friend sharply.

"What a mean thing to say!"

"No, what an honest thing to say. Lily, I simply will not stand for this any longer. You must not pine away over that man. You can do better than this. Where's the brave and bold woman who went to Bryn Mawr and came back so full of fire?"

Lily stared ruefully down at her hands folded in her lap.

"She's sitting here, all wet."

Mamie smiled at Lily's humor and shuffled over and sat on the edge of the bed.

"That's better. It's a good sign when you can joke about a broken heart. That means you're on the mend."

"I don't feel like I'm mending," said Lily begrudgingly.

"That's because the brain heals first. The heart will slowly follow. In the meantime, we need to get your body out of this mood and out of this room. That's why I stopped by. I've come over to invite you to an evening party at John and Lena Creasy's house. You know Mr. Creasy? He's the nice man who works at that little grocery store on the corner? Anyway, the Creasy's are having a few of the young people from church over for refreshments this evening. Lena's brother from up in Nelson County is staying with them over Christmas, and they wanted to have some people over to entertain him. Lena promised to make her famous apple pie. You can't turn down a slice of Lena Creasy's apple pie. And Ola Roberts has promised to play the piano for us. We can sing Christmas carols."

"I don't know, Mamie. I really don't feel like it."

Mamie smiled slyly. "Of course you don't feel like it. And that shouldn't influence your decision in the least little bit. It's simply the right thing to do. Say you'll come? I'm not leaving this room till you do."

She clearly had no choice. Mamie was much more stubborn than Virginia, and Lily knew it. It was a waste of time fighting Mamie McGuire!

"Alright. I'll come."

"Good. You won't regret it. We'll have a marvelous time. Ola Roberts and Vida Pearce are coming by to pick me up about seven. We'll swing by for you about half past. Sound okay?"

"That sounds fine."

"Well, I'll see you then."

Mamie carefully got off the bed and shuffled her way to the bedroom door. Before she opened it, Lily called out to her friend.

"Mamie?"

Mamie turned around and look expectantly at her.

Lily drew herself up in her bed and managed the smallest of smiles.

"Thanks."

*   *   *

Lily dressed half-heartedly and put on her makeup with complete apathy. She didn't care at all what she looked like. There wasn't anyone there that she wanted to impress. But she would try for Mamie. For her friend, she would put on a good appearance. She pursed her lips properly and applied a bright cranberry pink lipstick to her lips. Her hair had grown out considerably since Bryn Mawr. It was long again, but she had kept the bangs. She pinned up her hair in a fancy style and left a smart curl lying down on her forehead.

Well, she still felt totally horrible, but she looked good.

Mamie, Ola, and Vida drove up promptly at half past seven and blew the car horn. Lily drew her coat closely around her, stuffed her mittened hands in her coat pockets, and dashed out to the waiting car. Why did it have to be this cold, Lily thought shivering. It was biting cold outside. Utah had such a dry climate. Even when there were piles of snow outside, it never felt this cold in Utah.

The Creasys didn't live very far away, and on her own, Lily could have walked to their home. But due to Mamie's handicap, it was necessary to drive. And fortunately for them, Vida Pearce had a free-thinking father who allowed his young daughter both the opportunity to get a driver's license and permission to borrow his big black car. Lily sat in the back and didn't talk much on the ride over. But the conversation didn't lag a bit with her lack of participation. Ola, Vida, and Mamie chatted away nonstop.

They arrived at the Creasy's house and parked the car on the street. Lena had a beautiful pine wreath on the front door, and the living room curtains were pulled back to allow them a full view of a brightly-decorated Christmas tree. The four young ladies piled out of the car and hurried up the walkway to the front porch, with Mamie hobbling with them as quickly as she could. Lily held out her arm and allowed Mamie to hold on to it as they rushed to the door.

Ola banged on the door loudly.

Suddenly, Lily felt a wave of panic.

She felt the urge to turn and run back to the car.

She shouldn't have come. She should have stayed home, where it was warm. Where it was safe.

The door opened briskly, and Lena Creasy stood there smiling brightly.

"Merry Christmas Vida, Ola. Merry Christmas Mamie. Lily, so good to see you again. Merry Christmas, dear. Come in. Come in," she said, welcoming them to her house. She stepped back and motioned for them to enter. Ola and Vida went in first, and Mamie and Lily followed them.

They found John Creasy standing in the hallway grinning.

"Merry Christmas, gals. You all look like frozen icicles," he observed. "You better go in and stand by the fire and thaw out a bit!"

"Give me your coats first," ordered Lena with her arms extended. The ladies stripped off their heavy coats and hats and mufflers and piled them high on Lena's waiting arms.

"I'll put these in the back bedroom," she said from behind and almost underneath the stack of wool and fur. "You follow John into the living room. I'll be in presently."

John led them through two french doors into a cozy den with a fireplace and two sofas. Lily lagged behind the pack and was the last to enter the room and the last to see the fair-haired young man standing beside the fireplace mantle.

He had light blond hair and bright blue eyes. His face reminded her a lot of her brother Willie. A broad forehead, straight nose, and a mouth with a natural solemn expression. He was of medium build and height, and he held a cigar in his hand, which he puffed as he watched the ladies enter the room.

"Ladies," said John cheerfully, "I'd like for you to meet my brother-in-law, Mr. Levi Dameron. He lives up in Nelson County, near Lovingston now, but he's planning to move down to Lynchburg this spring to work at the barbershop on Fort Avenue. Levi, let me introduce you. This is Ola Roberts, probably the best pianist in our little church. Ola's extended family owns a furniture and piano business in town."

Ola giggled as she exchanged handshakes with Mr. Dameron, who made no verbal reply to this introduction but nodded his head in greeting.

"And this is Vida Pearce, who has a beautiful smile and unlimited access to her father's car. I recommend that you get well acquainted with her." Mr. Dameron dutifully took Vida's hand in greeting but still made no effort to speak. What a strange man this Mr. Dameron appeared to be.

John Creasy put his arm around Mamie and proudly presented her to Mr. Dameron.

"And this special young woman, Levi, is Mamie McGuire, who constantly inspires all of us." Mamie held her hand out to Mr. Dameron, who went so far as to greet her with an actual smile. But still he said nothing.

Now Lily was filled with both curiosity and disgust. Mr. Dameron was either deaf and dumb or terribly proud, and Lily severely doubted the presence of physical disability. Did he think himself too good to speak? Or was she being too hard on the man? Perhaps he was just terribly shy.

Mr. Creasy came over to Lily, took her by the arm, and led her over to the fireplace to where Mr. Dameron was standing.

"And this jewel of a girl," Mr. Creasy bragged with delight, "is our special sweetheart. Levi, may I have the pleasure of presenting Miss Lily St. John."

Mr. Dameron stepped forward and firmly took Lily's extended hand into his own and stared directly into her curious eyes. Lily felt somewhat uncomfortable at his intense attentions and then felt almost embarrassed as Mr. Dameron's muted tongue finally regained its powers of speech.

"Miss St. John, the pleasure is all mine."

7

September 1935

Lily got off the crowded bus on the corner of Main Street and Eighth Street. It was noon, and the downtown sidewalks were full of shoppers and businessmen. She looked around and up the side street to her destination, the tall tan-colored Allied Arts Building, a new skyscraper that towered over downtown Lynchburg. She clutched her handbag tightly and began her short walk up Eighth Street towards Church Street.

She wished desperately that Virginia could have come with her, but Virginia's stomach was bothering her again. Lily had often insisted that Virginia go and see a doctor, but Virginia had refused to go for so long, saying it was just nerves or indigestion. But during their last trip to the country, to attend the wedding of the daughter of Virginia's old friend Eliza, her sister's stomach upsets had grown much worse. Finally, with the combined influence of Lily's and Eliza's urging and protests, Virginia was persuaded to make an appointment with the family physician last week; and today she was meeting this doctor over at General Hospital for some x-rays and lab tests to try to figure out what was wrong.

Lily came up to the shiny revolving door of the Allied Arts Building and pushed through with firmness and determination. She squared her shoulders, ready to take care of this matter. Levi had offered to go with her, but this was her family business to take care of. And, besides, she didn't want him to miss a day's work at the barbershop. Levi had a good business working as a barber in a small shop on Fort Avenue, and they needed every extra bit of money he could earn to support themselves and their two little daughters. They had struggled successfully through the Depression, but the experience left Lily with too many lingering fears and concerns about finances.

Lily made her way over to the elevators, found the office that she was looking for on a directory posted on the wall, and pushed the up button. The elevator light soon blinked off and the doors opened with a cheerful little "ding." She boarded the car and pushed the button for the fifth floor.

The elevator doors soon opened, and Lily walked out into a long hallway. She went about halfway down the hall until she saw a door marked "Simon Crawford, Attorney-at-Law." She took a deep breath and went inside.

An attractive secretary sitting at a large oak desk greeted her promptly.

"Hello. May I help you?" she asked pleasantly.

"I have a noon appointment with Mr. Crawford."

The secretary looked down at an open calendar sitting on the corner of her desk.

"You must be Mrs. Dameron?"

"Yes, I am Mrs. Dameron . . . Mrs. Lily St. John Dameron."

The secretary stood and indicated to Lily that she should have a seat in one of the two large armchairs in the front waiting room area.

"Please make yourself comfortable, Mrs. Dameron, while I go tell Mr. Crawford that you are here. He is expecting you."

"Hello, Mrs. Dameron," said Mr. Crawford, as he invited her into his small private office. "Please come in. May I get you some coffee?"

"No, thank you." Lily sat down in a wooden chair in front of Mr. Crawford's large desk. Mr. Crawford went around the desk and took his seat in a bright red leather chair.

"I believe, Mrs. Dameron, that we talked on the phone briefly last week and that you sent me some materials in the mail for this interview."

Lily nodded her head and indicated that she had.

"If I remember correctly, I believe your neighbors, Fred and Mildred Price, referred you to me?"

Again Lily nodded.

"Yes, I've known the Prices for a long time. Fine family. Well, before we begin talking, let me pull your folder out so I can have all the documents that you sent right in front of me. My secretary just brought in the file."

He picked up a stack of files on the corner of his desk and sorted through them until he found the one he was searching for. He opened the folder and began looking through the contents.

Lily studied Mr. Crawford's features. He was a tall man, with thick dark hair and mustache. He had a very thin face, one of the thinnest that Lily had ever seen. How odd to be so thin in face and so thick in hair. And how did he ever find eyeglasses to fit so narrow a profile, she wondered as she stared at him.

"Now, I understand you are here in a matter regarding your brother?" he asked straightforwardly.

"Yes, my older brother William."

"Why don't you tell me what you know about the situation, and then we can decide what action to take."

Lily cleared her throat and began speaking.

"My sister, Virginia, and I need your help. We are desperately trying to find out any information regarding Willie. He is missing."

Mr. Crawford picked up one of several newspaper clippings from the file.

"No word since the hurricane hit Florida last week?"

"Nothing. Not a word."

"The accounts in the newspaper have been quite horrifying. Almost five hundred casualties? I understand that a large portion of the Florida Keyes were completely devastated and that President Roosevelt has declared it a national disaster area. When we spoke last week on the phone, you indicated that you had been contacted by the Florida Red Cross. Have you had any additional word from them?"

"We received a telegram yesterday. They report that he is still missing, but they are continuing efforts to search for him."

Mr. Crawford put the newspaper article down in the file folder and looked up at Lily with concern.

"I'm terribly sorry. I'm sure that you and your family are most upset. What would you and your sister like for me to do, Mrs. Dameron?"

Timidly, Lily pulled a letter out of her purse and unfolded it carefully.

"We would like to hire you to assist us in trying to get some information, anything really, from the War Department in Washington. I've written a letter that I would like you to send for us to Washington, with a cover letter from you attached. May I read this to you?"

Mr. Crawford nodded his head yes and leaned comfortably back in his chair while Lily began to read.

Gentleman:

As a last resort I am writing you to ask your assistance in locating my brother, William P. St. John, last heard of from Veterans Camp No. 5 Islamorada, Florida. Since the storm, the only information we have received has been through the Associated Press that his name was on the revised list from Florida, and through the Miami Red Cross that he was still missing. We have wired them several times, and don't doubt that they are doing all they can, but I thought maybe your department might get quicker results. We are almost frantic for word of him. I had two letters from him from Islamorada, the last one about the last of July saying they were building a bridge now, but later on they expected to start making shoes.

I understand that the War Department has finger-prints of all men who have seen service. My brother first joined the navy in Philadelphia in 1918. Served several terms in the navy on the U.S.S. Kansas and U.S.S. Dixie. Then in about 1929, he joined the army in order to get to go to Honolulu, and for a time was stationed at Schofield Barracks in Honolulu. He got his discharge from the army in 1932 in San Francisco, California, came here and worked in the shoe factories until work got dull and was laid off. In February 1935 was in a C.C. camp at Blackstone, Virginia. Then we next heard from him in Islamorada, Florida.

For identification he was about 5 feet 6 inches, weighed 150 pounds when he left here, has light brown hair, blue eyes, good front teeth, several jaw teeth missing, bathing beauty tattooed on arm, and bullet wound under skin near crown of his head. Slight scar somewhere near the eyes.

Any information would be greatly appreciated by my sister and me.

Thanking you for an early reply.

I am

> Yours most sincerely,
> Mrs. A. L. Dameron
> (Lily St. John)

Mr. Crawford extended his hand, and Lily promptly gave him her letter.

"This will do nicely," he said with assurance. "Very nicely. I'll have Mrs. Smoot type it up right away. Why don't we set an appointment for sometime next week, Wednesday perhaps, for you to come back and sign the formal letter? I'll have a cover letter written then which you can review. In the meantime, I'll do some work on finding a contact person in Washington. How does that sound to you, Mrs. Dameron?"

Until that moment, Lily had been in fairly good control of her emotions. She had steeled herself before leaving her house that morning. But a feeling of relief to finally have someone willing to assist her flooded her heart and brought forward an unexpected flood of tears as well. Lily wept openly. Mr. Crawford didn't seem too disturbed by her sudden display of emotions, but instead he calmly reached for a box of tissues sitting in the window sill and quietly handed them to her.

"Thank you so much," sniffed Lily gratefully when her outburst was finally over. "You have no idea what this means to us."

"I'll do my best, Mrs. Dameron. That I promise you. Let us hope that we can get you the information that you need and, God willing, that the news will be good and that your brother has been spared."

Mr. Crawford stood up and came around the desk to escort Lily out of the office. He walked with her up to his secretary's desk, and together they made an appointment for the following Wednesday afternoon at two o'clock. Lily bid Mr. Crawford and Mrs. Smoot an appreciative goodbye and left the law office with something she had not had for over two weeks — a small feeling of hope.

Lily boarded the return bus with every intention of returning straight home, but oddly enough, she found herself compelled to get off at an earlier stop in front of the old city cemetery instead. She walked quickly down the sidewalk, alongside the loud, rushing traffic, and through the huge black iron gates at the cemetery entrance. The September sun was shining high overhead giving off the warmth of a promising Indian summer, and the grounds were still green and wonderfully quiet. It was peaceful.

She had not been to this place in a very long time. As she strolled up a winding street, she tried to remember the last time she had come here. Mother's Day two years ago? Or was it three? Yes, it had been three. How could it have been that long? Why did it seem that as she got older, time passed so much more quickly?

The Lynchburg City Cemetery was an enormous place, with many rolling green hillsides and well-kept gardens. There were a few old sections that contained numerous large, carved stones topped with statues of angels and children. These monuments were Lily's favorite, and she usually made an effort to stroll past them whenever she visited.

The entire place was surrounded by a tall brick fence that helped shut out the noise of the outside world, and all along those brick walls were climbing rose bushes of red and pink and white. Lily walked quietly to one of the places she knew. There she looked down at the marker of Mr. Whitten, their former neighbor. He had died after she had gone out west, and Mrs. Whitten had gone to live with one of her daughters. It had been years now since they had heard from her. Lily wondered if she were still alive. Surely, they would have heard something.

Lily walked on until she came to the very back end of the cemetery. She knelt down between two stones, one flat marker that bore the name of her sister, and one raised white stone that bore the name of her mother.

Once again, as had happened in the lawyer's office, a wave of heavy emotion washed through her heart, and Lily openly gave vent to her feelings of grief and despair. Despite the sparkling sun overhead and the sweet smell of autumn roses in the air, Lily felt that she was surrounded by blackness. Everything seemed so dark. Mother was gone. Bessie was gone. And now, Willie was missing and probably dead.

And Virginia was ill.

She had never felt so alone in her life. So afraid of being alone. And so tired.

There were other things, too, taxing her strength. Raising two small children while working full time was a constant drain upon her nerves. And she and Levi were desperately trying to buy a house, but saving up that kind of money took time. They were currently sharing a house with Virginia, which despite Virginia's generosity, felt somewhat awkward and stressful.

"Oh, Mother," Lily whispered softly, "I wish you were here."

Lily leaned forward and touched her Mother's stone tenderly. As she did, a long forgotten memory stirred within her anxious mind. She pictured herself back in Salt Lake City, back at that little cemetery with Aunt Lizzie, having a discussion with *her*.

Eliza, I've brought a new friend for you to meet . . .

Lily smiled at the thought, almost laughed. Here she was doing just what Aunt Lizzie used to do. What would Silas think? Lily sighed. She hadn't thought of him in such a long time. He had married two years after she had left Salt Lake City, almost the same time that she had married Levi.

The two Decker sisters had kept up a correspondence with Lily for quite some time before and after her marriage. She could still picture Aunt Sarah fussing over preparing a fancy dinner, setting her beloved dining room table with the odds and ends of Aunt Lizzie's assorted china. And she could see Aunt Lizzie, sitting proudly in the sidecar of Silas' motorcycle, riding up and down the Avenue. Aunt Lizzie had been such a good friend. So had Aunt Sarah. And now they were both gone.

You'd like her. She's smart and strong and full of life. Just like you were.

Was I ever really smart and strong and full of life, questioned Lily bitterly? Maybe years ago, as an idealistic young woman, who had not yet really experienced the sorrows of life. Now she didn't feel very smart or strong at all. She felt only helpless and angry against the forces of nature and against the unexpected, things far beyond her control.

Lily bent her head over and sobbed again. Perhaps that was the greatest part of her despair, the difficult realization that the things that were breaking both her heart and her family apart were things that she couldn't control. She couldn't stop hurricanes and tidal waves. Or death from childbirth. Or consumption.

Lily felt a physical pain deep inside her chest, as if her heart would really break. And, in this moment that she believed she would completely give herself over to despair, she heard Aunt Lizzie's voice again speaking clearly through her pain.

You are a very special person, Lily St. John, placed on the earth in the days of restoration . . .

Lily opened her eyes and looked up at the sun shimmering above her in the bright blue sky. She blinked and shook her head. How could there be a special purpose in her life? What was so special about her life as a wife, a young mother, a garment factory worker?

Now you have to go back with that light.

Her light. The memory of Aunt Lizzie's words somehow encouraged Lily. With new resolve, she wiped the tears from her face and stood up. She would go back, back to her house and her life with some semblance of courage. She still didn't feel strong, but she would act strong. And, maybe, in the course of such acting, perhaps she would indeed become stronger. What was that saying? Fake it until you make it?

She stood up and blew a kiss goodbye to her beloved mother and sister and then paused a moment to smell one of the large, dark pink roses that graced the wall behind Mother's grave. The deeply-cupped blossom gave off a spicy fragrance that pleased Lily, and she gently removed a single rose petal and put it in the pocket of her sweater.

When Lily arrived home, she found Virginia seated in the living room in her favorite rocking chair, hard at work on a piece of embroidery. Lily gave her sister a kiss and inquired after the children.

"Mrs. Price brought little Peggy over when I returned home," replied Virginia simply. "I gave her a bottle and put her down for her afternoon nap, and I haven't heard a peep out of her since."

"Sometimes she takes an extra long nap in the afternoon," commented Lily as she looked at her watch. "I'll check on her in a minute. And Louella?"

"She's next door playing with the Finch's little girl."

"Good. And how are you feeling?"

"Fine," said Virginia without much conviction. Lily immediately doubted her sister's half-hearted response and sat down on the floor next to the rocking chair to further probe for the truth.

"Well, tell me, how did things go at the doctor's office. Did they do the tests?"

"Yes."

"And?"

Virginia finally put down her handiwork and looked directly at Lily.

"They found something."

Lily put her hand down into the pocket of her sweater and found the little rose petal. She squeezed it tightly in the palm of her hand. She would be strong. She must be strong.

"What is it, Virginia? What did they find?"

"Cancer."

8

August 1965

What was wrong?

Lily frowned to herself. Something just wasn't right. Something was missing, something important, something . . . what was it? She was having trouble putting her finger on it. Perhaps she should put her finger in it?

Puzzled, Lily leaned over the kitchen table and dipped her finger down in a thick apricot-yellow cake batter and then put her finger into her mouth to taste. It looked and tasted very dry, more the consistency of cookie batter than cake batter.

Surely she had forgotten something.

She went over to the kitchen counter and picked up the recipe card.

Applesauce Cake

1 cup butter	2 eggs
1 cup sugar	1 teaspoon cinnamon
2 cups light raisins	2 teaspoons cloves
1 cup chopped nuts	2 teaspoons nutmeg
1 teaspoon baking soda	pinch of salt
3 1/2 cups flour sifted	2 cups applesauce

"How stupid," she laughed at herself as she walked over and opened the pantry and picked up a large jar. "How can you make applesauce cake without the applesauce?" She opened the jar and measured out two cups of applesauce to add to the mixing bowl. She poured the sauce into the bowl, then put in the electric mixer and began mixing. There. That ought to do it.

Retirement was so enjoyable. After working for four decades in the factory, Lily relished each day that she had to spend quietly in her own home, doing the simple domestic things that gave her such pleasure. Over the years, she had gained quite a reputation within both her family and within her church circle for being an extremely good cook, and now nothing made her happier than creating a delicious meal. Admittedly, sometimes, she overdid it a little — well, maybe overdid it a lot — but she didn't mind the leftovers, and her family and friends didn't mind the enormous feasts that she prepared. A party for four meant making enough food to feed a family of ten. This cake, one of her very favorites, ought to do nicely for the church social this evening.

She also had a wonderful reputation for having a green thumb. Any flower flourished under her watchful eye. While Levi cared for the outside yard, she literally filled the inside of the house with her begonias and violets and baskets of hanging ivies and geraniums. Granted, it took a lot of work to keep everything watered and properly cared for, but she didn't mind. Plants made such good pets.

Lily put the mixer down and tasted the batter again. Perfect. She picked up the bowl and carried it over to the counter where she had two cake pans already greased and floured. She slowly poured and scraped the batter into the pans and popped them into the hot oven. Again, she consulted her well-worn recipe card:

Bake in oven at 350 degrees for one hour.

Lily set the timer on the oven for sixty minutes. Good. That would give her plenty of time to have lunch and then clear away the dishes. Then, while the cake was cooling, she could finish sewing the little blue calico dress for her women's circle project. They were going to send over their second batch of children's clothes to the African mission next week, and she wanted to get this dress done in time to ship with the other garments she had made. It was so nice of Louella to mail down those scraps of material last month. They were making up into the cutest little dresses and pants and shirts. Oh, how she missed her oldest daughter. Washington D.C. was too far away. She must remember to thank Louella when she wrote her next letter.

She started to open the refrigerator door to make herself a cold ham sandwich when she heard the front doorbell ring.

Now, who on earth could that be, she asked herself as she hurriedly wiped her hands off on her apron and dashed down the hallway to the front door.

Lily opened the door and was greeted by two young men, nicely dressed in dark suits and with properly-cut short hair, standing on her front porch.

"Good afternoon," said one man smiling at her, extending his hand in a very firm handshake. How nice, thought Lily with approval. Firm handshakes had long seemed to have gone out of style.

"Good afternoon," replied Lily.

"Mrs. . . . Dameron," continued the young man, reading the surname from the mail box. "My companion and I have an important message that we would like to share with you today. We are full-time missionaries from the Church of Jesus Christ of Latter-day Saints, and as the Lord's representatives, we . . ."

"My goodness gracious!" exclaimed Lily startled, her eyes opening wide in excitement.

The young men looked at her and at each other nervously.

"Latter-day Saints? Did you say Latter-day Saints? Why, that means you're Mormons, doesn't it?" asked Lily.

The young man who had begun their introduction answered and cautiously said that they were indeed Mormons.

"Oh, it's been so long . . ." Lily muttered to herself, as vivid images of the past quickly rose to the surface of her mind, sweet memories that she hadn't thought about in years.

"Ma'am," ventured the other young man mildly, "is everything alright?"

His question quickly brought her back to the present.

"I'm terribly sorry. It was just that seeing you made me think of some very dear friends that I knew a very long time ago. You see, I lived in Salt Lake City once, way back in 1925."

The two missionaries relaxed and glanced at each other with broad smiles.

"I'm from Salt Lake City," announced the first missionary proudly.

"You are?" Lily studied carefully the printed name tag that the young man was wearing on his suit coat. His last name was Adams.

"Elder Adams, did you, by chance, know any Deckers in Salt Lake City?"

"Tons of them," said Elder Adams.

"Really?" Lily paused, then she decided to invite the two young men into her home.

"Please come inside. Would you like some lunch?" she asked politely. "I was just about to make myself a sandwich."

Both missionaries readily accepted her invitation and stepped inside the doorway.

Lily led the way back to the kitchen. "Do you like ham? I cooked a ham last night. If not, I have some leftover meatloaf from the night before."

Elder Adams said he would like ham, and the other elder said he would like the meatloaf. Lily instructed them to have a seat at the table, which she immediately began clearing. She hastily put the mixing bowls and spoons that she had used for making the cake into the sink, took a wet washcloth and wiped off the table, then began pulling out meat, cheese, and bread from the refrigerator.

"Do you like potato salad?" asked Lily.

"I *love* potato salad," said Elder Adams happily.

"And how about jello salad? This cherry salad is my daughter Peggy's favorite. She was here last night with her family for dinner. They always come over for dinner on Thursday night. She has two little girls now, Rosemary and Heather. Rosemary's such a finicky eater. The only thing she ever wants to eat for dinner is Campbell's Bean with Bacon soup. Peggy thinks I spoil her, but I don't mind making Rosemary her soup along with dinner. I'd do anything for that little girl. Would you like some of the jello salad?"

"For sure," said the other missionary.

"Pickles, olives?"

"Great," said Elder Adams greedily.

Lily put all the food out on the table and then got plates, glasses, and napkins out for the missionaries.

"Why don't you fix your own sandwiches while I fix your drinks. Would you like some iced tea — no, wait, I remember, Mormons don't drink tea, do they?"

"That's right," said the other elder, who was already busy building a huge meatloaf and tomato and cheddar cheese sandwich.

More precious recollections flooded Lily's mind. "I remember that I had the hardest time at first not drinking tea while living in Salt Lake City. In the South, you know, we're raised on it. But Aunt Sarah got me used to drinking herb teas — spearmint and peppermint and chamomile."

"Aunt Sarah?" inquired Elder Adams, engaged in putting a large pile of potato salad on his plate.

"One of the Deckers that I knew in Utah. I'd like to ask you about the Deckers you are acquainted with while we eat. I can offer you milk or water."

Both missionaries chose milk, and Lily poured each of them a large glass. With both young men settled, she finally sat down with them and began fixing her own lunch.

"Oh, dear," said Lily a half hour later, when she and the missionaries finished their lunches and their discussion about Salt Lake City Deckers. It turned out that Elder Adams knew some of the Deckers from Aunt Sarah's side of the family. "I'm afraid Levi took the last of the chocolate cake with him to work this morning. I don't have any cake to offer you for dessert. There's one in the oven, but it's for my church social tonight."

"That's okay, Mrs. Dameron," said Elder Adams, as he leaned back in his chair and put his hand over his stomach. "I'm stuffed."

"Me, too," said the other missionary.

Lily went over to the refrigerator and made another search.

"Oh, how fortunate. There are still a few slices of the buttermilk pie Mrs. Wammack brought over Wednesday. Would you young men still have room for some pie and ice cream?"

Both missionaries found more room and accepted the offer of pie. Lily dished up the slices, topped each of them with a scoop of vanilla ice cream, and served them to her guests.

"So," said Elder Adams, with a mouth full of pie, "you lived in Utah for a whole year?"

"Well, nine months really. From January to September."

"Did you get to go up into the mountains," asked the other missionary after sipping his milk.

"Oh, heavens, yes. I went everywhere."

"Did you see Temple Square?" asked Elder Adams, who finished his pie first after just four big bites.

"Many times. And I heard the Mormon Tabernacle Choir sing, too."

"My grandmother sings in the choir," said the other missionary, taking his time with his pie.

"How wonderful," observed Lily sincerely. "We used to be able to hear them sing on one of the local radio stations years ago, but they don't broadcast it around here anymore. We don't hear much about the Mormon Church these days. Is there a Mormon Church in Lynchburg now?"

"There's a small branch," said Elder Adams. "It was started a few years ago. Tell me, Mrs. Dameron, do you know much about the Church?"

"I know a little," admitted Lily honestly. "From the time I spent living in Salt Lake City . . . and, of course, from the experience that I had as a baby."

Elder Adams and his companion looked very interested in what she was telling them.

"What experience was that, Mrs. Dameron."

"Well, I got very sick when I was a baby, sick enough that Mother thought I was going to die one night. My family was very worried and prayed for a miracle. And the next day, Mormon missionaries came to the house." Lily suddenly laughed. "My older sister Virginia always thought they were angels, but Aunt Sarah told me that they must have been missionaries. Anyway, they gave me a blessing and healed me."

Elder Adams looked quite excited, as if he were about to faint.

"And they left me a copy of the Book of Mormon."

Now the other missionary looked like he was going to faint.

"A copy of the Book of Mormon? Do you still have it?" he asked anxiously.

"Oh, yes, I still have it. It's upstairs in a closet. Mother wanted it to stay in the family."

The other missionary literally licked his lips in anticipation.

"Could we see it?" he asked breathlessly.

Lily stood up from the table and took off her apron.

"Why, of course, you may."

She excused herself and went down the hallway and up the stairs to the second floor. The book was somewhere in a box of old books in the back bedroom closet, Virginia's old room. Lily went into the bedroom and opened the closet door. A strong smell of mothballs assailed her nose. She used this closet to store old wool coats and some of Mother's old quilts. She really needed to spend a day doing some spring cleaning in this room.

She pulled the box down from the shelf and set it on the bed. She rummaged around for a moment till she found it. Carefully, she pulled the old book from the box and gently wiped the thick collected dust from its covers. She really hadn't looked much at this old book since she had returned from Salt Lake City years and years ago. She had offered it to Silas as a parting gift when he took her to the train station when she was leaving Utah, even though Mother had originally wanted her to keep it. Since she was leaving Utah, leaving Silas, she saw no more use for it. But Silas had insisted that she keep it. And so, she did.

She went back downstairs and handed the book to the missionary. His eyes were round with delight as he studied the outside jacket and as he opened it.

"Elder Adams!" he exclaimed with delight, as he read one of the first pages in the book. "It's a second edition! Can you imagine? It's a second edition!"

"That's right," said Lily. "That's what my friend Silas told me."

The missionary handed Elder Adams the book, and Elder Adams took it lovingly. Lily remembered fondly how Silas and Aunt Sarah and Aunt Lizzie had handled her book when she showed it to them. It clearly meant a lot to these young men.

"This is very special," said Elder Adams in awe, as he studied the book. He held the book for a few moments, then handed it back to his companion, who had held out his hand to view it again.

"Mrs. Dameron," said the other missionary boldly, "I was wondering if you would like to trade? I will give you a newer copy of the Book of Mormon if you would give me this one?"

"Elder!" thundered Elder Adams loudly in surprise, clearly disapproving of the other missionary's request.

"No, it's alright, Elder Adams," Lily responded kindly. She seriously thought about the missionary's request. Mother had insisted that this book stay in the family. Well, all the family were dead and gone now — Mother, Bessie, Willie. It had been twenty years since Virginia had died, and her estranged father had even passed away about ten years ago. So what difference does it make whether she had the original copy or a newer one? Besides, Lily had a tender heart and could hardly ever turn down a request.

"You may have it," said Lily softly.

"Thank you!" cried the missionary, hugging the book tightly.

"No, I won't permit it," said Elder Adams defiantly. "Mrs. Dameron, this is your book!" Elder Adams was clearly upset.

Just then, the buzzer of the oven timer went off. Lily's cake was done. She had to get back to work.

"Really, Elder Adams, my mind is made up," insisted Lily firmly. "Now, if you gentlemen will excuse me, I'll see you both to the door.

I need to finish with my cake and do some sewing before my husband comes home for dinner."

Lily immersed herself with her planned projects. She took the cake out of the oven and set it on the cooling rack. She cleared away the table and washed the luncheon dishes. She went into the dining room, where she kept her sewing machine, and finished the little dress. She then went back into the kitchen and made the icing for the cake. When she finished icing the cake and put it into the refrigerator, she picked up the new copy of the Book of Mormon, a hardback book with a black cover, and went to put it away.

Lily had to admit to herself as she started climbing the stairs that she was feeling somewhat guilty, guilty perhaps for being a bit short with the missionaries in making them leave so quickly. Had she been rude? This worried her. Why had she sent them away so suddenly?

And truthfully, she was now feeling a little bit sad over giving her old book away. Maybe Elder Adams was right. Maybe she shouldn't have done it.

But, it was too late now. No use crying over spilled milk. Lily went back to Virginia's room and put the new book into the cardboard box. She put the box away and shut the closet door.

It was now four o'clock. Levi would be home in an hour. She should start getting dressed so she would be ready to leave for dinner at the church when he got home.

She went into her bedroom. While she dressed, memories of Salt Lake City and her youth continued to flash through her mind, despite her futile attempts to think about something else. After combing her long white hair and putting it up in a bun, Lily went back into Virginia's room and went over to the chest of drawers. She opened the top drawer and pulled out a long, black photo album.

She sat down on the bed and opened the album.

Right in front there was a picture of her in knickers, standing by a rock in Emigration Canyon. If only she had taken a picture of Aunt Lizzie in the knickers that she had secretly purchased for her old friend! But Aunt Lizzie wouldn't let her. Lizzie only put them on when Aunt Sarah was out of the house on an errand, and she didn't want any evidence lying around for Aunt Sarah to find.

There was a picture of her and Mamie, dressed up in new spring dresses, standing in front of Aunt Sarah's flowering apricot trees. She had never tasted such sweet apricots anywhere else in her whole life.

There was a picture of her in a fancy flapper dress, standing on the steps of the Utah capitol building.

There was the funny picture of her on top of the ostrich! She should give this one to Peggy and her girls. This would make Rosemary and Heather laugh!

Lily turned more pages. She stopped at a page that had a picture of Willie in his army uniform. Her vision blurred as tears began to fill her eyes. This was the last picture Willie had sent to her. They never found Willie. After an extensive search for several weeks, the government had sent her a letter saying that Willie was officially presumed dead, his body lost at sea.

Then there was a picture of the four young women standing proudly in front of a telescope. Why, it was Charlotte and Helen and the others. What were their names?

Lily laughed. Here was a picture of her corrective gymnastics class, dressed in their white bloomers, lying on their backs with their legs in the air, doing a leg exercise.

And then there was a picture of the beautiful cloister garden, where she had walked in a lovely white gown, carrying a brightly lit lantern. The words of the old school song rang through Lily's memory, as if her adventure to Bryn Mawr had just been yesterday.

> Bryn Mawr, you called.
> We answer unafraid.
> Out of the factory
> we come to thee.
> Give us the tools,
> The tools of our trade.
> Give us the truth
> To set our spirits free.

The truth.

Her truth, Aunt Lizzie had said.

But what truth do I have to offer, thought Lily sadly?

And who would want it?

Lily closed the photo album and put it away. She looked into the mirror. She had cried off all her mascara and blue eye shadow. She would have to redo her makeup before Levi got home.

PART THREE

Rosemary

1

September 1971

"What's that?" asked Amy, bending over and looking intently at a small bed of white and yellow flowers. She gazed at one flower very closely and then took out the pencil from behind her ear and started to make a detailed sketch in her notebook.

"Chamomile," answered Rosemary with authority in her voice.

"It looks like a daisy," said Amy.

Rosemary crossed her arms and shook her head. "No, it doesn't. Not really. Look closer. Chamomile and daisies are very different. A daisy has fatter white petals and a small yellow center. Chamomile flowers have skinny petals and fat yellow centers. And chamomile smells nicer."

Amy reached out, picked a small flower, and sniffed.

"Smells like a daisy to me."

Rosemary groaned. Her best friend Amy may be a straight-A sophomore at Brookville High School, but she knew absolutely nothing about herbs and herb gardens.

"This is hopeless, Amy. Let's not do it. My dad offered to lend us some of his medical books. We could do a project on one of the systems of the human body instead."

"No way," Amy insisted sharply as she continued working on her drawing of the chamomile blossom. "Your sister Heather already did that last year in her sixth grade science class! Do you want to be a copycat?"

This statement was terribly unfair, for Amy knew how much Rosemary didn't like being compared to Heather. It wasn't easy having a gifted little sister with such a high IQ. Especially a haughty little sister.

Amy continued her argument. "I really want to do a report on your mother's herb garden and the medicinal properties of herb plants. We can look up how the Egyptians and the Orientals and the American Indians used herbs, and we have everything we need for a display right here!"

Well, there was no denying that. They were literally surrounded by numerous small three-foot squares of greenery. Mother was admittedly a garden nut. After she had taken a trip to visit a college friend in England four years ago, she came back to the states announcing they were going to turn their front yard into an English country garden. Dad was subsequently ordered to hire masons to build a brick wall to surround the front of the property, and Mother bought big picture books of English gardens in order to plan her garden. Every summer after that, Mother put in several new beds until she eventually achieved her goal. Rosemary didn't particularly enjoy her assigned chores in helping Mother weed the garden, but she did like spending quiet time there. It was very beautiful and very peaceful. And Dad didn't seem to mind the loss of the grass in the front yard. Now there was no need to mow.

"Well," said Rosemary relenting, "we will need to do the sketches of the garden first. Once the weather turns cold in October, everything will be gone."

"Then let's keep going. There's only a few more plants left to sketch in this square." She stood up and handed Rosemary the notebook and pen she had been using to draw a detailed blueprint of the garden. "Why don't you draw for a while and just let me look."

"Fine," said Rosemary with a sigh.

Mother's herb and rose gardens now completely filled up their front yard. And, thought Rosemary drily as she led her friend over to a small square of purple and white flowers, if it wasn't for the fact that their two-story tudor house was built beside Timberlake, the entire backyard would be filled with flowers, too. Fortunately, they didn't have a backyard. They had twenty feet of rock, crab grass, and gravel, then a dock, a boat, and water.

"How about this thing," said Amy, holding up the end of a fragrant bright green plant with magenta flowers.

"Bergamot."

"Berg-a-what?"

"B-e-r-g-a-m-o-t. The tall purple spiked flowers beside it are English lavender."

"Smells like my grandmother's cologne," said Amy sniffing.

"Mine, too," laughed Rosemary. "Let's look at the kitchen herbs in the next section. Maybe you have heard of some of them." The two girls walked over to the large square that was planted in front of the south wall of the brick fence. In the middle of the square was a small white statue of Saint Frances of Assisi, holding a small dove in his hand. Rosemary handed the sketchbook back to Amy and commenced identifying the plants.

"That big one is rosemary, my namesake. That skinny, frilly one is dill. There's basil, my favorite. We eat a lot of that in salad. Take one of the leaves and rub it between your fingers and then smell your hand. It's yummy. The tiny golden leaf one is lemon thyme, and that monster bush in the corner that is threatening to take over everything in sight is our run-away oregano."

Rosemary picked several leaves from each herb for her friend to smell and feel and see up close, then Amy dutifully drew and labeled the plants on her notepad.

"Oregano? Hey, isn't that what my Mom puts in spaghetti sauce? Neat!"

The girls' investigation of culinary herbs was abruptly interrupted by Heather, who called out to them from her second-floor bedroom window.

"Rosemary! Mother says you need to come inside and get ready to go to Teema's house. We're leaving in twenty minutes."

"Okay. I'll be right up."

"Mother said now."

"In a minute . . ."

"Mother said . . ."

"Okay, okay. I'm coming," yelled Rosemary back loudly. "I better go. Besides reading books and being brilliant, Heather's greatest love in life is to tattle. If I don't go inside right away, she'll run and blab who-knows-what to Mother."

Amy grimaced. "Poor Rose. Must be awful living with a goody-two-shoes genius."

Amy and Rosemary made their way back to the front porch, and Amy put her notebook into her bookbag. "I'll see you tomorrow at school. Maybe we can go to the library during study hall and find a book that talks about Egyptian medicine."

"Sounds good," said Rosemary.

Amy pulled a shiny magazine out of her bookbag and handed it to Rosemary.

"I got the new issue of *Tigerbeat* last week. Have you seen it? There's a real long article about the Osmond brothers. There is a page with a big picture and information on each one."

Rosemary excitedly grabbed the magazine and flipped through the pages until she found the page with the picture of Donny Osmond, her favorite.

"Can I borrow it? I promise to give it back to you tomorrow."

"Sure," said Amy, putting on her bookbag. "I've already read the part about Jay! Three times!"

"Rosemary," a smug voice called out from above, "Mother says come inside the house *immediately!*"

"Okay!" Rosemary yelled back.

Rosemary angrily walked with Amy over to the driveway where Amy's dark blue bicycle was parked and said goodbye to her friend.

"Hey, Rosemary, how come you call your grandmother 'Teema?'" asked Amy.

"That's totally my invention," conceded Rosemary as she watched her friend get on her bicycle. "When I was a real little girl, I couldn't say the word 'grandma.' It came out 'Teema' instead, and the name stuck. Everybody calls her that now."

Amy grinned.

"What's her real name?"

Rosemary laughed. "In this family? What else but a name of a flower."

"Your baby brother isn't named after a flower," observed Amy.

"Mother had an herbal name all picked out: Sage Coleman. But Dad put his foot down on that one, and Michael Christopher got named after Grandpa Coleman instead."

"Lucky for Michael. So, let me guess your grandmother's real name. Daisy? Hyacinth? Rose?" asked Amy happily.

"No, more elegant than that."

Amy shook her head and gave up.

Rosemary smiled. "Lily."

Rosemary loved going to her grandmother's house for dinner. For as long as she could remember, ever since Dad had finished his residency and settled down into his own practice, their family had gone over to Teema's house every Thursday night for dinner. They went on Thursday since that was Dad's office day. He did surgery on Monday, Tuesday, and Wednesday. And he played golf religiously on Friday.

Rosemary was especially close to Teema. Aunt Louella had twin boys, Richard and Ryan, who were five years older than she was. But she had been Teema's first granddaughter, and that fact had cemented a very close bond between the two of them. When she was very little, Mother had let her sleep over on Friday nights with Teema. Teema would make Rosemary her favorite dinner. Then they would watch television together in the living room and sleep on the pull-out sofa bed. On Saturday, Teema would take Rosemary over to the Pittmann Plaza, a shopping center that had been built directly behind the house. Teema and some of her old lady friends from the Parkview Methodist Sewing Circle met there every Saturday at the S&W Cafeteria for lunch. The old ladies would make a fuss over Rosemary, which she now confessed that she liked, and then

Teema would take her shopping at the Murphy's Department Store for some little treat, which she liked even more.

Now that Rosemary was fourteen, she didn't spend the night with Teema anymore. She was too old for that! But she loved going to her house for supper. Teema was the greatest cook, and what she cooked for their family of five could easily feed an army of ten. A typical Teema supper would include two meats, Dad's favorite corn pudding, some sort of greens for Mother, hash browns for Rosemary and Heather, tossed salad, jello salad, and at least two desserts. It was too early to tell what she would be cooking up for little Michael, but it was bound to be good.

When they arrived at the house, Rosemary saw that Dad's car was already parked out front. He must have finished up at the office early. Mother parked their station wagon behind his car, and she carefully got Michael out of his car seat. Mother handed Michael to Rosemary while she gathered up the diaper bag and her purse. Heather marched on ahead of them, her nose firmly planted into her new Jane Austin book. Rosemary didn't like it when Heather read Jane Austin. She thought it made her sister "peevish" — at least that's the word Heather used to accurately describe her own mood. Well, she should know. She knew everything.

Rosemary carried Michael inside the house and found Teema waiting for them in the kitchen. She greeted Rosemary with a kiss and held out her hands for the baby, which Rosemary promptly handed over.

"Oh, Mother, dinner smells wonderful. I'm simply starved."

Teema smiled at Mother.

"Well, Peg, sit down at the table and I'll fix you some iced tea. Dinner's almost ready. Why are you so late? I was beginning to get worried about you."

"Sorry. Michael spit up just as we were leaving the house, so I had to go back in and change his clothes."

"This precious angel?" said Teema, adoring her grandson.

"Yes," said Mother, "that precious angel."

"Impossible," said Teema heartily.

"Very possible and probable," contradicted Dad, as he entered the kitchen. He had been sitting in the large easy chair in the corner of the dining room, reading Teema's latest copy of the *Enquirer* newspaper. Dad wouldn't be caught dead ever buying one of those newspapers at the grocery store, but he never failed to read Teema's copy before dinner. Dad walked into the kitchen, put the copy of the *Enquirer* down on the kitchen table, and held out his hands for the baby. "However, Peg and I have come to regard it as a shower of liquid love. Now, let me see my sweet and often smelly son."

Dad took Michael back with him into the dining room, and Mother and Teema settled down at the table to talk while waiting for the potatoes to finish baking. Heather was nowhere in sight, but Rosemary figured she had escaped to the backyard to sit under Grandpa Dameron's apple tree and read. Rosemary decided to go outside on the front porch and sit in one of Teema's white wicker rocking chairs and read Amy's magazine while waiting for supper.

Rosemary excitedly opened the magazine and flipped through the pages until she found the article about Donny Osmond that she had seen earlier. She really liked Donny. She had first seen him about two years ago on the Andy Williams Show, dancing and singing with his brothers. Now the Osmond brothers were big pop stars, and all of Rosemary's friends were wild about them. Rosemary could have just died when Amy told her that the Osmonds were coming next month to the Roanoke Civic Center for a concert. Their parents had gotten them tickets, and Rosemary's parents had promised to take the girls down for the concert. It was only three weeks away!

Rosemary began reading the article. It was written in a question/answer format.

Question: What is Donny Osmond's favorite color?

Answer: Purple.

Well, purple had always been Rosemary's favorite color since she was three years old. At that age, she had demanded purple shoes. Donny wore purple socks. It must be a sign.

Question: What color are Donny's eyes?

Answer: Brown.

Disappointing, if one were really truthful. Rosemary preferred blue eyes. But, she sighed, she guessed she could learn to live with brown.

Question: What religion is Donny Osmond?

Answer: Mormon.

Mormon?

Rosemary paused.

She had never heard of "Mormon" before. What a funny name for a religion. It didn't sound anything like Baptist or Methodist or Catholic. Was that Christian? The section about Donny didn't say anything else. There weren't any further details at all about what a Mormon was. Rosemary looked through the rest of the article with the interviews of the other Osmond brothers, but there wasn't anything else about Mormons.

Intrigued, Rosemary took her magazine and went back inside the house. In the kitchen, she found Teema standing beside the stove, stirring a pot of gravy, while Mother was now holding Michael and feeding him his bottle. As usual, Mother and Teema were having some sort of discussion about plants.

"Peggy, I want to order one of those antique scented geraniums like you now have in your living room. The one that smells like strawberries. What's it called?"

"Countess of Scarborough," answered Mother without hesitation. Mother knew her plants.

"Mother," interrupted Rosemary meekly.

Mother looked up. "Yes, what is it, dear?"

"Mother, what's a Mormon?"

A funny look immediately crossed Mother's face.

"Why in the world would you want to know that?" she asked with concern.

Rosemary held up the magazine in her hand and pointed to the full-page picture of Donny Osmond.

"Donny Osmond is a Mormon."

Mother instantly relaxed.

"Oh. I see. Well, I don't really know much about Mormons, Rose. But your grandmother does. She lived in Utah once, and she's had some dealing with Mormons."

Rosemary looked over at Teema, whose face had flushed pink from standing over the hot burner. The gravy was done, and she was pouring it out of the pan and into her white china gravy boat.

"Teema, what's a Mormon?"

Teema finished pouring the gravy and set the hot pan back down on the stove before she answered.

"Mormons are very good people, Rosemary. I lived with some very nice Mormons once long ago. Some people might try to tell you that they're a cult or not Christian, but don't you believe them. Mormons are good Christian folks."

Mother put down an empty bottle and raised Michael up to her shoulder to pat his back for a proper burp.

"Mother, tell Rosemary about when you were a baby and how you were healed."

This sounded like a real interesting story, and Rosemary immediately sat down at the kitchen table to listen. Teema took off her apron, hung it on the back of her chair, and sat down with her daughter and granddaughter. She took out a white handkerchief that she always kept down in the front of her dress and patted her flushed face. She then began her story, telling Rosemary all about how she was born in the country, how her mother Louella brought their family to Lynchburg, and then how she got sick. Rosemary listened breathlessly as Teema told her about how the two missionaries appeared and gave her the special blessing and healed her. Then Teema told her about her Book of Mormon.

"Do you still have it," asked Rosemary completely in awe.

Teema sadly shook her head and told Rosemary about the visit from the other pair of missionaries.

"How horrible!" gasped Rosemary fervently. "He shouldn't have asked you to give him your book. It was *your* book."

"Well, no use crying over spilled milk," reflected Teema resignedly. "What's done is done."

Rosemary's eyes widened.

"Teema, do you still have the other book? The one that awful missionary traded with you?"

Teema smiled.

"Come with me."

Rosemary followed Teema up the stairs and to the back bedroom. She stood anxiously as Teema opened the musty closet and pulled out an old cardboard box. She set the box on the bed and thumbed through the books inside until she found it. She pulled out a small black book with gold letters on the front. She handed it to Rosemary and said simply, "Here. You can have this."

2

October 1971 – March 1972

The lights darkened suddenly around Rosemary.

She grabbed Amy's hand and held it tightly. The overwhelming sound of several thousand young women's voices starting to scream filled her with emotion, and even though she and Amy had solemnly promised that they wouldn't do it, they were literally on the edge of their seats screaming, too. Way down in front of them, multicolored lights of electric blue, red, and green began to flash sporadically across the stage. A white spotlight focused on a large glittering ball hanging over the center of the Coliseum. The ball began to turn, and thousands of tiny glimmering lights floated across the audience. Next, they heard the sound of an electric guitar, slowly, ever so slowly, begin to play long sustained single notes, rising up a musical scale. As the notes rose in pitch, the screams in the building rose in loudness and fervor. Finally, Rosemary heard an announcer's voice speaking above the noise. "Ladies and gentleman, the Osmonds!"

All the multi-colored lights on the stage went black, then numerous bright white lights flashed on, and Rosemary saw five young men standing on the stage. The young girls in the audience in the Roanoke Coliseum went wild, yelling and screaming louder than ever, as the Osmond brothers, dressed in solid white fringed outfits, began singing and dancing across the stage.

"One bad apple don't spoil the whole bunch girl . . ."

Rosemary and Amy yelled unashamedly as they watched their teen idols, Rosemary yelling Donny's name and Amy yelling Jay's name. Rosemary couldn't believe it. She was actually in the same building as Donny Osmond, within a couple of hundred feet of him. Admittedly, their seats were pretty terrible. They were way in the back and way up in the bleacher section. But that didn't matter very much. They were here! And he was right there!

Rosemary held up the pair of binoculars that her father had given her when he had dropped them off at the Coliseum. Mother and Dad had elected not to join them. They decided to go out to dinner at the Ground Round instead and would pick them up outside when the concert was over. Too bad Heather didn't want to come. She claimed to not like the Osmonds. It was juvenile, she said. She chose to stay home with Teema and Michael. Well, thought Rosemary drily, Heather doesn't know what she's missing!

Once the concert got started and the first few songs were over, the noise in the Coliseum settled down to a much more subdued roar. Rosemary unselfishly shared the binoculars with Amy, and they took turns watching their favorite Osmond brother perform.

Rosemary had just handed the binoculars over to Amy again when she took notice of the security guards who were standing literally everywhere on the floor below and in the front aisles up in the bleachers. The guards on the floor were not allowing any of the girls to go up front near the stage. However, the guards up in the bleacher sections were allowing girls to walk around closer to the stage to take pictures. The guards must have figured that this was relatively safe. It was a good long drop from the aisle up in the stands to the stage below. She watched several girls go around and take pictures and then come back to their seats. In a wave of courage, Rosemary grabbed Amy's camera and jumped out of her seat.

"Hey, where are you going?" cried Amy startled.

"Up front," Rosemary yelled back excitedly.

She raced around the walkway along the upper deck and smiled happily at the big fat guard standing at the spot right beside the stage. She held up her camera, and the guard smiled and motioned that she could go ahead. She leaned over the metal railing a bit to get a closer shot and took the picture. She was so close she could hardly stand it.

She took several more pictures and then she stood still for a minute, taking it all in. *Just wait till Heather sees these pictures. She'll be pea green with envy.*

Suddenly, quite unexpectedly, it seemed to Rosemary as if the noise of the building slowly faded out for a few moments, as if she had been submerged in an airtight bubble. And then she felt this warm, tingling feeling fall over her, beginning at the top of her head and slowly flowing through her body.

It was a very peaceful feeling and an odd one. How strange to feel this calmness, this quiet, amid such excitement and hysteria. Then Rosemary heard something. It wasn't a voice, really, but a sentence floated clearly and distinctly through her mind, like a printed sentence would run across a television screen with a weather bulletin.

They have something that you must have. They have something you need.

The impression and the feeling then faded away as quickly as it had come, and Rosemary was once again keenly aware of the battling sounds of the screaming and the pop music in her ears. She clutched her camera tightly and hurriedly back to her seat. She found Amy anxiously waiting for her.

"Well?" asked Amy fervently. "Did you get it?"

Rosemary handed the camera back to Amy.

"Yes," said Rosemary with an odd, solemn voice. "I got it."

The ride back to Lynchburg took about an hour and then they had to drop Amy off at her house, so it was well past midnight when Rosemary and her parents finally pulled into their driveway. There was a light on in the living room. Teema must still be up. She didn't have to wait up, for they had a guest room ready for her. But Teema always waited up. She was a real worry-wart when it came to her family.

"How was the baby?" asked Mother after greeting Teema and giving her a kiss on the cheek. Teema was sitting on the sofa, reading an Agatha Christie mystery. She and Mother traded Agatha Christie mystery books back and forth all the time. Both women could read one in a day, which just amazed Rosemary. She wished she could read a whole book in a day.

"Fine. Just fine. I fed him supper about six, and he ate real good. He doesn't seem to like the strained carrots, though."

"Do you blame him?" said Dad with a grin.

"Stop it, Brett. When did you put him to bed, Mother?"

"He took his bottle about eight and then I put him down. Haven't heard a peep since."

"And Heather?"

"We spent a quiet evening in here reading. I started the new mystery you gave me, and she read something about Egyptian pyramids, I think. I let her stay up till eleven. Hope you don't mind."

"That's okay. Tonight was a special night for everyone. We had a wonderful dinner in Roanoke, and Brett took me over to the new shopping mall. We'll have to take you there sometime soon, Mother. There are dozens and dozens of stores under one roof. It's quite something. Brett seems convinced that shopping malls will be the thing of the future."

Teema turned and looked at Rosemary, who was being awfully quiet.

"And did you have a nice time?"

Rosemary nodded her head in answer to Teema's question and found some remaining energy to relate the details of the concert to her grandmother.

"I think," said Mother putting a strong arm around Rosemary's shoulders, "that this one is plumb tuckered out. I'm surprised that she hasn't lost her voice after all this carrying on. Rose, why don't you go on to bed. I'll get Mother settled in her room."

Rosemary didn't linger to question her mother's request but wearily went up the stairs. She put down her pocketbook and her picture program from the concert on her dresser. She undressed and went into the bathroom to brush her teeth and wash her face.

After she finished getting ready for bed, she went back to her bedroom. Just recently she had gotten her own room. Mother had moved her sewing things down into the family room and had put Heather into her old sewing room. Mother thought it was important for them to have their own rooms now that they were getting older. For one thing, it cut down on arguments.

Tonight, Rosemary was very glad to have her privacy, because she wanted to keep the light on for a while. She didn't want to go to sleep just yet. She sat down at her little writing desk and wrote a letter to her girlfriend Mary Ellen. In the letter, she described the concert in detail and her excitement over seeing Donny Osmond in person. She and Mary Ellen had been friends since first grade, and after Mary Ellen's family moved out west to Montana they become pen pals.

After she finished the letter, she knelt down by her bed and said her prayers, the Lord's prayer and another short prayer she had learned in vacation Bible school last summer. Then she crawled into bed and pulled the covers up around her. It was late September and still fairly warm at night, but Mother had already put a blanket on her bed. Rosemary nestled down into the blanket and stared up at the ceiling, recalling many of the scenes from the concert in her mind.

Rosemary remembered the funny feeling and impression that she had felt at the concert. What made her feel that way? She didn't know, but she knew it had been real, very real.

They have something that you must have.

What did the Osmonds have that she needed? It was then that Rosemary remembered the article she had read at Teema's house and the black book that Teema had given her. Rosemary slid out of bed and went over to her small bookshelf. She picked up the small black book and carried it back to bed with her. Maybe this is what the Osmonds have that she must have, that she needed — something written inside this book.

Rosemary propped up her two pillows, leaned against them and opened the book. She quickly thumbed through the book. Drat. No pictures. Disappointed, she turned to the front of the book and read the first page.

"A Few Interesting Book of Mormon References."

This page had a list of questions and places in the book where one could go for answers. Heather would love this. And, because she knew Heather would love it, Rosemary decided to skip this page and go immediately to the next. This looked like a title page.

THE

BOOK OF MORMON
An Account Written by
THE HAND OF MORMON
UPON PLATES
TAKEN FROM THE PLATES OF NEPHI

Nephi?

What a funny name, thought Rosemary to herself. Wonder how it's pronounced? Rosemary read the rest of the title page with interest. It sounded a lot like her Bible. She turned and saw the copyright date of her book. It was 1948 by George Albert Smith as Trustee-in-Trust. Her book was sure an old book! But not as old as Teema's first book. She frowned about that. What a rotten fellow to steal her book. Some missionary he turned out to be!

Rosemary settled down in her warm blanket and flipped through the next few pages until she got to what looked like the beginning of the book, the First Book of Nephi. There was that funny name again. Well, she wasn't too sure if she would understand this book, but she felt strongly that perhaps the answer to her funny experience tonight would be found within its pages. She vowed that she would read a page each night before she went to bed.

After making that decision, Rosemary began to read.

*   *   *

Rosemary was true to her promise. For the next six months, each night before turning out the light and going to sleep, she would read one page in her Book of Mormon. To be honest, she didn't comprehend very much of what she was reading. She did recognize the passages from Isaiah, which began on page seventy-four. That part she really didn't understand. But who understands Isaiah? Nobody in her parents' Methodist church, that's for sure. They always skipped Isaiah — most of the Old Testament for that matter — in her Sunday school class. Her class mainly read Matthew, Mark, Luke, and John. Anyway, she kept on reading faithfully each night.

She didn't really know how it happened, but slowly another impression began to form in Rosemary's mind. This book was true. Even though she didn't fully understand what she was reading, she knew that she felt very good when she read it. There was a quiet peaceful feeling that came over her as she read. And although she didn't know any Mormons personally or know anything at all about the Mormon Church, she also felt impressed that she must join the Church. And soon.

Rosemary fretted over this.

How was she going to present this idea to her parents? After all, she was fourteen, not legally of age to do something so drastic as change her religion. She would have to have their permission first.

But what was she going to say?

"Okay, Mother, I'll plant the new sage and oregano plants this afternoon after school, and say, could I join the Mormon Church?"

No, that wouldn't fly.

Perhaps this was not the right thing to do now. Perhaps she was too young. She could wait until she was eighteen. Then her parents couldn't say anything. It would be totally her decision. But the feeling that she needed to join the Church now kept nagging at her.

She didn't say anything about it to Amy, but she did write a long letter to Mary Ellen that began, "Mary Ellen, you probably think I'm crazy, but I want to join the Mormon Church." It was about two weeks later, in mid-March, when Rosemary came home from school and found a letter from Mary Ellen waiting for her in the mailbox.

Mother's blue station wagon was not in the driveway. Rosemary remembered that Heather had a dental appointment that afternoon, so that's where Mother was. Rosemary got the mail out of the mailbox and went inside the empty house. She dumped her books on the hall steps and went back to the kitchen to get a drink and a snack. She poured herself a glass of milk and helped herself to a couple of chocolate chip cookies. She sat down at the kitchen table, opened Mary Ellen's letter, and began to read.

> Dear Rosemary:
>   I was very surprised when I read your last letter, and I wanted to write to you right away. No, I don't think you are crazy for wanting joining the Mormon Church. I am going to join the Mormon Church in August! I never told you, but I have been going to the Mormon Church for the past two years with my uncle and aunt. They are Mormons. Mother has said she will let me join the Church on my birthday when I turn fifteen . . .

Rosemary stopped reading the letter and let it fall to the table. Her best friend in the world was joining the Mormon Church. This revelation fueled her own desire to become a Mormon and gave her the resolve to approach her parents with her request.

It seemed like an eternity before Rosemary heard the sound of the station wagon pulling into the driveway. She hurried to open the side door, and Mother and Heather walked in, each carrying a brown paper bag of groceries.

"Rosemary, could you help me carry in the rest of the groceries? And Heather, could you get Michael?"

"Mother, I want to ask you something . . ." began Rosemary anxiously. Now that she had decided to say something, she couldn't wait to ask.

"In a minute, dear," Mother answered with a wave of the hand walking out the door. "Groceries first."

"But it's really important!"

Mother turned and raised her eyebrows.

"Can't it wait for a few moments?"

Reluctantly, Rosemary said it could. All three of them went back to the car. Heather got Michael out of his car seat and took him into the family room to put him in his playpen while Mother and Rosemary made two trips to carry in all the groceries. Once the groceries where in, Mother began unbagging, putting things out on the kitchen table. It was Rosemary and Heather's job to then put the food away in the cupboard or in the refrigerator.

"Okay," said Mother. "What is it that you want to tell me."

Now that she had Mother's attention, she felt a bit flustered at first. Where to begin? Best to just come out with it.

"Well, I got a letter from Mary Ellen today, and she says that her mother is letting her join the Mormon Church. And I want to join the Mormon Church, too. I want to be a Mormon."

Mother stopped unbagging. Heather stopped putting away. Both stared. Then Heather spoke. Sarcastically.

"Oh, brother. You're really nuts."

"Heather, that's enough," said Mother mildly. It was obvious that Mother was a bit shocked at Rosemary's request. Normally, she would correct Heather with a much firmer and louder voice. So Heather ignored her and kept on.

"I know why you want to be a Mormon. You just want to join the Mormon Church because Donny Osmond is a Mormon!"

"I do not!" cried Rosemary in her own defense. "That has nothing to do with it."

"Oh, yes, it does."

"Does not!"

"Does too!"

"Does not!!!"

"*I said, Enough!*"

Mother had recovered, voice and all.

The girls instantly quieted and awaited their doom.

"Heather, go in and tend to Michael."

"But . . ."

"Now."

Heather knew better than to defy Mother in that tone of voice. She quickly grabbed her milk and bowl of potato chips and immediately left the kitchen, leaving Rosemary alone. Mother sat down at the kitchen table and indicated that she wanted Rosemary to do the same. Rosemary sat down promptly.

"So," Mother said with a not-very-pleased voice, "tell me why you want to join the Mormon Church?"

Rosemary took a deep breath and told her Mother the whole story — the experience at the concert and reading Teema's book and the feelings she had been having and Mary Ellen's letter.

"Let me see it."

Rosemary handed the letter over to Mother, who read it carefully.

"Well, I don't know what to say, Rose."

Mother paused.

"I think we better discuss this with your father."

"Have a seat, young lady."

Rosemary entered the small office and sat down in one of the two oversized green leather chairs that stood in front of Dad's big oak desk. Mother followed her into the room and sat in the other chair. Dad went around and took his seat in the red leather swivel chair that Mother and her parents and his parents had chipped in and given him as a gift when he graduated from medical school.

"So," Dad began with an ominous voice, "tell me about it."

Rosemary told her story again, right up to the point where Heather started challenging her motives.

"I don't want to be a Mormon, Dad, because of the Osmonds! That has nothing to do with it. Don't believe Heather. She just wants to ruin things. She hates me." Just remembering how Heather had taunted her made Rosemary fume. She sank down in her chair and pouted.

"Now, I wouldn't say that, Rose. Heather's just envious of you."

This statement took Rosemary by complete surprise.

"Envious? Of me? But she's the brilliant one. What do I have that she would ever want?"

Dad sat back in his big chair, folded his arms, and took a real hard look at his daughter before speaking.

"To begin with, you are a natural extrovert, full of life. No one is a stranger to you. Heather is by nature an introvert. She has a hard time meeting people and making friends. I would guess she envies your ability to make friends and to be with people."

"She has friends, Dad," Rosemary said drily.

"Oh, really? Name one."

"Allison."

"Mary Ellen's little sister. But they both live out west now. No, that doesn't count. Name someone in the state of Virginia."

Rosemary thought. She thought hard.

"Mrs. Newsome."

Dad looked puzzled. Mother took this opportunity to say something.

"The new librarian at the downtown library."

Dad grimaced. "That also doesn't count. She's over twenty-one and married. Name someone single and under sixteen, please."

Rosemary huffed and sat and thought. She hated to admit it, but Dad was right. Heather didn't really have any close friends to speak of, which was something that Rosemary hadn't particularly noticed until now. She really hated it when her parents were right.

"Now, let's name a few of your friends. I can start with a few. There's Mary Ellen . . ."

"She doesn't count. She's out of state," interjected Rosemary haughtily.

"My mistake. Scratch Mary Ellen. Well, there's your best friend Amy and then there's Mary Kay and Patti and Laura and Jenni and who's that new girlfriend at the dance studio?"

"Tracy," offered Mother.

"Yes, that's it. Tracy."

"Don't forget Ann and Debbie in her algebra class."

"Thank you, Peggy. Let's see," Dad mumbled as he started counting with his fingers, "that's eight so far. Any more you'd like to add?"

Angrily, Rosemary shook her head. They had her but good.

"The point is, Rose, that you have a wealth of friends. A high IQ doesn't guarantee anything in life. So, try not to be so hard on your sister, okay?"

"But she's hard on me!" cried Rosemary bitterly.

"I know, but try to be patient with her. Promise you'll try?"

"I'll try," muttered Rosemary.

"Well, that got us off track. Let's get back to the subject at hand. I want you to know that I do take this very seriously, Rose. I don't believe Heather's comments. You are a very serious young lady, and I trust you. And religious beliefs are a very personal matter. I would be lying if I said this didn't upset me, this idea of your leaving our church. But I guess you are getting old enough to decide for yourself what to believe."

Rosemary looked up at her father in disbelief. Was he really going to give her permission to go to the Mormon Church? It was almost too good to be true.

"I trust you, Rose, but I feel somewhat remiss in letting you go off and join a church that I know nothing about."

Rosemary felt her heart sink. He wasn't going to say yes.

"I think," said Dad practically, now holding a pencil in his hand and doodling on a scratch pad on his desk, "I would feel better about this if I knew something about this Mormon Church."

"Brett," Mother responded thoughtfully, "why don't we invite our new minister over, Mr. Mahon. Perhaps he could tell us about the Mormon Church."

Dad looked up and smiled broadly at Mother.

"Splendid idea, Peggy. We'll let Mr. Mahon tell us what he thinks about the Mormons!"

3

March 1972

Wednesday seemed to be the longest day of Rosemary's entire life.

She didn't sleep well the night before, and she awoke anxiously that morning at five-thirty without the aid of her alarm clock. This was the day that their new minister was coming over to talk to her parents about the Mormons. Her immediate fate rested in the hands of this man who had just arrived at their Methodist Church this past year. She didn't know him very well at all and could not predict what he might say, which made her extremely nervous.

She lay in bed and worried about it until six-thirty, the usual time that she got up on school days. Preoccupied with her fears, she apathetically dressed and fixed her hair and then went down to breakfast. There was a regular routine worked out for breakfast in their family. Monday through Friday you were on your own, which for Rosemary translated into cold cereal, pop-tarts, or buttered toast. On Saturday mornings, Mother usually treated everyone to an old-fashioned southern breakfast of scrambled eggs, bacon, hashbrowns, sliced tomatoes, and juice. Then on Sundays, Dad would take over the kitchen and whip up either his homemade pancakes or his homemade waffles.

Rosemary poured herself a bowl of Cheerios and a glass of orange juice and sat down at the kitchen table. She ate her breakfast quickly, wanting to avoid all family members if possible. She mostly succeeded since Dad had already left for the hospital and Mother was upstairs nursing Michael. Heather showed up just as Rosemary was putting her bowl in the dishwasher, and Rosemary managed to leave hurriedly, thus avoiding getting into a prolonged discussion with her younger sister over that night's planned meeting. Rosemary put on her jacket, grabbed her bookbag and left the house to wait for the bus down the street. Since she was out rather early, it proved to be a long wait, which only added to her frustration.

Rosemary went through her six periods of classes with little interest. Instead, she watched the clock in every class, anxious for the school day to be over. She thought she would just about die in sixth period geometry. Mrs. Wilkens was boring enough as it was on regular days, but today her teacher seemed to be talking in slow motion while demonstrating on the board the latest theorem outlined in their textbooks. At long last, the bell sounding the end of sixth period and the end of the school day rang out over the school intercom; and Rosemary dashed out of the classroom and out to the waiting bus.

When she got home, she found plenty of things to occupy her time for the remaining few hours. She had to finish up her geometry homework, which she didn't finish in class, and there were three Robert Frost poems to be read for English class tomorrow. It was her night to set the table and do dishes, so before and after supper she stayed busy.

At long last, the grandfather clock in the hallway chimed seven o'clock and the front door bell rang.

This was it.

Rosemary rushed to the front foyer just as Dad was opening the door. Mother was upstairs again, putting Michael down in his playpen and giving Heather strict instructions in watching her baby brother while they met with Mr. Mahon. To Rosemary's delight, Dad had asked Heather to watch Michael, which meant Heather would not be downstairs contributing to tonight's discussion. Heather had already flaunted her advanced IQ at dinner by telling Mother and Dad the results of her recent research at the junior high

library on the topic of Mormonism. Heather seemed totally fascinated with an historic Mormon leader named Brigham Young and his
colonization efforts throughout Mexico and western Canada. Mother
and Dad seemed quite interested. Rosemary was quite annoyed.
Thank goodness Heather would be out of the way this evening!

"Good evening," said Dad warmly, greeting Mr. Mahon and
inviting him into the house.

"Good evening, Mr. Coleman. Hello, Rosemary," said Mr.
Mahon in a friendly voice as he stepped inside. The gust of cool
night air followed the minister into the house. It wasn't spring yet,
and the air outside still held a bit of winter chill in it. Mr. Mahon
wore a light tan raincoat over his Sunday black suit. He was a short,
round man, with dark wiry hair, dark eyes and a double chin.

"The weather man is calling for thunderstorms tonight. That's
a sure sign that spring is on the way," Dad commented as Mr. Mahon
took off his coat. The minister handed it promptly to Dad, who
opened the hall closet and hung it up.

"I'm not in a hurry," Mr. Mahon said thoughtfully. "I enjoy the
transition. March and October are my favorites parts of the year."

"Well, then, you're going to love living in Virginia. If any state
in the union can transition well, it's the Old Dominion! Wait till
you see our dogwood trees and azaleas in full bloom. And if you need
any help landscaping, feel free to call Peggy. The only thing she likes
better than digging up her front yard is digging up someone else's.
Please come in and make yourself comfortable," said Dad, indicating
that they would go into the formal living room. Mr. Mahon went
first, and Dad and Rosemary followed closely behind.

Rosemary loved their formal living room. There were white
french glass doors that separated this room from the rest of the house.
It was a quiet place to retreat to indoors if you wanted to be alone.
Mother had decorated this room in soft pastel shades of pink, blue,
and yellow. It was a friendly room. It was a comforting room.

Mr. Mahon sat down on the sofa, and Dad sat down in one of
the two big striped chairs directly across the room from where Mr.
Mahon sat. Rosemary sat down on the other end of the sofa.

"My wife will join us in a minute," Dad said. "She's putting the baby down."

"How is your little boy doing?"

Dad smiled proudly. "Terrific. Cutting teeth and drooling and trying to sit up."

"All at once?" asked Mr. Mahon laughing.

Rosemary tried not to fidget while listening to the humorous conversation over Michael's growth and development. Mr. and Mrs. Mahon also had a new baby boy, and he and Dad were enjoying comparing notes. But it was hard not to be restless. She wanted to get to the real purpose of this meeting. She wanted to talk about her!

Mother finally appeared, rushing in to greet Mr. Mahon with a pleasant handshake, and took her seat in the other striped chair next to Dad.

"Well," Dad began, changing the topic with a much more serious tone of voice, "I guess you are wondering why we invited you over tonight, Mr. Mahon. I wasn't very specific about the nature of the matter when we talked on the phone. It seems that we are in need of some information and your counsel."

"I hope I can be of help," Mr. Mahon ventured without hesitation.

"Our daughter, Rosemary, has come to us with the request to join another church — the Mormon Church."

Dad paused. Rosemary stared at Mr. Mahon's face, trying to see his reaction. He raised his eyebrows sharply in response to Dad's statement. A negative sign? Rosemary bit her lip. At least Mr. Mahon didn't jump out of his seat or act totally shocked or instantly start arguing against the idea. A positive sign?

"I see," said Mr. Mahon softly.

"It's a rather unique situation, I confess," Dad continued firmly. "Perhaps the best way to begin is to let Rosemary tell her story."

Rosemary did not expect this turn. She thought Dad and Mother were going to do all the talking. A bit startled, she smiled weakly, swallowed hard, and started speaking.

"Well, Mr. Mahon, you see, well, it all begins in 1902 . . . ."

Mr. Mahon looked very confused.

"I beg your pardon?"

"When Teema was born," said Rosemary in way of explanation.

"Teema?"

"Rosemary, there's no need to go into all that part, " Mother began impatiently.

"Hush, Peggy," Dad ordered practically. "It's her story. Let her tell it."

Rosemary continued. "When my grandmother — that's who Teema is — was a little baby, she got very sick and these Mormon missionaries came and healed her and left her this copy of the Book of Mormon. Do you know about the Book of Mormon?"

Mr. Mahon leaned back on the sofa and folded his hands quietly in his lap.

"Yes, Rosemary, I've heard of the Book of Mormon."

The minister's voice was plain and unemotional, so Rosemary couldn't discern anything regarding the opinions he had about the book.

"And?" prompted Mr. Mahon, eying her closely.

"And then she grew up and worked in the factories, which sent her out to Utah to live. She stayed with some real nice Mormons, two old ladies named Aunt Lizzie and Aunt Sarah. Do you know any Mormons, Mr. Mahon?"

"Rosemary, don't bother Mr. Mahon with so many questions," interrupted Mother critically.

"I don't mind her questions really, Mrs. Coleman. Yes, Rosemary, I've known a few Mormons in my day. Continue, please. I assume that you got a hold of this old Book of Mormon and read it yourself?"

Still no indication which way he was leaning, thought Rosemary bitterly.

"Oh, no, sir. That book was stolen."

Mr. Mahon's eyebrows really went up high this time.

"Stolen?"

Dad jumped into the conversation again. "I think stolen is not quite the right word, Rose. Perhaps 'lost' might better describe what happened."

"No, Dad! Teema didn't lose it. That awful missionary took it from her!"

Mr. Mahon seemed to be getting more and more interested in this amazing story.

"More missionaries? The same ones who left the book?"

Rosemary shook her head violently. "Nope. The first missionaries who came long ago in 1902 were good ones. The awful ones came just a few years ago."

Next, Rosemary carefully told about the visit of the second set of missionaries and the copy of the Book of Mormon that she now possessed. She had already decided to minimize the Osmond part of her story, not wanting Mr. Mahon to get the wrong idea like Heather had done. That could ruin everything. Instead, she told about the peaceful feelings she felt when reading the book and her strong desire to join the Church.

"As you can see," Dad said after Rosemary finished speaking, "my daughter feels quite strongly about this matter. And my wife and I take her request seriously. Rosemary is our oldest child and a very responsible young lady. I think she's old enough to make her own decisions, and I believe my wife agrees with me."

Mother nodded her head that she did. This display of trust touched Rosemary's heart deeply. Even if they didn't give her permission, at least her parents believed her. It was one thing to be loved. It was quite wonderful to be trusted.

"But my wife and I don't know any Mormons ourselves and don't know anything really about this church. So, we wanted to get your counsel on the matter. What do you think we should do?"

The suspense of the entire day seemed to well up in Rosemary's chest, and she felt as if she might faint or explode waiting for his answer. Mr. Mahon took his time in responding. He stared at his hands for a moment or two, then looked up at her parents with a very solemn stare.

"I find it a strange coincidence," he said slowly and deliberately, "that you should ask me such a question. When I was in seminary, studying for the ministry, one of my classes gave the assignment to study another religion in depth. And I chose the Mormon Church."

Rosemary could hardly move. She could hardly breath. And she could hardly believe her ears at what the minister said next.

"Mr. and Mrs. Coleman, if you let your daughter join that church . . ."

Mother and Dad leaned up at the edge of their seats. Rosemary practically fell off of hers.

". . . she will turn out just fine. The Mormon Church teaches very high moral standards of conduct. There is a strict law of health called the Word of Wisdom, which prohibits drinking coffee, tea, and alcohol. They prohibit smoking. They place much emphasis on marriage and family. They even have a program called "Family Home Evening" one night a week where the family spends time together. In my experience, Mormons are an honest, kind, Christian people. I must admit I feel somewhat awkward in giving my blessing in having one of my flock join another church, but I wouldn't be honest if I didn't tell you my true feelings about the Mormon Church."

"Then you approve of her request? She has your blessing?" Dad asked marvelling.

Mr. Mahon turned and looked steadily at Rosemary.

"She has my blessing."

4

February 1987

Rosemary leaned over the bed, gently opened the small eyelid of her patient, and shined the tiny bright white light of her pocket flashlight quickly across the child's pupil. Nothing happened. The large black pupil remained fixed and dilated, as wide and dark as one of the centers of Mother's garden daisies. Rosemary closed the one eye and repeated the same procedure in the other eye. She got the same result.

She wearily stood up and glanced over at the anxious nurse standing at the foot of the bed.

"Have they sent up the CT scan?" asked Rosemary in a depressed voice. The nurse nodded and left the small room within the pediatric intensive care unit to retrieve the films. While she waited, Rosemary leaned up against the wall and closed her eyes. She had been on call all night. It had been a busy evening, with three new admissions to the ICU, and she was totally exhausted. Why did children get sick and suffer trauma in the middle of the night? She yawned and stretched. What she would give for a few hours sleep.

The nurse quickly returned and handed the large cardboard film packet to Rosemary, who pulled the shiny square black films out and placed them up on the lighted wall display. The films showed a tiny skull with small hairline fractures alongside the left ear and grey brain tissue filled with a sizable amount of small black dots. The dots meant edema. The brain was swelling with fluid.

Rosemary pulled the films off the wall and handed them back to the nurse.

"Jill, call Audiology. I want an auditory brainstem response evaluation stat to determine if there is any brainstem function left. As soon as that's done, call EEG. We'll need a brain death tracing."

"Yes, Dr. Coleman," said the nurse solemnly.

"And get some new blood gases on bed four," added Rosemary as she left the small enclosure and went out to the long counter space in the open area of the Pediatric ICU. She pulled out two hospital charts from a nearby rack and sat heavily down in a comfortably-padded swivel chair. She hated death. As a Mormon, she intellectually accepted it as a part of life, but as a pediatrician, she considered it her avowed enemy. And tonight, the enemy had won.

She opened one of the charts and began the laborious process of looking through the many test results obtained during the night in order to make her running notes and to be prepared for rounds at ten o'clock. Dr. Martin, the attending physician, had gone downstairs to his office for a little breakfast and morning nap. But for her, the pediatric resident on call, naps and breakfast were looking extremely doubtful. She sighed and started reading through the cryptic admit notes from the emergency room. However, her study was soon interrupted by a cheery male voice.

"Good morning, Dr. Coleman."

Rosemary looked up to see Dr. Rick Williams entering the Pediatric ICU with a tray of hot food from the hospital cafeteria. Rick was hands down the most handsome resident in the University of Virginia Medical Center. He had curly black hair, deep blue eyes the color of sapphires, and a beguiling smile that could talk a charge nurse into anything legal and many things illegal. He had money, charm, and personality, and his dress and manner turned just about every female head in the hospital. He was drop-dead gorgeous, and he knew it. He was also one of the finest physicians that Rosemary had ever worked with and was the chief resident in Pediatrics.

"Morning, Rick," Rosemary said half-heartedly. She was tired and angry and didn't really feel much like talking.

Rick sat down in the chair next to hers and put his tray down on the counter. The delicious smell of hash browns and bacon almost made Rosemary faint. She had missed breakfast.

"You look hungry," he said bluntly.

"An accurate diagnosis," Rosemary replied drily.

Rick took out the small plate which held several hot biscuits and divided his breakfast and promptly gave half to Rosemary. Rick may be vain, but he wasn't stingy.

"Here. Eat."

"Don't be silly. That's your breakfast. I'll grab a doughnut later."

Rick shoved the small plate of hot food over.

"You'll do no such thing. Eat. Doctor's orders."

Gladly, Rosemary gave in and greedily fixed a bacon biscuit and ate it promptly.

"Looks like you've had an exciting evening," observed Rick airily, looking around the unit and seeing three of four beds occupied. "I go off service for twelve hours, and you open up a head trauma hotel. How do you do it? Do you advertise?"

"That's . . . not . . . funny," Rosemary mumbled, her mouth filled with biscuit.

Rick took a big gulp of orange juice and then handed the glass over to her. "So what've we got?"

"Car accident in rooms three and four. Brother and sister. Neither one in car seats, of course. Both went through the windshield, and both sustained closed head injuries. Little girl is doing okay at the moment. The little boy had some problems breathing about three this morning. Dr. Martin put him on the respirator, and we're getting a CT scan on him within the hour."

"Anyone else hurt in the accident?"

"Yes. The father was killed. Mother is in adult ICU with a punctured lung and two broken legs."

Rick grimaced and shook his head sadly. "Terrible. You know, since graduating from medical school and working in ICU, I've started driving like an old lady. Nice and slow."

Rosemary smiled at his comment. She related. She seemed to be driving slower these days as well. She picked up some hash browns with her fingers, poked them into her mouth, and then continued her review of the admissions.

"Room two is an abuse case. Two-year-old hispanic female."

Rick finished eating his biscuit with two big bites and said, "Oh, that explains it."

"Explains what?"

"The foul mood everyone is in. I thought the unit clerk and the respiratory therapist looked awfully sour when I came in. And our group lab techs that I saw down in the cafeteria weren't talking. They were just sitting at their table scowling, and you know that that bunch is never quiet."

"Do you blame them? According to the E.R. report, mother's drunk boyfriend got mad at her and pushed mother and baby down two flights of stairs. Mother will survive. Baby, I'm afraid, will not. Baby was flown in by helicopter about eleven last night. She arrived comatose."

"What are her vital signs?"

"Pupils have been fixed and dilated since midnight. I just checked them again. CT scans show massive edema. She's been unresponsive to touch and sound since admission. I've just ordered ABR and EEG tests. Once we have the test results, Dr. Martin can determine if and when we can remove life support."

Rick finished eating his hash browns and took a last bite of his last biscuit before speaking.

"Well, there is at least one bright spot in this nightmare," he said.

"What's that?"

Rick leaned over and put his arm playfully around Rosemary's shoulders.

"You. You're looking as beautiful as ever this morning."

Rosemary wrestled away from his grasp and stared at him coldly in protest.

"Oh, sure! I've had only two hours of sleep and haven't had a shower as you most surely can surmise. My hair is in a pigtail, and I'm not wearing my contact lenses. I have on the same pair of surgical scrubs that I put on yesterday morning, along with last week's smelly socks that I found in my locker. I'm covered with blood and numerous body fluids that I'd rather not think about, and you say I'm beautiful? I'll have Jill get bed number one ready. I think you must be suffering from a head injury as well."

Rick sat back and laughed heartily, his handsome smile beaming at her despite her scorn. His blue eyes sparkled merrily.

"Beauty, my dear Rose, they say, is in the eye of the beholder."

Rosemary frowned. She was not going to be taken in by his charm. She knew full well the reason for his attraction to her. Rick could have any available woman in the hospital. Come to think of it, he could probably have many of the unavailable ones as well. All except for one. Rose.

Over the past few years, Rosemary had learned the hard way that dating outside the Church was a painful dead-end street. Somehow she had managed to get through four years of BYU without getting married, which had been a terrible blow to her ego. She had gone to BYU with definite plans to date madly her freshman year, get engaged her sophomore year, get married her junior year, and have a baby before graduating. Obviously nothing went according to plan. However, she had resigned herself to being happy whether or not she was married. Eventually the Lord would provide.

When she went down to Lubbock, Texas, to Texas Tech Medical School, she had decided to try dating outside the Church with the intent of converting a future mate.

Big mistake.

After suffering the biggest heartbreak of her life while completing her third and fourth years at the Health Science Center campus in Amarillo, Texas, she vowed never again to go down that road. From now on, she would only date other Mormons. Active, worthy, available Mormons. So, when she came to Charlottesville, Virginia, she had been the only girl at the University of Virginia who did not care whether he lived or breathed.

And this bothered him no end.

"Well then," said Rose standing up, "I suggest that you have an eye exam as soon as possible." With that, she picked up her clipboard and walked over to room four to check on one of her patients. She went into the room and checked the readings of the heart monitor, then pulled out her stethoscope to check the little boy's heartbeat. Rick followed her into the room and shut the door. Rose ignored him and focused her attention on listening to her patient's chest.

Rick picked up the end of the stethoscope and spoke quietly into it.

"Rose, why don't you give me a chance?" he asked impatiently.

"Stop that!" She pulled the stethoscope out of his hand and resumed her exam. She took her time in listening to the injured child's heart while Rick anxiously stood beside the bed.

"Answer me," Rick insisted when she had finished. She made a few notes on her clipboard and then faced her colleague.

"Rick, we've been over this before. I only date Mormons."

"Then I'll become one," he said simply.

At this, Rosemary pushed him aside and laughed out loud.

"You don't think I would?" he asked, appearing hurt. Rosemary severely doubted the sincerity of his pain.

"No, I don't think you could. For one thing, you would have to give up coffee, and I happen to know that on average you down at least three cups before eight a.m. on good days and at least five on bad ones. I don't know why you bother drinking it. We could hook you up and feed it to you intravenously."

He ignored her sarcastic remark.

"I would give up coffee for you," he ventured soundly.

"You wouldn't be giving it up for me, Doctor. You'd be giving it up for God. How about beer?" she asked wickedly.

This was a tough one. Rick bit his lip.

"See," she said triumphantly, "it would be too hard. You couldn't possibly . . ."

"No," he said straightening like a soldier with firm determination. "I could give up booze. I mean, hey, I'm a doctor. I shouldn't drink the stuff anyway. Why, giving up liquor would be setting a good example to my patients."

Rosemary eyed him suspiciously.

"May I remind you that you are a pediatrician? The majority of your patients are three years old and under."

Rick would not be swayed.

"Then I'll be setting a good example for their parents."

Rosemary checked the settings on the ventilator and made note on her chart of the child's current blood pressure and temperature readings from the wall monitor. Then she put down the chart and faced Rick with a smug smile. She had saved the best for last.

"And sex? Could you manage to abstain from everything except hugging and kissing until you were legally and lawfully married?"

By the look on his face, she knew that she had won and left the room quite pleased with herself, not bothering to wait for his reply. As she sat back down at the counter, the unit clerk notified her that she had a call waiting on line one.

"Hello, this is Dr. Coleman."

"Rose . . ."

Rosemary happily recognized the voice on the other end of the line immediately.

"Dad! Good morning! What a surprise! How are you?"

Her father didn't return her friendly greeting right away, and the long pause made something in her belly instantly clinch tight. Something was wrong.

"Rose, you need to come home."

"Dad, what is it?" she said in a soft, frightened voice. In the corner of her eye, she saw Rick approaching her quickly with a real look of concern on his face. She looked away and down at the many papers scattered on top of the counter.

"It's Teema, honey. Grandpa Dameron came home this morning after taking a walk to the Plaza and found her in the kitchen . . . " Her Dad's voice suddenly choked up with emotion, and Rosemary felt tears filling up her eyes. No, God. No.

"She had a heart attack, sweetheart. I'm afraid she's gone."

Rosemary let the phone drop out of her hand. She looked up at Rick's face briefly and then put her head down on the counter and began to weep uncontrollably. The shock that she felt, along with her lack of sleep and stress, overwhelmed her. She barely heard Jill pick up the phone and finish the conversation with her father, but she did feel Rick's strong arm around her shoulders once again.

This time, she did not pull away.

"You didn't have to drive me," Rosemary said in a voice that was quiet and subdued. It had been a bit awkward how Rick had insisted on taking her to the funeral, but she had agreed and now was quite grateful that she had. She was glad to have his company on this most painful of days.

"Shut up, and you're welcome," Rick replied in a cheerful voice.

They were traveling down Route 29, the twisting four-lane highway that connected Charlottesville and Lynchburg. She gazed thoughtfully out the window at the scenery, watching the barren trees that lined the road quickly pass by. Everything looked so dead. She wished it were spring.

They were approaching Lovingston, a small town that sat nestled between two small mountains of the Blue Ridge. She smiled as she gazed over at the quaint little southern city. It reminded her a lot of Logan, Utah. All it needed was a temple on top of the small hill that rose up in the center of town.

Rosemary shifted herself around in her seat and looked over at Rick to speak to him.

"I'm still amazed that you were able to get off service. Mind telling me how you did it?"

"Dr. Martin owed me a favor," said Rick matter-of-factly.

"Really?" Rosemary said with some interest, willing to talk about anything that would get her mind off the upcoming funeral service. "An attending physician in debt to a chief resident. I thought it was usually the other way around."

Rick's mouth parted into a small grin.

"Remember the blonde that Dr. Martin showed up with at the Christmas party?"

"Uh huh. Oh, I see. I don't think I want to hear this."

"You're right. You don't. But thanks to my infamous connections in the UVA nursing school, I'm here and I'm completely yours for the day. So get used to it."

Rosemary smiled at him. Who would have ever thought Rick Williams could be so nice? And who would have thought that she would ever let him be so nice to her? Well, it was a blessing she thought as she leaned back in her seat again and watched the road ahead. His ever-present humor had helped her through the most difficult parts of yesterday and was easing her pain today.

She reluctantly thought about the previous two days. She now felt somewhat embarrassed over her outburst in the ICU, but it was very understandable. Rick had held her gently until her tears had stopped, then he had taken her over to the empty unit in the ICU with strict instructions to lie down and to rest. He returned minutes later with a tranquilizer and a glass of water, which she took without argument. Her hands were literally shaking when she took the pill, and she quickly calmed down and fell into a much-needed sleep.

She had called home that evening to talk to Mother, who was holding up remarkably well. Mother told her of the funeral plans, and it was then that Rosemary announced her decision that she would not come home until the day of the funeral. She wouldn't come sooner. It was too hard, too painful. She didn't want to see Teema at the funeral home. She couldn't stand the thought of seeing her beloved grandmother lifeless. And truthfully, she dreaded going to the funeral. Mother did not protest. She understood.

"So, tell me, Dr. Coleman," said Rick, interrupting her sad thoughts, "what are your views on life and death."

His unexpected question seemed to come of the blue and surprised her.

"My what?"

"You know, your beliefs on the afterlife, heaven and hell, all that kind of stuff."

"Rick, you're not serious."

"I'm quite serious. I'm going to a Mormon funeral, my first mind you, so I think I should be prepared. I want to kneel and to pray at all the right times."

His assumption, a very natural one, stung her. The fact that she was still the only member of the Church in her family was a little sore spot in her heart that today loomed large. If she were married and had a family of her own, maybe it wouldn't be so important to her. But she was alone in life and alone in the Church, and today she felt it deeply.

"I'm the only Mormon in my family, Rick."

Rick turned and stared at her.

"But I thought . . ."

"My parents are Presbyterian," she said mildly.

"So I'm going to a Presbyterian funeral?"

"No, Methodist."

"But you just said . . ."

"My parents joined another church when I was in college."

"Oh, I see. I'm disappointed. I was looking forward to seeing what this Mormon Church is all about. Oh, well, in the meantime, give me the Big Picture."

Rosemary hesitated for a moment. She wasn't exactly in the mood to give a missionary discussion on the plan of salvation on the way to Teema's funeral. Yet, oddly enough, given her grandmother's role in her own conversion process, it was somehow strangely appropriate. And it would be a good reminder of what she herself believed.

For the next thirty minutes, Rosemary described her beliefs to Rick, beginning with the pre-existence and slowly explaining in detail about the purposes of life, physical death, the spirit world, and the resurrection. Rick seemed sincerely interested, listening mostly and asking a few pertinent questions.

By the time she finished her discussion, she felt very peaceful. Teema had lived a very good life, a rich and abundant life. Now she was in a better place, in a much better world. That thought gave Rosemary a lot of comfort, and in her mind's eye, she recalled a photograph taken of Teema and her family when Teema was just a toddler. Great-grandmother Louella was sitting in a chair holding Teema in her lap, and Great Aunt Virginia, Aunt Bessie, and Uncle Willie were standing around her. Now Teema was with her family again, with her beloved mother and brother and sisters.

Rosemary's attention came back to the present as they crossed the big cement bridge that extended over the James River into downtown Lynchburg. She gave Rick directions where to turn, and they quickly made their way through downtown, up Fifth Street, and over to Park Avenue, to the small red brick Methodist church that had been Teema's place of worship. This building held so much of Rosemary's own history. Her parents had been married in this little church, and she had been christened there as an infant. Teema had taken her there to vacation Bible school when she was a little girl, and she had helped Teema prepare the annual Christmas luncheon for her Methodist Women's Sewing Circle in this building many, many times.

Rick parked the car and helped her out, offering a strong arm for her to lean upon. They walked into the church and found her family waiting for her.

It was early. The funeral was not to begin for another hour, but Mother and Dad had arranged for all of them to meet there when Rosemary arrived. Mother held out her arms to Rosemary, and Rosemary embraced her. Both of them began to cry. It felt so good to cry with Mother. Rosemary hugged Dad, then Michael. She could hardly believe how tall her little brother was. At sixteen, he was almost as tall as Dad. Michael held a long-stemmed red rose in his hand which he gave to Rosemary.

"It was too early to get anything from Mom's garden," he explained shyly, "so I got you this. I know how much you loved the red roses in Teema's backyard."

She hugged Michael again and cried again. Strange how she could feel such pain and such love at the same moment.

Then she reached out for Heather, who stood there with her husband and two little boys. Time had quieted their old rivalry, and Heather was now a close friend. Heather took Rosemary by the hand and led her into the empty sanctuary.

A beautiful silver grey casket stood at the altar. Rosemary held Heather's hand tightly as they approached the coffin. It was all that Rosemary could do to look down at the tiny figure, the small, graceful white-haired woman who had been her sweet grandmother and who had once been the young adventuresome lady who had gone to Bryn Mawr and Salt Lake City and San Francisco. Rosemary reached out and touched Teema's petite hand, the hand that had sewn thousands of factory garments for employment and children's clothes for orphans in Africa for charity. Those hands had labored tirelessly to cook and clean and provide for her beloved family.

Tears flowed as Rosemary took Michael's rose and placed it into Teema's hand.

"For you, Lily Dameron," she said softly.

5

April 1988

It never ceased to amaze Rosemary how startling the Washington temple appeared from the beltway. The approach was dramatic coming from either the north or south. Driving south from the Maryland side, the temple seemed to slowly arise in front of your car, appearing to float mystically on top of the forest of trees below. When driving north from Virginia, as she was doing now, the temple suddenly appeared out of nowhere as the eight-lane highway veered sharply to the left. Rosemary noted with amusement several black lines that streaked the highway in front of her. She wondered as she signaled to take her exit how many cars had wrecked on the beltway as a result of surprise in suddenly seeing this majestic temple.

The building left her view as she got off the beltway and began driving through the park which was directly below the temple. It was a warm, beautiful, sunny spring day, and the park was filled with people. She passed joggers and bicyclists and young mothers pushing small children in their strollers. It was not until she neared the end of the park that the tall, white marble structure reappeared, its golden spires sparkling brightly in the sun.

It was a Saturday morning, so Rosemary didn't bother trying to park directly in the temple parking lot. She knew from past experience that on Saturdays the parking lot would be full. Instead, she drove her car directly to the stake center located right next to the temple and parked her car there. She didn't mind the walk over, for there was a small path that went through a wooded area between the two buildings.

The grounds of the Washington temple were always lovely, but this time of year was Rosemary's favorite. The driveway going into the temple parking lot was lined with delicate pink dogwood trees, which were in glorious full bloom. Clouds of pink flowers hung overhead as Rosemary slowly approached the temple. Below the trees, bright pink azaleas edged the drive with their own spectacular beauty. As if there weren't enough color, large crimson-pink tulips rose up gracefully beside the sidewalk and around the bubbling water fountain in front of the temple.

The landscape was breathtaking, and Rosemary paused by the fountain to take in the loveliness of the surroundings. The sound of the falling water seemed to sing to her heart. Six months from now, she and Rick would be married in this temple. Rosemary glanced down at the diamond ring that sparkled on her finger. Who would have ever dreamed that Rick Williams, handsome playboy doctor, would eagerly take the missionary discussions and then successfully give up coffee, beer, and all immoral expressions of intimate premarital affection? Who would have ever dreamed that he, of all people, would have been baptized and then would accept a calling to teach the Sunbeam class in Primary? Rosemary chuckled to herself. If Rick could be converted, it was proof positive the Church was true!

She entered the temple and handed her recommend to a very elderly man dressed in white sitting at the desk. He smiled at her, carefully examined the recommend, and handed it back as he wished her well on her day at the temple. She walked around the wooden divider behind the recommend desk and entered the walkway that led into the temple.

Gathered around several sofas and chairs within the connecting walk were several couples from her ward in Charlottesville. It was their ward temple day, and they had gone up to the temple much earlier that morning for an early session. Four couples were waiting for Rosemary — Laura and Steve, Melissa and Jay, Diane and

Douglas, and Renée and Brad. They greeted Rosemary warmly, and together they walked into the temple.

Before them was a large mural painting of the second coming of Christ. The resurrected Lord was placed in the center of the painting, dressed in white robes with his arms outstretched. On his right hand, people from different nations and from different eras of history knelt in worship and praise. On his left hand, scenes of destruction were painted with figures of people struck down in fear and remorse.

Rosemary stared at the painting for a moment or two, then she walked over to the small office on the right side of the front foyer. The sign overhead read "Family File." A bright-eyed young woman stood behind a counter and welcomed her as she approached.

"Can I help you?" she asked.

"I have some names in the family file," answered Rosemary.

"What name is it under?"

"Coleman. Rosemary Coleman."

The temple worker opened a file drawer and flipped through a series of small card packets until she came to Rosemary's file. The young woman pulled the packet out and walked back to the counter and handed it to Rosemary.

Silently Rosemary pulled the cards out of the file to check to see if all of them were there. One by one, she sorted through the cards.

"William T. St. John, Louella Smith, Virginia Florence St. John, Bessie Lee St. John, William P. St. John, Lillian Ruth St. John."

Carefully, Rosemary distributed the cards out among her friends, keeping one special card for herself. Tightly holding Teema's card in her hand, Rosemary followed her friends over to the winding staircase at the end of the building.

As Rosemary changed clothes in the women's locker room, she smiled as she thought back to the day that she received her own endowment in the Salt Lake temple. What a disaster that had proven to be.

Admittedly, she could see now that the Salt Lake temple had been a wrong choice; for when she arrived, there were ten weddings taking place in the temple that day. In addition, there were two sisters preparing to leave on missions, and a family being sealed. The place was too crowded.

As she and her roommate Susan, who was serving as her escort, were walking from the bride's room to a small room where they were to hear a talk from the temple matron, a tiny little temple worker stationed in the hall for the purpose of giving directions stopped them and extended her hand in greeting.

"Congratulations, sister. You make a beautiful bride."

Rosemary pulled back her hand and stared at the small woman with tall white hair and thick glasses.

"I'm sorry. I'm not getting married today."

The little lady's eyes then widened, and she beamed a broad smile at Rosemary.

"Oh, you're going on a mission! How wonderful!"

Rosemary crossed her arms and smiled back politely.

"No, I'm afraid I'm not going on a mission either."

The tiny temple worker looked distressed.

"Then why," she asked bemused, "are you here?"

Rosemary sincerely wanted to educate this woman on the subject, but Susan gave her a look that forbid such a dialog. Quietly, she and Susan proceeded on to their next destination.

Rosemary excitedly opened her heart and mind for the ceremony, relishing every lovely word. However, she could not help becoming irritated at the young bride sitting directly in front of her. The young girl was adorned in a dress that reminded Rosemary of something Scarlett O'Hara would have worn at a garden party in the movie *Gone with the Wind*, an ornate showy gown with rows and rows of lace and a monstrous hoop skirt. As the ceremony progressed from room to room, the entire company was repeatedly held up by the lack of cooperation from the hoop skirt.

The complete disinterest of the bride and her mother toward the ceremony itself infuriated Rosemary. They were obviously more concerned about how the bride looked than what she learned. The mother anxiously arranged and rearranged the lace draped across the girl's thin shoulders, and the girl spent half of her time glancing across the isle at her intended, smiling, giggling, and blushing. It was enough to make Rosemary sick. But she refused to let their actions affect her experience. This was one of the most important days of her life. With awe and wonder, she moved through the beautiful rooms of the temple, embracing each covenant with her whole heart.

Rosemary finished dressing and left the locker room, she wondered happily if Teema would meet any funny little temple workers on the other side of the veil today? If so, Rosemary had no doubts as to Teema's ability to handle them.

She took her seat in the crowded sealing room. She looked around this particular room, a large sealing room which was decorated in shades of greens, blues, and purple. Each of the sealing rooms in the Washington temple were done in different colors. She had seen rooms of peach, pink, blue, and lavender, but she had not been in this room before. This larger room was usually reserved for weddings. The walls and chairs were covered in a light silk tapestry, and the cushions surrounding the white marble altar and the drapes along one wall were done in a dark green velvet. An elegant cloth of hand-woven white lace hung gracefully over the altar.

The room was filled with about thirty people, a variety of unknown patrons who were working on their family files and members of Rosemary's party. One of the usual disadvantages of being single, Rosemary mused, was not having help in doing one's genealogy and temple work. It took a handful of people to do the sealing work, and she had no one. But today, that wasn't really true. She had her ward family.

The temple sealer arrived in the room and took his seat at the head of the altar. He pulled a small table closer in front of him and began sorting through several stacks of cards. When ready, he welcomed them to the temple and congratulated them for the work that they were doing.

Once he had finished his little address, he reached for a very large stack of cards belonging to a dark-haired sister named Giberson. He understood that Sister Giberson had a long trip ahead of her that afternoon. Would anyone mind if her names were done first?

Rosemary did not object. She had all day, and she welcomed the time to sit quietly in the temple, away from her seemingly endless responsibilities at the hospital, away from life. Besides, it was one of her pet peeves to rush around while serving in the temple. "Rush" and "busy" and "hurry" were words she disdained while in the house of the Lord.

Rosemary sat still and calm as the Giberson party knelt down at the altar and began their work. Rosemary watched awhile with interest, but then she let her gaze wander upward to the sparkling crystal chandelier that hung high over the altar. The lights of the chandelier that danced in her eyes had almost a tranquilizing effect, and she found her mind, her awareness, drifting far away as vivid images came brightly to her mind, images that seemed very real.

She pictured: a beautiful room similar to this one, a room filled with light and vivid color and peace. In this room, several people gather, standing anxiously around an altar. There is a fair-haired young man and a lovely young woman with long blond hair. There are two noble women standing side by side, both with long, dark black hair pulled back in thick braids. These four people, all dressed in temple white, are excitedly talking to another woman, a petite young lady who has just entered the room.

There are embraces of deep affection, tears in greeting, and smiles of joy. Two male personages unexpectedly enter the small room, and the people around the altar suddenly turn and look at them. One man, tall and angelic, leads the other man carefully by the arm. The man that he assists is newly dressed in white and newly released from his own personal spiritual prison. He stands unsure, marveling at his new condition and at the people standing before him.

The first to greet him is the fair-haired young man. Of course it must be him, the happy soldier lost so long ago to his family, the son named after him, the man who was once the little boy so friendly and playful and loving. Willie walks up to his father and throws his arms around the man's shoulders in an affectionate greeting.

"Father, how good to see you again," says Willie softly.

The man awkwardly puts his arms around the son whom he has not seen in almost a hundred years.

Bessie approaches next. Gone from her face are all signs of the resentment and bitterness that she harbored in her heart for years. Somehow, sometime, those scars have been healed here, just as her father was healed of his mortal compulsion to drink. The man looks almost afraid as she approaches. The hand that last touched him with an angry slap is now placed gently upon his cheek.

"Welcome back, Father," says Bessie.

A look of pain crosses the man's face as Virginia steps forward. On Virginia's face is a look of radiant happiness, for all that was denied her in mortal life has been abundantly given to her in this sphere. In such happiness, how can she withhold pardon? Virginia rushes forward, unwilling for her father to suffer another moment longer.

The daughter that cast him out so long ago takes her tearful father into her arms and holds him in a tight, accepting embrace.

"Papa," she whispers, "don't be afraid. All is forgiven. All is forgiven."

The man looks with awe and wonder as the petite young lady approaches, and Rosemary feels her own tears fall as Lily takes her father's hands into her own in greeting.

"Father, I'm your daughter, Lily."

The man gazes at the young woman that he never knew in mortality, then closes his eyes in deep emotion as Lily steps closer and kisses him sweetly on the cheek.

His children step aside now as the man turns and faces the remaining woman in the room. Louella steps toward the man who loved and left her, but he rushes instantly to her, perhaps not feeling worthy that she should come to him. He drops to his knees and bends his head in shame, covering his face with shaking hands.

"Oh, Louella, I'm so sorry. I'm so sorry," he exclaims through his tears.

Slowly, Louella raises her delicate hands and places one upon his head, gently stroking his hair, calming him as she would a heartbroken child. Then she takes the other hand and places it under his chin and lifts it up to face her. The man looks up at this remarkable woman as if she were an angel of the Lord. He waits for his hell to end at last.

And it ends with a single word.

"William," Louella says softly.

In her voice is the sound of pardon, and William St. John rises and embraces her, weeping.

"Sister Coleman? Sister Coleman?"

The voice of an impatient temple sealer immediately brought Rosemary back to her present surroundings. Had she been daydreaming? Surely. Yet the images had been so real.

"Sister Coleman, we're ready to do your names. Will you and two members of your group go and kneel at the altar, please?"

Rosemary got out of her seat and went over to the altar with her friends Jay and Melissa by her side. Humbly, she knelt down and reached out her hand.

Since it was Saturday, the traffic on the beltway was quite minimal, so Rosemary had no trouble getting out of the city. She took her time driving back, rolling down the car window and enjoying the smells and the warmth of the spring air. Her thoughts were quite scattered as she drove out of the nation's capital.

The circle was complete.

A copy of the Book of Mormon, like a small seed planted over eighty years ago, had finally flowered and saved a distant harvest of souls. A good family, once torn apart by war and disease and alcohol and death, were now bound together through eternal priesthood power.

It was perfect.

Well, almost perfect, for somewhere out there lived a returned missionary in his late fifties or early sixties — that horrible, terrible, awful missionary — with an old Book of Mormon on his living room shelf, Teema's precious Book of Mormon.

Someday, when I die, thought Rosemary with determination, I shall face the Lord and obtain the name and whereabouts of this atrocious elder. If he is dead, I will go to the Spirit Prison where he lives in eternal punishment for his crime and will give him a good piece of my mind. If he is alive, I will come back from the dead and haunt him for the rest of his living days.

Such thoughts of revenge were perhaps not in accordance with the sweet spirit of the day, but they pleased Rosemary very much and made her trip home most enjoyable.

Afterword

This work is a fictionalized account of the actual events that led up to my conversion to The Church of Jesus Christ of Latter-day Saints. The story of the lives and the deaths of my great-grandmother, Louella Smith St. John, and her four children has been presented in accordance with historical information obtained from conversations with my mother and my aunt and from my grandmother's records. Some information was related to me by "Teema" herself while she was still living. However, in order to preserve the privacy of myself and my immediate family, our names and some of the places that we have lived have been altered.

At the turn of the century, there was not a Mormon congregation — ward or branch — in Lynchburg, Virginia. In fact, the Mormon Church was first organized in Lynchburg in the late 1940s. As a student at the University of Virginia, I learned that there were some members of the Church living near Charlottesville in the late 1890s. In addition, I have learned that there were also members of the Church living in northern North Carolina at the turn of the century. It is possible that the two elders who healed my grandmother and who placed the Book of Mormon in Louella's hands were from one of these locations.

Attempts have been made to identify the names of the elders who came and took away the original Book of Mormon. They would have been missionaries serving in the Roanoke, Virginia, mission. My mother relates that the book was still in my grandmother's possession at the time of her marriage in 1955. My grandmother retired from the sewing factory in the early 1960s, so we estimate that the book was lost sometime between 1960 and 1971. In the course of writing this book, my aunt revealed to me that grandmother's original Book of Mormon was a rare second edition copy. To this date, all efforts to locate the elders and the book have failed.

About the Author

Denise Anne Tucker was born in Lynchburg, Virginia, and was raised by a family who effectively taught her how to clean house, to sing, and to garden. She joined the Church during her high school years. She attended Brigham Young University where she failed to marry, but did manage somehow to earn a B.S. and master's degree. After a brief interlude of life in Texas, she returned home to earn her Ph.D. at the University of Virginia. These days she can be found in Greensboro, North Carolina, where she spends her time teaching at the local university, growing roses in her backyard, and searching for recruits for the ward choir.